Escape to the Wildey

Book 1

David Kempher

Otter Rock Productions

To my mother, Virginia Kempher
for the love behind the money she left on the kitchen table before going to work on those warm Illinois summer mornings while I slept in, so that when I woke I could make my...
Escape to the Wildey...

Created with Vellum

Prologue

Hear my soul speak,
Of the very instant I saw you,
Did my heart fly at your service...
–Shakespeare, The Tempest Act 3, Scene 1

October 1968
Edwardsville, Illinois

Ninth-grader Ethan Krieger gazed down the hallway of his high school at Nona Riley talking to a girlfriend as she thrust her books inside her locker. Nona, considered by most to be the prettiest and most popular girl in school, fascinated Ethan and his interest in her went well beyond Nona's physical beauty. He liked the way she walked, her style in clothing and Nona's slow, careful, sly way of speaking reminded him of Lauren Bacall in a movie that he had once seen. A bit reserved, Nona, a smart student like Ethan, didn't always have her hand in the air. However, when called upon by the teacher, she produced not only a reliably correct answer, but could also shrewdly analyze, compare, and contrast as well. At home in the classroom, it seemed obvious to everyone that she had a future in whatever she decided to do.

One day, when Nona smiled at Ethan with her piercing dark brown eyes, it seemed as if the entire room glowed and afterwards, whenever he heard her laugh, Ethan found himself wanting to laugh with her as if she floated on a perfect spring breeze, like an angel.

However, while Ethan had no problem mingling with girls as lab partners or classmates, when it came to the strange new tingly feelings within him, like many other fifteen-year-old boys, he suddenly became shy and apprehensive. So, when he considered the idea of asking Nona out on a date, in Ethan's mind it appeared certain that when she turned him down, the whole school would know about it immediately, and that they would be merciless in their ridicule. It drove Ethan into a better safe-than-sorry hiding place that tortured his romantic adventurous soul every time he saw Nona.

But, today, Friday afternoon, Ethan had finally gained control of his teenage cowardice. A Three Stooges double feature plus cartoons played at the Wildey Theater in their small town on Saturday afternoon, and Ethan steeled himself to ask Nona to go out with him before she left school. Inhaling one last nervous deep breath, he walked towards her.

"So, what's playing at the Wildey this weekend?" asked Nona as she pulled her coat from the locker and put it on.

Cynthia shrugged. "Nothing, just a stupid Three Stooges double feature."

Nona secretly adored The Three Stooges and loved their comedy, but she didn't want to seem uncool to her girlfriend.

"Yeah, you're right, they're really stupid," responded Nona semi-derisively as she picked up her books. Holding them against her blossoming chest, she turned and saw tall, handsome Ethan Krieger standing behind Cynthia. Smiling up at him, Nona liked the way his soft brownish-blond hair caressed the top of his ears and his steel-blue eyes shone whenever he looked at her. Nona, playing with a small silver cross on a chain around her neck, couldn't help herself. A warm, excited feeling raced through her body whenever he was around. A nice feeling that her religious mother reminded her on many occasions good girls didn't have.

Ethan and Nona stared at each other while Cynthia watched.

"Ethan. Did you want something?" asked Nona, hoping he did.

Ethan, with Nona's Three Stooges comment blaring in his mind like a trumpet, shook his head. At that moment, he felt like everyone in the school was judging him, laughing at his foolishness and audacity for believing he had a chance with the smartest, prettiest, most popular girl in school.

"No...uh...nothing," answered Ethan sullenly, and to Nona's disappointment, quickly retreated in the direction he'd come.

Ethan had walked thirty feet down the hallway when blind, relentless courage kicked in and he decided that no matter what he had to endure, he *would* ask Nona out this weekend to something, anything. Then, as he turned around, he saw Nona talking to Kenny Peters, the most popular boy in school, and in that instant, Ethan knew his moment had passed.

Part One

Fifty-Five Years Later

Chapter 1

Escape

June 2nd, 6:30 a.m.
Olympia, Washington

Wearing Nikes, jeans, a black polo shirt, and a light baby-blue fleece hooded jacket, seventy-year-old Ethan Krieger kept his wary eyes on alert as he walked at a steady quick pace down Plum Street in Olympia, Washington. He had timed his departure perfectly. This early in the morning, the streets were almost empty.

The spring sun had risen almost an hour earlier, and the tree-lined four-lane street and its surroundings glowed through a drifting fog that had almost cleared. On the horizon to the west hovered a few dark, ominous clouds, prodding him onward. Heavy rain had been forecast for later. But with a little luck, Ethan hoped that he would be far away by the time the expected droplets fell.

Past the Japanese Garden, a stoplight commanded the interchange to Interstate Five North. To the right, Plum Street merged onto Henderson Boulevard. Only half a mile further, the on-ramp to Interstate Five South beckoned through the haze. Ethan scratched his beard for a moment and considered his options before he decided to turn right.

On his back, Ethan carried a small pack. Inside, he had stuffed only a change of underwear, socks, and an extra shirt, along with his shaving kit. Looped over his shoulder and across his chest, he clutched a messenger bag tightly against him. Tucked away among other things inside lay his Glock, ready for use in case of trouble.

Tall fir trees shrouded this portion of the road, and Ethan's bald head soon grew cold in the shadows. Reaching inside his fleece jacket pocket, he pulled out a black stocking cap, thrust it upon his head and, given that old habits die hard, folded it military style, so that the edges were all even.

Ten minutes later, Ethan reached the on-ramp to I-5 South, as Henderson Boulevard curved east into Watershed Park to eventually meet Olympia's sister city, Tumwater. Standing at the side of the road, he slid off his pack and dropped it to the ground. Ethan looked around and, seeing no cars, sat sullenly on his pack, keeping his messenger bag close against him wondering if he were doing the right thing.

"Maybe I should just..."

But then his stubbornness fought back...

"No! No! No!" he told himself. "I'm not turning back now!"

Ethan had no intention of acceding to their wishes, voluntarily or involuntarily. Years earlier he had made a vow to himself regarding what he would do under these circumstances. So long as something, anything, burned within Ethan's soul, he wasn't going to let anyone gradually extinguish what remained of the flame—no matter how well-meaning.

Opening his messenger bag, he popped a lozenge from a blister pack and sucked on it. Gazing at the tall green trees and the numerous varieties of colorful pink and purple wild spring flowers beside the road, Ethan inhaled a long, deep breath of cool morning air. A thousand memories, good and bad, sped through him, and Ethan felt a rush of absolute certainty that the right thing laid before him on the road in back of him. Pulling a piece of cardboard from his pack he unfolded it and got ready to hold it up if a car approached. On it, written in large letters, it read...

East

Just then, in the distance on Henderson Boulevard, Ethan spotted an older model white Ford Sedan turn towards him. Still resting on his pack, he held up his sign. But then, deciding he would look less threatening, Ethan stood and held the sign against his chest while he smiled. As the car approached, it slowed and turned off onto the side of the road in front of him. Picking up his pack, Ethan trotted to the driver's side of the sedan, trying not to look too anxious. Inside sat an attractive older woman about his age, dressed in blue jeans, a flannel shirt, and a Mariner's baseball cap over her long greyish-white ponytail. The top two buttons on her shirt were unbuttoned, exposing a hint of bra along with a touch of cleavage.

She smiled at Ethan while his eyes explored the subtle curves of her face for a moment.

"Where you heading, handsome?" asked the woman.

"East," replied Ethan, smiling back. "To a small town in Illinois called Edwardsville."

The woman seemed puzzled.

"Why?" she asked.

Ethan studied the woman's face while he contemplated how to answer that question. He didn't want her to leave without him. Figuring he had nothing to lose, Ethan decided it best to be honest.

"I'm escaping," he confessed.

"From where?" she asked. "From jail?"

"What's left of my family wants to put me in one of those homes, or as they're called now, 'assisted living communities,'" explained Ethan. "I refuse to spend what time I have left in this world imprisoned in one of those smelly hellholes."

"What's your name?" asked the woman curiously.

"Ethan Krieger," he answered.

The woman stared at Ethan for a moment in stunned silence and made an immediate decision.

"Get in," ordered the woman.

Ethan picked up his pack and walked to the other side of the car. Throwing his pack into the back seat, he slipped into the passenger seat.

The woman quickly drove onto the on-ramp and headed south onto I-5. The legal speed limit was sixty-five, but she zoomed to eighty, and Ethan buckled his seatbelt.

"My name is Mary, Mary Katz," she said. "So handsome, what's your story? Why are you running?"

Mary swerved into the left lane to pass a semi without putting on her turn signal, making Ethan a bit nervous. She multiplied his apprehensions when she merrily pulled in front of the honking semi, again with no signal.

"I lost my balance and fell down the front steps of my house yesterday and hit my head on the sidewalk," said Ethan, watching Mary drive. "It wasn't the first time, and I didn't get hurt. But while I was resting on the couch, I overheard my nephew talking to my niece. They were going to go to court today to get a power-of-attorney over all of my affairs based on multiple falls. They think I'm not able to take care of myself on my own anymore."

Ethan patted his messenger bag.

"But I beat them to the punch," said Ethan, grinning. "I pulled my entire life savings from the bank yesterday and this morning and... well...I'm escaping their clutches."

He laid back on the seat and relaxed as Mary slowed down.

"But as soon as they get their court order today, they'll have the police out looking for me."

The sedan reached the speed limit.

"So, why are you hitchhiking?" she asked. "Don't you have your own car?"

"I do," replied Ethan. "But I left it. The first thing they'll do when they can't find me is have the police out looking for that vehicle. It's slower, but hitchhiking makes it harder to find me. Also, since I left my car behind, hopefully they'll concentrate their search in Olympia for a while."

"So beautiful, what's your story?" asked Ethan.

Mary gripped the steering wheel tightly.

"It's funny that I should run into you," said Mary, "because my relatives want to do the same thing with me."

"Put you into one of those hellholes?"

Mary sped up.

"Yes," she snarled. "And they started last year by taking away my license. Said I was a terrible driver!"

Their speed reached ninety.

"Said I was going to kill myself and maybe someone else when they really just wanted me to be dependent on them!"

"So, you're driving without a license?" stated Ethan, looking at the cars they were whizzing past.

"Yes! What about it?"

Ethan motioned his hand towards Mary's tense grip on the steering wheel.

"Well, since we're both on the lam," cautioned Ethan calmly, "and you're driving without a license, maybe we shouldn't give the cops any reason to pull us over."

Ethan smiled at Mary, calming her, as she slowed down to the speed limit.

"Mary," said Ethan, "I have a proposition for you."

"Umm," said Mary, smiling delightfully. "You're not in the car five minutes and already you're propositioning me."

She shook her chest and winked

"What do you have in mind, handsome?"

Ethan liked Mary. She was fun.

"The authorities will probably be looking for us individually," said Ethan slyly. "But they probably wouldn't give a second glance to two people traveling together. It wouldn't fit their profile. I have money and you have a car. How would you like to team up and run away together?"

Mary felt something warm glow within her that she hadn't felt in a long time, and wondered if she was dreaming.

"That's a good starting proposition," said Mary, grinning, "but I might expect more later."

She winked.

"Duly noted!" replied Ethan. "So?" he asked. "Deal?"

"Deal!"

Mary held out a hand and they shook.

"Now, are you hungry?" asked Ethan.

"I will be soon," said Mary.

"Good," said Ethan. "I'm going to put an address into the GPS on your car. If we're going to be running away together, we're going to need a few things. When we get there, wake me up. I got up very early this morning and I need to take a nap."

Ethan typed a Portland address into the on-board GPS while Mary watched. The computer determined a route on the screen for Mary. Then Ethan lay against the window and went to sleep almost immediately. Mary gazed at Ethan while he slept.

"Ethan trusts my driving while he sleeps," said Mary softly, and she smiled.

Portland

Mary tapped Ethan on the shoulder and he awoke with a start.

"Where are we?" yawned Ethan as he stretched.

Mary pointed to a building next to a bicycle shop in a quiet tree-lined neighborhood of South Portland next to the river.

"Fernando's Mexican Restaurant."

"Good," commented Ethan as he rubbed the sleep from his eyes.

"I'm not a big fan of Mexican food," said Mary.

"That's ok," Ethan said, smiling. "We're not here for the food."

Ethan got out of the car and Mary followed him inside the restaurant. Ethan requested a booth and the waiter handed them menus. As the waiter began to leave, Ethan stopped him.

"Could you let Fernando know that Ethan Krieger and a friend are here to see him?"

The waiter nodded and left.

"Who is Fernando?" asked Mary.

"Someone I work with," replied Ethan. "I think he can help us. At least I hope he still can."

A few minutes later, the waiter returned and asked Ethan and Mary to follow him. The waiter led them through the kitchen to a stairway at the back, and pointed to a door at the top that connected to the next building.

"You don't need to knock," said the waiter, "he's waiting for you."

Ethan and Mary climbed the stairs and opened the door. A Hispanic man their age, with a large, bushy mustache and eyebrows met them at the doorway and embraced Ethan.

"Ethan," said the jovial man. "I hope you're here to pick up the software for Operation Tyrannosaurus, because I just finished it!"

"Oh my God. I completely forgot about that," remembered Ethan, lightly hitting himself on the side of the head.

"How could you forget?" asked a puzzled Fernando.

"Sorry," said Ethan. "I've had a few other things on my mind lately."

He turned towards Mary.

"Oh, I see," said Fernando.

"Fernando," said Ethan. "I'd like to introduce my friend, Mary Katz."

Mary held out her hand, but Fernando, to her surprise, embraced her instead. Then, holding Mary at arm's length in front of him, he examined her.

"She's too beautiful to be just a friend," said Fernando, smiling.

Ethan smiled at Mary.

"She is beautiful," commented Ethan while Mary blushed. But then he quickly changed the subject.

"We need your help," said Ethan. "I need your special back-back-backdoor into the cyber records world."

Fernando motioned to several seats in front of his desk and Ethan and Mary sat while Fernando leaned on the edge of his desk.

"So, what do you need?" asked Fernando.

"A new package for each of us," replied Ethan.

"Why?"

"Our relatives want to put us in one of those homes. We're not willing to go, and before they force us, we're escaping."

Fernando shook his head.

"Ah, relatives!" said Fernando. "I know they mean well but...well —fuck them! I'll do this for what it's going to cost me to keep you two out of one of those hellholes."

"Thank you," said Ethan. "So, how much is it going to be?"

"The computer networks have gotten better, faster, and more secure. But I can still work the system," said Fernando. "It has made my contacts a lot more expensive. So, twenty thousand."

"For both of us," said Ethan.

"No," said Fernando, shaking his head, "each. I wish I could do better, my friend, but this is at cost. I have people to pay."

Ethan thought for a second and then nodded.

"Ok," replied Fernando. "Why don't you two go have some lunch on me? By the time you're done, I'll have you inserted into the system and your new papers ready. Also, on the house, I'll give you a couple of throwaway cell phones that can't be traced to your new package."

Ethan and Mary started to get up.

"By the way," asked Fernando, "which direction are you heading?"

"East," replied Ethan.

"Good. Avoid San Diego," advised Fernando.

"Why?" asked Ethan.

"I was just notified the other day that a former friend of yours lives there," said Fernando.

Ethan became curious.

"Who?"

"Susanna Rybkanowski," answered Fernando.

Ethan snarled as he looked up at the ceiling and memories flooded through him.

Mary nudged Ethan's arm. "Who is Susanna Rybkanowski?" she asked. "An ex-wife?"

"You would think that," said Fernando with a laugh, "given how she feels about him, but no."

Ethan shook his head still thinking.

"No. Just an old...uh...acquaintance," said Ethan. "During one of my assignments, she escaped."

Mary made a mental note to ask him later what he meant by *assignments.*

Then something occurred to him.

"How the hell did she end up in San Diego?" said a confused Ethan. "She should be in prison somewhere."

"After your encounter with her, she saw the writing on the wall and knew it would only be a matter of time before you caught up with her," said Fernando, "so she turned state's evidence, or so we thought. I'm hearing some disturbing things about her. After getting all the information they could from her, the higher authorities allowed her to retire to a San Diego suburb with a new identity. Odds are very slim that you would run into her, but just in case, I thought I would give you a heads-up."

"Thanks. I appreciate it," said Ethan. "What name is she going by these days?"

"Clara Barton," said Fernando, chuckling. "The authorities had a weird sense of humor when they assigned her a new identity."

Mary quietly analyzed Ethan while Fernando walked behind his desk and turned on his computer. Then he pointed to a door at the side of the room.

"Before you eat lunch, I need to take pictures of you two. You should shave," said Fernando. "You'll find a razor, scissors, and a towel inside."

Ethan nodded and headed for the bathroom.

Meanwhile, Fernando motioned Mary to a chair.

"What do you need pictures for?" asked Mary.

Fernando eyed her through the lens of his digital camera.

"For your new identities."

"How are you able to do this?" asked Mary. "What were you and Ethan involved in?"

Fernando grinned.

"Turn a little bit more to the left," he requested.

A few minutes later, Ethan emerged from the bathroom. Mary strolled to him and boldly stroked her hand against his newly-shaven cheeks to feel the smoothness.

"You look much better," said Mary as she cocked an eyebrow. "I like it."

Fernando took a few pictures and Ethan and Mary went downstairs to eat while they waited. Mary ordered a salad and Ethan shrimp enchiladas.

Mary studied Ethan across the table. She liked his face without the beard. In it resided strength and confidence. She wondered exactly what he had been involved with to be able to do what he was doing, but decided she had plenty of time to ask him about that later.

"Why do you want to go to Edwardsville?" asked Mary as she took a bite of salad.

Ethan reached inside his jacket and pulled out a piece of paper and handed it to Mary. She looked down at an old picture of the Wildey Movie Theater from his hometown.

"I want to go there one last time," said Ethan. "It went out of business in the eighties, but the city has since renovated it and returned it to its old glory. I want to see one last movie while I have some popcorn, sip a soda, and munch some Milk Duds."

"But why, after all these years?" asked Mary.

"Because the best moments of my life were spent there," said Ethan. "And something is telling me that's where I need to be."

He looked at Mary and chuckled.

"I know, pretty pathetic when the time you spent at a movie theater from your childhood contains the best memories of your life."

"No, not really," said Mary, studying him. "We all have things that are special to us."

After they were finished, the waiter took their plates and told them Fernando was ready.

Upstairs, Fernando laid out their new birth certificates. When he handed them their driver's licenses, social security cards, and passports, he explained that while he'd kept their first names, it would be best if they traveled as a married couple, and he'd given them the same last name: Jones. He also turned over a flash drive.

"If you decide you still want to do Tyrannosaurus, notify me and insert this into any computer in their system," he said to Ethan. "On the screen it will show a file with letters in Microsoft Word. Invisible, behind it, is the Tyrannosaurus program. Once someone, anyone, logs in, it will break through the rest of security and then merrily go on its way. However, this takes time."

"How much time?" asked Ethan.

"You'll need to distract them for thirty minutes," replied Fernando.

While Ethan counted out forty thousand dollars, Mary imagined herself and Ethan in the balcony at the Wildey theater and wondered if he was a good kisser.

The Columbia River

According to the map, the quickest route to Edwardsville from Portland started by traveling east along the Columbia River on Interstate 84. After lunch, Ethan volunteered to drive while Mary rested. They made it as far as The Dalles, eighty-five miles away, when together they decided to find a place to stay for the night. Since they were traveling as a couple, Ethan, using cash, rented them a room with two queen beds at a Motel 666.

When they made it to the room, Ethan lay on the bed to take a quick nap before supper. An hour later, Ethan woke to find Mary sitting on the edge of the mattress, watching him.

"How do you feel?" asked Mary.

"Better," yawned Ethan as he stretched his arms. "You hungry?"

"Yes," answered Mary, patting him on the leg. "But I've already taken care of supper. I thought we could stay in tonight and watch the NBA playoffs on TV."

She glanced at her watch. "The game starts in five minutes."

"You've taken care of supper?" asked Ethan.

"It's a surprise."

Just then they heard a knock on the door.

"That must be our surprise now," said Mary.

She walked to the door and opened it. On the other side stood a pizza delivery lady, who handed Mary a large box and a two-liter bottle of diet Pepsi. Mary set it on the bed, took five dollars from her pocket and handed it to the delivery lady while she closed the door. Then, picking up the remote for the TV, she handed it to Ethan.

"Our game is on channel six."

After pouring Ethan a glass of soda, Mary sat on the bed next to him and opened the box. An NBA playoff game, a pizza, and a beautiful woman beside him. Ethan couldn't be any happier.

"Hope you like pepperoni," said Mary, handing him a piece.

Ethan munched a bite.

"Delicious!"

"What's your favorite pizza?" asked Ethan as he chewed.

"My favorite pizza," said Mary shyly, "involves pepperoni, with ... uh...lots of anchovies and jalapenos."

Ethan stared at Mary. Mary was taken off guard by Ethan's perplexed silence.

"What?"

"That's my favorite pizza too!" blurted Ethan. "I love anchovies and jalapenos."

A big smile stretched across Mary's face.

"Really?" asked Mary.

"Really," said Ethan, grinning back at her.

Mary couldn't stop smiling as she ate.

Ethan took another bite. Suddenly a thought entered his mind.

"You gave the driver a five-dollar tip," said Ethan as he chewed.

"Yeah," said Mary. "What about it? Too much?"

"No. That's not what I'm thinking," replied Ethan. "How did you pay for the pizza bill?"

"Oh, I gave them your credit card over the phone," said Mary. "I hope you don't mind. I maxed out mine months ago."

Ethan thought for a few seconds.

"Oh shit," said Ethan in a frenzy. "Get all our stuff and the pizza into the car."

"Why?" asked a confused Mary.

"Trust me," said Ethan. "Just do it right away. I'll be back."

Ethan ran out the door and around the building to the hotel front desk.

"Do you have a road map of the United States?" asked Ethan.

The desk clerk picked up a box under the desk and shifted through it until he found a map and handed it to Ethan.

Ethan pointed to a can of pens.

"Can I borrow your yellow highlighter?"

"Sure," said the clerk and Ethan plucked it from the can.

When he returned to the motel room, Mary had everything in the car. Ethan spread the map on the bed. Then taking a highlighter, he quickly drew a route on the map from The Dalles north into Canada, and around the Great Lakes, ending in Montreal. Carefully refolding the map, Ethan dropped it on the floor next to an end table.

"Let's go," said Ethan.

Mary confused, stood still.

"We need to go now," repeated Ethan with emphasis.

Taking Mary's hand, Ethan led her out the door.

Ethan drove the car out the parking lot, and just as they got a hundred yards onto the main road, a police car zoomed past them on the way to the motel. Taking the on-ramp to I-84 West, Ethan drove the car back towards Portland.

"What was that about?" asked Mary. "How did the cops know where we were at?"

"The pizza," said Ethan. "They were probably tracking my credit cards, and the pizza joint told them where they delivered the pizza. We can't use our credit cards anymore. If you need money, I'll give you cash."

"Oh shit," said Mary. "I almost got us caught."

"Do you have a personal cell phone?" asked Ethan, watching the road and scrutinizing the rearview mirror.

"No. Just the throwaway Fernando gave us," said Mary. "I knew better and left my own at my house."

"Good," said Ethan.

"Where are we going?" asked Mary, looking down the road.

"The map I *accidentally* left is a red herring," replied Ethan. "Hopefully, they'll be looking for us along the route that I drew. Meanwhile, we're going to head in the opposite direction and take the long way around the country. Tomorrow we'll ditch the car and get another."

Ethan looked at Mary's jeans and flannel top.

"In the meantime, we're going to have to blend in."

"What do you mean by blend in?" asked Mary.

"Do you like to shop?" Ethan asked.

"Well...uh...yeah," said Mary.

"Good," responded Ethan. "Let's get you into some other clothes. On the positive side," he added, "since we're heading south, I might as well feed the dinosaur in Anaheim. Maybe that's what I'm supposed to do. Maybe someone's guiding me in that direction."

"You mean Operation Tyrannosaurus?" asked Mary.

Ethan felt a sudden twinge of pain and grimaced as he rubbed his abdomen.

"What's the matter?" asked a concerned Mary.

"I have reflux disease," said Ethan, taking short, shallow breaths. "Heartburn has kicked in. Probably from the pizza."

He pointed to his messenger bag.

"Inside my bag are lozenges in a blister pack. Could you get me one?"

Mary opened the bag and in the dark, she quickly felt around what were obviously bundles of cash, until she found the blister pack. Popping out a lozenge, she handed it to Ethan and he sucked on it. A minute later, Ethan felt better and Mary, relieved, relaxed.

When he reached Portland, Ethan took the back roads and cut across to the coast using Highway 26. In Cannon Beach he used his new Ethan Jones driver's license to rent a nice room at the Brazen Hussy Hotel on the bottom floor with a patio that opened up onto the beach, just in case they needed a quick exit.

While Mary took a shower, Ethan strolled down the block to another hotel and exchanged license plates with a Cadillac. Mary and Ethan were both bushed when he returned, and they went to sleep almost immediately.

Chapter 2

The Watcher

June 3rd, 6 a.m.
Cannon Beach, Oregon

Nestled in a forest of tall coniferous trees, Cannon Beach is a northwest Oregon community located along a narrow strip of land that extends three miles down the coast between Highway 101 and the Pacific Ocean. Inside the town boundaries reside numerous hotels, restaurants, and boutique shops. However, Cannon Beach's main draw is the romantic atmosphere that floats through the air in the hotel rooms, streets, and on the beach. Rain or shine, everywhere you look, you see couples holding hands, celebrating anniversaries, birthdays, made-up special occasions, or just vacationing with their husband, wife, boyfriend, girlfriend, or somebody else's wayward spouse.

Halfway down the beach, Haystack Rock, a 235-foot ancient monolith, juts out of the ocean, majestically dominating its surroundings, like a king of old holding court. During low tide, the young and the not-so-young alike are drawn to its tidal pools, which are teeming with starfish, and the outcrops that provide refuge to flocks of puffins, not realizing that the rock is alive and watching them.

Watching the watcher, a hundred yards down the beach in the early dawn light, Ethan sat in the sand just outside their hotel room with a blanket covering his bare shoulders. Looking upward, he wondered if Haystack Rock thought about how this gift of life below it, so powerful in its love, could also be so devastating in its darkness. He inhaled a breath of cool morning ocean air into his lungs and, closing his eyes, sighed deeply. Then, reaching into his pocket, he popped another lozenge from a packet and sucked on it while he watched the fog delicately dance around the crest of Haystack Rock like an ethereal crown. The colors of the world, though dull in the overcast morning light, seemed bright and alive everywhere Ethan looked, and the sound of the ocean and the wind played like a symphony upon his ears.

Meanwhile, inside their room, Mary woke and her eyes searched for Ethan on his bed. Not finding him there, she sat up and looked around. She spotted him sitting outside, looking lonely, but at peace to her.

Pulling her pants on over her underwear, Mary slipped into her shoes, opened the patio door and stepped outside with a blanket. When she reached Ethan, she sat beside him and pulled the blanket over her.

"What are you doing out here?" asked Mary.

Ethan looked upwards at the clouds breaking apart in the sky.

"Just enjoying the dawn," he said with a sigh. "If one lives a long life like you and I have, you take the mornings for granted. You forget how wonderful they are. It's like everything is brand new. All the mistakes that you made the day before, or the day before that, are wiped clean, forgiven, and you get another bite at the apple. Sunsets are sad and signal an end, but dawn, now that's... a new beginning."

Ethan inhaled another deep, refreshing breath into his lungs, as if he were being baptized by the sin-forgiving air, and exhaled as Mary watched. Ethan fascinated Mary. He wasn't like other men she had known. He didn't seem to take aging as a curse to be mourned. Instead, he seemed to be enjoying, even celebrating, the experience. But something worried Mary.

"You know, eventually, they're going to catch up with us," said Mary, staring at the beach. "Somehow, we'll slip up, or someone will see a bulletin on TV, or a cop will spot us and that will be the end of it."

"Then we can't slip up," advised Ethan.

He looked at Mary.

"How about making an agreement between us. First, if one of us gets caught, the other one will come to the rescue."

Mary nodded. Not sure how she would do it, she agreed anyway.

"Ok."

"Second," said Ethan, "as long as we're together, we'll live our lives unafraid of being caught."

Mary liked that.

"Ok."

"And third," said Ethan. "I like you, and with the time we have left on this Earth, let's have some fun together."

Mary turned to Ethan and smiled.

"Where do you want to start?"

"I know a local restaurant called the Lazy Susan where we can have a great breakfast," said Ethan. "Then, let's do a little car shopping in Newport and find you some clothes."

Mary smiled.

"It's beautiful," she said, looking at Haystack Rock. "Would you believe I've never been down the Oregon coast?"

"Never?" repeated an incredulous Ethan.

Mary shook her head.

"Well then," Ethan said. "You've found the right tour guide."

9:15 a.m. San Diego, California

Tall, willowy Erika Barton strolled into Starbucks. Her ebony black hair swung back and forth on her shoulders, while her brown eyes smiled at everyone she passed. At the counter, she ordered a triple tall Americano and a cherry croissant, and used her phone to pay. Sitting by a window on what had turned into a beautiful San Diego morning, Erika wanted to enjoy the exquisite weather while she did research for the novel she was writing.

Erika had worked with computers since receiving one as a present on her eighth birthday, and had been known early on in her life as a master hacker and a child prodigy. Just after she graduated from high school, she formed her own company, bankrolled by her grandmother, to assist other companies in upgrading their online security. But while she had grown rich during the last ten years, she had also outgrown her fascination with computers and electronic devices. Gradually, they had turned into mere tools, not unlike a wrench, or a pair of scissors. Now at twenty-eight, Erika wanted more out of life. She wanted to write and make up shit that people enjoyed and she wanted to sell her company and move on.

Erika set her laptop on the table and opened it up. After entering her passcode, her computer automatically interfaced with the Starbucks network. As her email accounts updated, Erika took a bite of croissant and a sip of coffee, while she dreamily gazed out the window at the golden hills in the distance. Erika giggled because... she was in love.

Several days earlier, Erika had met an artist named Joanna at an exhibition. She liked that Joanna had no interest in computers, but more importantly, Erika liked the way Joanna's eyes gleamed whenever she looked at her. They had a date that evening for dinner. Erika's mind wandered as she thought about Joanna's smile and the sexy way she spoke to her. Just then, she noticed the small red light flashing on an icon in the upper right-hand corner of her computer desktop.

"Oh shit," she muttered.

Meanwhile, on the Oregon Coast

Ethan and Mary sat on the beach a few minutes longer and silently watched as dawn rolled over the wooded hills behind Cannon Beach to illuminate the rocky sentinel observing them down the beach. Finally, Ethan rose to his feet and held out his hand to Mary to help her up. After Mary had finished in the bathroom and dressed, it was Ethan's turn. When she heard the water turn on and the shower door close, curiosity overcame Mary and she quietly cracked open the bathroom door to peek in.

Through the steam in the bathroom, Mary admired Ethan's naked, seventy-year-old but still muscular body from behind. Unlike her two former overweight husbands, he obviously took good care of himself. Though he did look a little gaunt and bit pale, she wrote it off as the stress of the last several days. Mary started to wonder... but then Ethan, almost as if he were reading her mind, turned to soap himself and she looked downward and wondered no more. Mary smiled and nodding her head in approval, she quietly closed the door. Outside, she cupped her breasts through the material of her flannel shirt and bounced them while she confirmed to herself that they still had their persuasive power. Then, looking around the room, she remembered that in her haste to leave, she had forgotten to pack a suitcase. She would need a change or two of clothing—something sexy and alluring that would beckon to Ethan's *better angels.*

After eating breakfast at the Lazy Susan, Ethan and Mary headed south on HWY 101. Ethan wanted to drive. He had something special that he wanted to show Mary.

The road south from Cannon Beach began by tunneling through a thick forest of deciduous trees. By the time Ethan and Mary had reached Arcadia Beach several miles further on, the forest had transitioned into tall stands of fir and pine trees, dotted with a heavy undergrowth of elderberry bushes sporting large clumps of bright red berries. As the road curved and wound up and down, the hilly coastline teased Mary with glimpses of the Pacific Ocean on her right until, after passing Oswald West State Park, the road headed upward towards the sky to the Neahkahnie Mountain Overlook.

Ethan pulled over into a parking area at the top.

"Come on," he said. "I have something I want to show you."

They got out of the car and, as they walked to a short stone wall, Mary gasped. The sun had cleared away the clouds, and from the overlook 500 feet up, they could see twenty-plus miles of coastline in the distance. Looking below Mary saw five miles of beach hugging the town of Manzanita. To her right rippled the endless blue of the Pacific Ocean.

Mary grasped Ethan's hand.

"This is so beautiful," said Mary, smiling up at Ethan. "Thank you for showing it to me."

Ethan looked down at the hand holding his. The warmth of Mary's grip felt good. Letting go, he reached his arm around Mary's waist. Mary leaned against Ethan as she gazed at the horizon. Seconds later, a cold breeze blew across the parking lot and Ethan felt Mary shiver. She turned to hug him. Closing her eyes Mary sighed into Ethan's warm chest while her fingers caressed his back.

"Mary," said Ethan, having second thoughts. "Maybe we shouldn't..."

Mary, anticipating Ethan's defenses, kneaded her fingers deeper into his back.

Ethan stopped talking and enjoyed her touch.

"How does that feel?" asked Mary.

Something deep within Ethan surrendered, and fifty years of being on guard slipped away in that moment as he molded Mary firmly against himself.

"Good," he replied.

Lizard Valley Retirement Village, San Diego

As Erika drove through the gate to her grandmother's retirement community, she thought about what she was doing. Ten years earlier, when she had bankrolled Erika's company, her grandmother's only request in return, besides paying her back, was for her granddaughter to constantly monitor the web for any mention of a man named Daniel Rickman and locate him. When Clara later suggested Erika use facial recognition software using pictures she had of him, because Rickman probably wasn't his real name, Erika instantly became suspicious.

When Erika began the search, she felt relieved when she found nothing, but still she had concerns. Modern facial recognition software had the ability to analyze through a person's age and disguise to determine who they were using only a few characteristics. This immediately signaled one thing to Erika—governmental agencies. Only a select few had the ability of embedding photographs online to the point of preventing recognition and foiling facial software. Also, the simple fact that he was a ghost in the digital age sent up more red flags telling her not to go any further. But still, her grandmother *had* bankrolled her company, so Erika's computer continued the search over the years, albeit on automatic.

Earlier that day, when the man she had been searching for popped up with an Oregon State driver's license entered into the system under the name of Ethan Jones, Erika cross-referenced last names and databases, and came up with something interesting. Just a few minutes later, someone the same age had been entered into the Oregon DMV system at the same location under the name of Mary Jones. It seemed like too much of a coincidence. Erika wondered if this man was an old flame of her grandmother's.

"If so," mused Erika, "she was going to be disappointed."

Searching further, Erika found a registration and checkout for Ethan at the Brazen Hussy Hotel in Cannon Beach using his Oregon ID. From the registration, she also had the make and model of the car he drove. Since he had requested two key cards, she also knew he probably wasn't traveling alone.

However, all this was just too strange for Erika—a probable government ghost suddenly appearing out of nowhere. Erika wanted nothing more to do with it. But every time she debated not telling her grandmother, she remembered her promise and kept driving.

~

As tall and thin as her granddaughter, at sixty-four, Clara Barton generously participated in her retirement community. Every day at lunch, she helped deliver meals to those no longer able to fix them for themselves. In the morning and afternoon, she checked in on her neighbors to see that they were ok and she made sure they always had fresh flowers. Clara waited for her granddaughter in her garden when she arrived.

"So, what do you have for me?" asked an anxious Clara in a heavy Russian accent as she motioned to some chairs around a patio table. Erika sat and looked at Clara.

"Is this man an old flame?" asked Erika scrutinizing her grandmother to see her reaction.

Clara hesitated for a few seconds and then shook her head. But then...

"Uh...maybe."

"That's not very convincing," said Erika. She rounded her hand and stroked her finger in and out like a piston.

"Did you two ever...?"

"Why do young people nowadays always have to be so graphic?" grumbled Clara.

"You didn't answer my question," said Erika sternly.

"Ok, we fucked!" exclaimed an annoyed Clara. "A lot! And," she added sarcastically, "in as many positions as we could, like two horny rabbits. But the fact that we fucked is not why I'm looking for him!"

"Why then?" asked Erika.

Clara leaned forward, and taking her granddaughter's hand in hers, she smiled into her eyes.

"Because my dear," confided Clara. "He's my true love."

Chapter 3

Pink Elephants and Red Pilots

Highway 101, Oregon

Ethan drove because he wanted Mary to appreciate the countryside of coastal Oregon. At least that's what he told her. While beautiful scenery treated the eyes around every turn, in reality, Ethan didn't want Mary distracted on a narrow, unfamiliar highway that curved along cliffs with few guard rails. Besides, this time of year, numerous cross-country bicyclists peddled along the road, paying little attention to the cars whizzing past them. It would not be good for the two of them to be picked up by the police because Mary cleared a couple of bikers off the highway and into the ocean while she tried to glimpse a lighthouse.

Mary didn't mind. She enjoyed watching Ethan drive as much as she enjoyed the scenery. She appreciated Ethan's confidence, and, how at the right moments he knew how to make her laugh. She noticed that he always seemed to have his head on a swivel, searching, scrutinizing, watching out for her, for them. She also noted the way he looked outwardly at the world around him. As if everything appeared new and wondrous, something to be cherished and appreciated. And she especially liked the way he gazed at her, with that goofy grin of his, when he thought she wasn't looking.

Ethan, conflicted, couldn't believe his luck at running into Mary, and he wondered about it. Through his years of training and experience, he had learned not to believe in coincidences or convenient facts. He turned to gaze at her.

"But there she is," his brain said.

Ethan decided at that moment, for once in his life, not to question fate, though he knew there were things he should tell her about himself. His heart struggled in a major battle with his conscience, while strange, giddy feelings that he had long forgotten bubbled inside of him.

Past Manzanita, the road curved gently along the coast. When it reached Tillamook, it took a thirty-mile jaunt into the farmlands of the countryside before intercepting the coast again at Lincoln city. Past the tourist-overrun beaches of Lincoln City, the coastline became craggy, strewn with lesser minions of the sentinel of Cannon Beach, and crowded with walls of driftwood that had washed ashore like the bleached bones of long leviathans.

Depoe Bay, a small community located approximately halfway between Lincoln City and Newport, was built on a fortress of ancient lava rock. The city boasted two things: being the whale-watching capital of the world, only disputed by Iceland and Australia, and having the world's smallest harbor. At only five acres, with a thirty-foot entryway conveniently carved out of the rock by nature, that claim was not disputed. It was also one of the few places left where you were required to park at an angle on the street. The town's most-important industry by far was tourism, and along the main thoroughfare resided numerous shops designed to attract only the most discriminating refrigerator magnet and keychain collectors.

As Ethan drove through Depoe Bay, he spotted a shop with a parking space in front and quickly pulled in.

"Why are we stopping?" asked a puzzled Mary.

Grinning like a little kid, Ethan pointed to the sign in front of the car.

"Ice cream."

Mary frowned.

"I don't know," she said, looking down. "It's a little early in the day and ice cream's not very good for my figure."

"Hell Mary. We're seventy years old," responded Ethan jovially. "What have we got to lose?"

Chuckling, Ethan wagged a friendly finger at Mary while he studied her body. "I remind you that you also promised we were going to make this escape fun," said Ethan. "Besides, I think you have a wonderful figure that a few ounces of ice cream couldn't possibly hurt."

"Ice cream, hmmm," she said enjoying the compliment while envisioning something a little more touchy-feely regarding fun. But, she decided, looking at Ethan, if he wanted, they could start with ice cream.

"Ok," said Mary. "You've convinced me."

They got out of the car and walked inside the fragrant establishment, holding hands while Mary glanced at Ethan. Inside, Mary pointed at the menu whiteboard.

"I haven't had a banana split since high school," said Mary. "Would you like to share one with me?"

"Sure," replied Ethan, and he ordered a banana split from the skinny blonde woman in her early twenties standing behind the counter. They sat at a nearby table, and a few minutes later the woman brought the banana split to them, along with two long spoons. The young lady scrutinized them curiously and, for a reason she couldn't explain, she impulsively asked...

"Are you staying in the area for a while? Or are you just passing through?"

"I think we could stay a few days," said Ethan, gazing at Mary. "What do you think?"

"Yes, a few days." Mary nodded as she savored both Ethan and a spoonful of vanilla ice cream sweetly laced with chocolate and caramel.

"My uncle has a really nice vacation house that you can rent for the next several days; it's on the coast just north of Newport," said the girl. "His reservation this morning canceled on him at the last minute and I know he could use the business. It's on a cliff overlooking the ocean. Big picture windows. Terrific views of the Pacific. Large wood fireplace. He calls the place Camelot. Oh," she added, "and a hot tub. Believe me. You two will love it." She smiled. "Only problem is that it only has one bed if there's anyone traveling with you."

Before Ethan could say anything, Mary jumped in.

"That's not a problem," said Mary. "We'll take it."

Ethan, surprised, looked at Mary.

"Good," said the girl. "I'll call my uncle. What time should I say you're going to be there?"

Ethan glanced at his watch.

"It's ten now, and we have a few things to do, so how about..."

Ethan looked at Mary. "Five o'clock?"

Mary nodded and looked upward.

"What's your name?" Mary asked.

The girl held out her hand.

"Kathy. Kathy Hugmeister, but my friends call me Kat." She pointed behind the counter at the girl who had just walked in from the back.

"That's my identical twin sister Kit," Kat said, grinning. "We're known as the Kit-Kat twins."

"Good to meet you, Kat," said Mary. "I'm Mary, and this handsome fellow is Ethan."

Ethan shook her hand. Customers walked in and Kat excused herself to help her sister behind the counter.

"I'll call my uncle and arrange the reservation. I'll get you the address and phone number before you leave," said Kat as she left.

Ethan watched her walk away and then turned towards Mary.

"I'm a little surprised," said Ethan.

"Why?" asked Mary slyly. "We are traveling as husband and wife. It would look a little suspicious if we said we had to have separate beds."

Ethan thought a moment.

"Hmmm," he murmured. "I guess you're right. It might blow our cover."

"And I'll bet you're good under the covers," she whispered very softly to herself.

The outright intense randiness she felt, especially between her legs, surprised Mary. She had been sexually excited in her life, but never to the point where she wanted to tear someone's clothes off them.

Ethan took a bite of ice cream and closed his eyes, so he could savor it without distractions.

"I'm glad you suggested a banana split," he said. "I haven't had one of these since high school."

"Me neither," said Mary, as she imagined Ethan without his shirt on.

Mary scooped up a spoonful of banana and caramel. "Keep your eyes closed," she whispered. "And open your mouth."

Ethan, did as instructed, while Mary held the spoon to his lips.

"Now slowly," said Mary, "slide that onto your tongue."

Mary watched as Ethan reached out his tongue and carefully slid the creamy sweetness into his mouth, while she caressed an erect nipple through her flannel shirt with her free hand.

Ethan opened his eyes and smiling at Mary, found himself inhaling a deep appreciative breath of air into his lungs.

"So," said Ethan. "There are several new car dealerships in Newport. What do you feel like driving?"

An hour later, an excited, eager-to-car-shop Mary watched as Ethan drove past Gloria Faith Honda on Highway 101 in Newport.

"Hey, I thought that's where we were going?" said Mary.

"No. Not yet," replied Ethan as he put on his signal to turn left. "First, we need to ditch this car."

"Can't we just leave it on a side street somewhere?" asked Mary.

Ethan shook his head. "After a few days a cop will figure it is abandoned and run the plates or VIN number," he said, watching for an opening in the traffic. "And then there goes our red herring ruse. They'll know we're in the area."

Spotting a gap in the traffic, Ethan quickly pulled into the parking lot of Leave-It-and-Forget-It Storage. He turned to Mary.

"Now here's how we're going to do it," said Ethan. "You're going to store your car. Cops won't look for it here. Use your Mary Jones name and, when you fill out the registration, use Fernando's address in Portland in case they have address confirmation software."

"Oh, and—" added Ethan, "they might ask you about insurance while it's being stored. Tell them USAA."

"What do I do if I'm asked why I'm storing it?" said Mary.

"They probably won't care, but just in case they do, change the subject or give him a compliment," said Ethan. "He'll forget about the original question and, in his mind, he won't remember that you didn't answer the question. Worst-case scenario, make something up or just flirt with him."

Ethan handed Mary $2000.

"Store it for a year."

Mary stuffed the money in her front jean pocket, along with her new driver's license, and got out of the car. Walking to the business office door she opened it. Standing behind the inside counter stood a stout woman in her fifties with a purple crew cut, sporting around a dozen piercings on her face. She greeted Mary.

Mary turned to look at Ethan sitting in the car and then back at the storage manager while she hoped she didn't have to flirt.

Ten minutes later, Mary emerged from the office holding paperwork and the code to the electronic lock on the fence surrounding the complex.

"How'd it go?" asked Ethan as Mary sat next to him in the car.

"Fine," said Mary sarcastically. "I think I have a date later."

"A date?" said Ethan a little puzzled.

"Yeah," said Mary. "Lizzie Borden, the lady watching us from inside with all the piercings..."

Mary turned and noticed Lizzie observing them from the office window. Mary waved.

"...told me she got off at five and that she would be at the Pink Elephant Bar downtown if I was interested. I can only guess what kind of bar the Pink Elephant is!"

"So," said Ethan, being very careful not to laugh. "Are you interested?"

Mary turned and self-righteously punched Ethan in his upper arm with her fist. Ethan winced a bit while Mary turned and pointed.

"We're in space five three two."

Meanwhile, from the office window, Lizzie watched Mary and Ethan with great interest.

"Hmmm," she wondered aloud. "They aren't getting along. Maybe the cutie will be at the Pink Elephant tonight."

Lizzie felt lazy. She had the next week off and she didn't feel like entering shit into the computer.

"Besides," she said, "the cutie might not want to store her car for long if she breaks up with him and comes to the Pink Elephant tonight."

She threw the paperwork on a growing pile to be entered the next day, when her co-worker showed up.

Lizard Valley Retirement Village, San Diego

"Your true love?" said Erika. "That's so sweet."

But then she thought a moment.

"Hey, wait a minute," said Erika, leaning across the patio table.

"This guy obviously is, or was, a government spook. How the hell did you get involved with him?"

"We met at an outdoor café in Vienna, in the spring, twenty years ago," recalled Clara as she looked into the distance. "Your grandfather had died the year before, and I had just taken over his import/export business. I was alone, lonely and he was beautiful, strong, confident. He told me he was a teacher on sabbatical. I believed him. The affair lasted almost three months. Then one day he was gone, and I never saw him again."

"Did you look for him?" asked Erika.

"For several years," replied Clara. "But found nothing. I contacted the school he said he was on sabbatical from. They did have a Daniel Rickman on sabbatical, but his picture didn't match. Finally, I gave up and stopped looking."

A big smile rolled across her face.

"That is, until today."

Erika remained cautious.

"He's a government agent, Grandma," said Erika. "It might be dangerous to contact him."

"Nonsense," scoffed Clara. "He's several years older than me. He's probably retired by now and hardly dangerous. At least not to me."

"What if he's with someone now?"

"Then, he can at least tell me why he left me alone in Vienna without even saying goodbye," said Clara. "He owes me that."

Clara reached out for her granddaughter's hand.

"Please, Erika," pleaded Clara. "Please help find this man. Help me get some closure."

Erika reluctantly nodded. "Ok, Grandma," she assured her. "I owe you. I'll help you find him. But if things start going south, we're getting out of there fast."

"Yes, we will," said Clara. "I promise."

Newport, Oregon

Using the key code, Ethan opened the gate and parked the car in the assigned space. Before throwing his backpack and messenger bag over his shoulder, he pulled out a lozenge and popped it in his mouth, along with a couple of pills while Mary watched him.

"Your reflux acting up again?"

Ethan nodded as he groaned and felt his stomach.

"What are the pills for?" asked Mary.

"They're for nausea," said Ethan. "Sometimes the reflux and the lozenge together make me sick."

He leaned against the car.

"I just need a moment to rest."

A few minutes later, Ethan felt better, and they started walking towards Gloria Faith Honda a block away on their side of Highway 101. When they arrived, Mary stopped at the showroom door and pointed at a decal on the door.

"Oh no," she groaned. "This place is owned by fish people."

"Fish people?" asked Ethan.

"Yes, fucking fish people!" replied an irate Mary, waving her arms. "Gloria Faith. I should have known, evangelical fucking Christians. I'm way too familiar with them and their hypocrisy. Fuck them. I don't want to go in there. Just look at the doofus fucked-up misogynistic president they saddled us with. They have absolutely no moral credibility. None!"

"Well, we have two choices," said Ethan. "Either we go in and buy a car, or we hike two miles across the bridge to the Toyota dealership."

"Please Mary," pleaded Ethan. "You'd be surprised how quickly morality goes out the window when it comes to making us a deal on a car."

Mary looked at a pale Ethan. Reaching to his hair, she pushed a few strands behind his ear as she smiled sweetly at him.

"Ok," she said, "but let's at least have some fun with these people."

Ethan smiled and nodded. "Duly noted," he said with a flair of his arm as he opened the door for her. "Lead on, fair maiden, to the promised land."

As they entered the showroom, a slim young African-American salesman, bald with a long Fu Manchu mustache, immediately spotted Mary and Ethan, and quickly jogged across the room to intercept the prospective customers before any other salesperson might see them. He held out his hand. "Hi, my name is Barry, Barry Height. Interested in a new car?"

Mary threw her arms into the air.

"Hallelujah, thank the Lord, a salesperson," Mary cried out, while Barry shook Mary's energetic hand. "Praise the Lord!"

"Can I help you?" asked Barry.

"Yes, but first we need to pray," scolded Mary.

She took Barry's hand in her left and Ethan's in her right.

"Bow your heads," ordered Mary.

Barry looked at Mary for a moment and then bowed his head, along with Ethan. Mary squeezed their hands tight and very sincerely and loudly...

"Our Father who art in heaven, hallowed be thy name. Thy kingdom come, thy car deals be done, on Earth as it is in heaven. Give us this day a great deal; and forgive us our turn signals, as we forgive those who forget to use their turn signals against us; and blessed be this salesman, so that he may lead us to a new car with a special leather option package and a sunroof. Amen.

"Oh, and Lord, before I forget," she added, "I'm not getting any younger. A seat warmer for my tush would be nice too. Amen again."

Mary let go of their hands and with a big maniacal grin on her face looked at Barry while Ethan tried very, very hard not to laugh.

"So, what do you have for us?"

"That depends," said Barry. "What are you looking for?"

"Something big and beautiful," exclaimed Mary, waving her

hands. "Something our Father in Heaven would buy for his son as a welcome home present the second time he walks the Earth."

She held out her hands, palms up, and looked towards the ceiling.

"Something Ethan and I could drive to the Rapture in!" Mary passionately exclaimed.

"Oh, and also..." she continued in a whisper, "something large enough in the back for my husband and I to fornicate in."

Ethan bit his lip, and let Mary do all the talking, afraid to say anything lest he roll on the floor laughing.

Barry looked around the showroom and pointed to a red Honda Pilot SUV at the side, staring majestically at them. He walked them over and around the Pilot.

"This," he said, "has everything Jesus could ever want. Special touring package with internet hookup, leather seats, seat warmer, and..." he added, "...a sunroof worthy of our Father in Heaven himself."

"Let's see the back," said Mary.

Barry walked to the trunk and opened it. He motioned inside.

"It's roomy and has the full package, complete with speakers for music, and a DVD player," said Barry. "Large enough for any activity you desire."

Mary smiled and turned towards Ethan.

"Honey, what do you think?" asked Mary. She wiggled a little. "Would you like to experience the Rapture in there with me? It looks large enough for you to stretch out your legs."

Mary pointed.

"And look! It has electrical plugins for all our blessed toys. We can use the electric forgiveness whip!"

Ethan peered inward.

"I don't know," he said. "It looks a little hard on the knees."

Barry smelled opportunity.

"They custom-make a four-inch air-mattress for these cars now that blows up using the electrical outlets," said Barry. "If you decide you want this car, I'll throw in a mattress, along with a set of fitted silk sheets.

"And two sets of pillows," asked Mary.

"Two sets?" said Ethan.

"Yes," said Mary, "I want to be comfortable while you perform God's divine plan for man and wife."

"Oh."

"I intend to submit myself to God's will often," Mary said, nodding her head enthusiastically up and down.

Ethan walked over to the car's sticker and examined it.

"How quick can you have the paperwork done if we pay cash?" asked Ethan.

"We'd have to call your bank and have them put a hold on the funds from your check," said Barry. "So, maybe two hours."

"What if I handed you this amount in real money, and just between you and me, afterwards an extra two for you personally as a tip?" replied Ethan. "We're a little anxious to get on the road and fornicate a little."

Barry, excited, stared at Ethan while he thought of all the bills he could pay with the two thousand and his commission.

"Forty minutes. Tops!"

"The clock's running," said Ethan.

Barry rushed off to his office and Ethan turned to Mary.

"Did my little honey-bunny have fun?"

Mary wrapped her arms around Ethan and squeezed tight.

"What do you think?"

"I think you're the perfect partner for Operation Tyrannosaurus," said Ethan.

"Tyrannosaurus?" asked Mary.

"We'll talk about it later," said Ethan.

Half an hour later, Barry and Ethan stood in the manager's office counting out money, while Mary sat in the gleaming red Pilot in the parking lot, vrooom-vrooming behind the steering wheel, anxious to get going. As Ethan glanced out the window at Mary and smiled, one of the dealership mechanics, a mid-twenties six-foot-six menacing hulk of a man named Artie, peeked in.

"The mayor's car is done," said Artie, staring at the pile of cash on the table and then at Ethan.

"Good," said the manager. "I'll give her a call."

Artie thought a second.

"My wife's not doing too well," said Artie. "Can I have the rest of the day off? Pete says it's ok. All the work is covered."

"No problem," said the manager. "I hope your wife feels better."

Ethan turned around to the manager, who was signing some papers as Artie left.

"I'm kind of curious," said Ethan. "That fish sticker on the front door. Does it get you more business?"

The manager seemed confused.

"Fish sticker?" he said.

"Yeah, the evangelical Christian sticker on the front door," said Ethan.

The manager shook his head.

"A customer stuck that on our door as they left yesterday," said the manager. "We're a very secular business. Someone should have scraped it off this morning."

"But the name, Gloria Faith Honda..." said Ethan.

"Gloria Faith is the owner of the dealership," said the manager. "If you want to meet her, she also owns and manages the Pink Elephant Bar downtown."

Ethan looked out the window and laughed.

"Do me a favor and don't mention the sticker to my wife. I'll do it later."

Chapter 4

Christian Charity

Newport, Oregon

Mary drove across the Yaquina Bay Bridge and down the coast several miles, enjoying her new SUV toy, before Ethan reminded her that she also needed some new clothes. Turning around against traffic without, of course, using a turn signal, Mary headed back to Newport and Nye Beach.

Located a half-mile off Highway 101, one could easily miss Nye Beach. Bordered at one end by a shopping area featuring artsy shops, funky boutiques, and trendy restaurants, the beach, voted several times the most romantic spot to kiss on the Oregon Coast, was only a mile long. On any given day, one could smell fresh baked goods and watch couples holding hands while dining at any of the several outdoor cafés, as a refreshing sea breeze from the Pacific drifted between the shops. However, the streets were narrow and parking could sometimes be a problem.

Ethan guided Mary off Highway 101 at 3rd Street. When they reached the Nye Beach shopping area, they circled around until Mary finally found a deserted side street with no houses three blocks away and parked. After they got out and started walking, Mary stopped and turned around to admire her new Honda Pilot. Ethan had put the pink slip and registration in her name. No one had ever given her such a wonderful present. Euphoric, she reached down and gripped Ethan's warm hand tightly and, intoxicated with him, swung it as they headed towards Nye Beach. She intended to dress very deliciously for her man.

As they entered the Beach Drive turnaround, they came across Bettie Wage's Dress and Undergarment Boutique. Ethan balked when Mary started to pull him inside.

"Maybe I should just give you some money and take a walk while you're shopping," said Ethan.

Mary shook her head. "No. Un-ah." She smiled. "I want to model clothes for my amazing *husband*." She winked. "I need to know what you like."

Ethan looked at Mary happily gripping his arm and allowed her to guide him through the door. Inside, they were greeted by the owner, Bettie.

"Hello," said an effervescent Bettie. "What can I do for you today?"

Ethan motioned towards Mary with his hand.

"This beautiful woman lost all her clothes in a fire," announced Ethan. "She needs a new wardrobe."

Bettie lit up and looked at Mary.

"I think you'll like what I have to offer," said Bettie. "A lot of it I designed myself."

"Is there somewhere private where Ethan can sit so I can model for him?" asked Mary as she clutched Ethan's arm. "What he thinks matters a lot to me."

"Yes, of course," said Bettie, studying Ethan. "There's a chair and a couch by the dressing room in the back."

Bettie motioned for Ethan and Mary to follow her. After Mary made sure Ethan sat comfortably on the couch, she turned to Bettie "Where would you like to start?" asked Bettie.

Mary whispered in her ear and Bettie smiled.

While Mary stripped in the dressing room, Bettie brought her some clothes and hung them inside before leaving to help another customer who she had just heard come in. A few minutes later, the curtain to the dressing room opened and Mary, wearing only a skimpy pair of sheer pink panties and a matching lacy push-up bra, emerged. Ethan gulped.

"So, what do you think?" grinned Mary, posing provocatively in front of him. "Do you like it?"

Ethan stared at Mary, wondering what to say. He wondered, at first, if he should leave, but found himself paralyzed by her beauty and sexuality, and unwilling to move away. Sexual feelings were very familiar to Ethan—he had harnessed them to do his job all his life, but this giddy euphoric feeling racing through his body electrified him. However, despite his attraction, a small part of Ethan still headed for his inner redoubt to make a last stand.

"Mary, what are you doing?" asked Ethan cautiously.

Mary strolled to Ethan and, wrapping her arms around his neck, sat on his lap. Then leaning down, she nibbled the top of Ethan's ear and savored feeling him shiver against her.

"I thought that was obvious," whispered Mary warmly into his ear. "I'm seducing you."

"What if I don't want to be seduced?" sighed Ethan as her lips magically started breaking down his defenses.

Mary gently kissed the side of his forehead and lingered with her tongue.

"The time for you to say *no* has come and gone," said Mary wetly.

She wiggled her bottom and felt him grow against her.

"Time for you to surrender to the inevitable," she breathed. "Before you go to sleep tonight, you *will* be my lover!"

Ethan took a deep breath, looked at Mary and with only a little hesitation, let go of a lifetime of self-enforced, disciplined restraint.

Reaching downward, Ethan slowly drew his finger across the sensitive surface of Mary's outer thigh while he felt her tremble.

"Well, I guess," acknowledged Ethan slyly, "if that's the case, then I better start seducing you back."

"Yes, you should," giggled Mary as she hopped off his lap and scampered to the dressing room to try on something new.

Over the next several hours, Mary delightfully tried on one article of clothing after another. After Mary posed, Ethan would give her a yea or nay, and then find an excuse to lightly tease, touch, or stroke Mary before she headed back, a little more aroused, to the dressing room to try on something else.

Ethan noticed that Mary wasn't extravagant or overly frilly in her tastes. She liked simple, subtly alluring items, but leaned practical in her style. By the way she watched his eyes while he evaluated her clothes, he had the feeling she already knew what he was going to say before he said it.

Finally, Mary had enough clothes to fill a large suitcase and emerged from the dressing room wearing a colorful floral peasant blouse atop gray cotton pants and sandals. In front of Ethan, she unbuttoned the top three buttons of the blouse and spread the brocade, so he could see a hint of his future.

Meanwhile, Bettie gathered up Mary's purchases and gave Ethan a tally. After paying, there were too many boxes for them to carry at one time, so Ethan and Mary picked up a few and left to get the Pilot and bring it around to pick up the rest.

As Mary and Ethan approached the Pilot on the side street, Ethan noticed an old blue sedan parked a car-length behind them. Inside sat Artie, the mechanic from the dealership. Ethan walked to the rear of the Pilot and opened the trunk. As he set the boxes inside, he heard a car door open and close. Ethan counted the footsteps. Then suddenly he turned and while his left hand gripped the barrel of the gun Artie held, his right-hand slapped Artie's wrist, dislodging his hand. Before the surprised Artie could react, Ethan slammed him twice on the side of the head with the butt of the gun. Blood sprayed in the air while Mary screamed and Ethan smashed his boot against the side of Artie's knee. Artie's legs buckled from the pain and he fell to the ground, holding his bleeding head and shrieking knee. Ethan loomed over him and pointed the gun at his temple.

Panic-stricken, Mary stared at Artie bleeding.

"Mary!" barked Ethan to get her attention. "Go inside the car. In my pack you'll find a small hand towel!"

Hesitating for a second longer, Mary rushed to the backseat of the car. Her shaking hands searched inside his pack, and she ran back to Ethan.

While he held the gun on the groaning Artie, Ethan, with his free hand, took the towel from Mary and dropped it on him. Artie held the towel it to his bleeding face.

"Ok," shouted Ethan, "why the FUCK were you trying to rob us? You're obviously just a God damn amateur! I could never have done that to a professional!"

Artie looked up through the blood in his eyes.

"Please mister," he pleaded, "don't hurt me anymore."

Ethan put the barrel to Artie's head and twisted it against his temple.

"Why were you trying to rob us?" he snarled. "Answer me!"

"I needed the money," choked Artie.

"What for?" asked Ethan.

"My wife had a heart operation two months ago," gritted Artie through the pain. "Our insurance only covered so much. We still owe fifty thousand."

"Why don't you just declare bankruptcy?" asked Ethan.

"She might need another operation next year," grimaced Artie, rolling on his side. "She can't work and right now, with all this debt, even with me working overtime, we haven't been able to afford all the medication she needs. We've had to start rationing. I'm scared I might lose her."

"Is your wife at home now?" growled Ethan.

"Yes," answered Artie.

Ethan turned to Mary still in shock.

"Mary!" barked Ethan to get her attention.

She looked at him and Ethan handed her his phone and turned back to Artie.

"Give her your home phone number!" said Ethan.

"Why?" asked a panicked Artie.

Ethan pointed the gun at him.

"Give her the phone number, or I'll blow your fucking brains out!"

Artie stuttered out the number.

"What's your last name?"

"Thompson."

"Now, Mary," said Ethan slowly. "I want you to call Ms. Thompson. Say you're the hospital. Ask how she's doing. Then confirm how much he owes and whether she's taking her medication in prescribed doses."

Mary hesitated.

"You can do it," assured Ethan, patting her on the shoulder.

Mary looked at Ethan, nodded, and tapped in the number. The phone rang and...

"Yes. Is this Ms. Thompson?" asked Mary cheerfully. "This is the hospital calling. We're just following up to make sure you're doing ok. You are. Good. We also just want to confirm the balance of what you think your remaining bill is, for our records. Ok, good; that matches up with what we have. One final thing we want to confirm. You are still taking all the medication that was prescribed for you in the recommended doses? ...Ok, thank you. Sorry to have bothered you. Have a nice day."

Mary turned to Ethan.

"He's telling the truth," said Mary. "And by the way, his wife hesitated when I asked about the medication; he's probably telling the truth about that too."

Ethan frowned downward at Artie.

"Are you going to kill me?" asked Artie.

Ethan shook his head.

"Three weeks ago, I might've," said Ethan. "You're just lucky I recognized you as the mechanic from the Honda dealership."

"But you were looking out the window," said Artie. "I didn't think you even saw me."

"I see everything," growled Ethan.

Ethan looked over at Mary watching him and then back down at Artie.

"Ok, this is what we are going to do," said Ethan. "I'm keeping the gun and you're going to go home, and every morning, when you look in the mirror and you see that nasty scar on your cheek, you're going to thank God for another day on this Earth. Then, you're going to cherish your wife and take care of her and be thankful to have someone to share that life with."

Ethan reached inside of his messenger bag and pulled out six packets of hundred-dollar bills and threw them on the ground in front of Artie.

"That should take care of your bills, plus extra for your wife's medications and to get you patched up," said Ethan.

Ethan walked away with Mary following him. Artie, still holding the cloth to his face, started to get up.

"But..."

Ethan turned.

"Don't fucking say anything!" growled Ethan pointing his finger at Artie. "Not one damn word! I'm still pissed off with you for endangering Mary!"

Ethan and Mary got in the car and drove away.

Artie stood, and bending over, picked up the six packets of cash. He looked at the red Pilot disappearing down the street, then at the money in his hands and back up the street.

"Thank you," whispered Artie.

Then the big guy fell to his knees and sobbed.

Lizard Valley Retirement Village, San Diego

"If anything else surfaces, I'll call you immediately," said Erika.

"Keep a light bag packed," warned Clara. "We might have to leave quickly."

Erika nodded and glanced at her watch. Clara noticed.

"What's your hurry?" asked Clara. "I thought maybe we could talk for a little while longer. You know, like we used to."

Erika hesitated for a moment, not wanting to tell her grandmother, but then decided to just be honest.

"I have a date tonight," said Erika, "and I need to go home and get cleaned up."

"What's his name?" asked Clara while Erika grimaced.

"Grandma, you know I don't date men."

Clara shook her head. "I keep hoping you'll abandon your sinful lifestyle and return to the light of the Lord. Back when I was in Russia, we had no gay people."

"Oh right," said Erika laughing sarcastically. "Isn't that the country where all the porno by law must involve at least one species of barnyard animal?"

Clara frowned at Erika. "Erika honey, please," she pleaded. "It's sinful, immoral, and perverted. The Reverend Jimmy Bob Swindle says, unless women like you repent, hellfire awaits you. I don't want you to have that to look forward to. I want to see you on the other side."

Ten years earlier, Clara had converted from Russian Orthodox to born-again evangelical Christian when she saw the Reverend Jimmy Bob Swindle on TV and then attended services at his Diamond Cathedral in Anaheim. His charismatic voice lifted Clara to a place that worried Erika, not to mention the thousands of dollars in seed offerings that she gave his Prosperity Ministry. Erika could not understand how the fifty-room mansion Jimmy Bob lived in, complete with private golf course and riding stable, not to mention the five private jets he owned, or the expensive vacations he took with his pink-haired wife, didn't give her grandmother something to think about.

Several years earlier, when the cops pulled him over and they found a kilo of cocaine in the trunk, the Reverend Jimmy Bob's lawyer managed to get all charges dropped on a search warrant technicality. Then, in grand style, Jimmy Bob revealed to his congregation on TV that he had merely borrowed the car from a friend, whom he couldn't legally mention because of slander laws; and that the hooker in the backseat wearing fishnet stockings and no underwear, well, he thought she was simply a hitchhiker, to whom, Jimmy Bob, out of Christian charity, had given a *ride*. Jimmy Bob then solemnly swore on the Bible that he had no idea she was a sinful lady of the night, and his congregation seemed willing to give him the benefit of the doubt on all charges. Afterwards, Jimmy Bob delivered a sermon on the sin of greed and the need to give seed money of thyself, especially to his Supernatural Seed of the Lord Prosperity Ministry. His parishioners, feeling guilty for having ever doubted him, contributed a record amount afterwards.

Erika kissed Clara's cheek.

"I'll call you as soon as I have something," said Erika, and she left.

Marina District, San Diego

Meanwhile across town, five-foot-six, short pink-on-blonde-haired, brown-eyed Joanna put the finishing touches on the painting she had been working on in her studio and stood back to examine it. All day, all she could think about was her date with Erika that evening. She hoped working might distract her. It didn't. Though she had only spent one evening with Erika...

"Love at first sight," mused Joanna. "It's so cliché."

But then she sighed, "and oh so wonderful..."

That evening, Erika had suggested taking her to the Wharf Seafood Restaurant nearby and Joanna wondered what to put on.

Should she wear her slinky black top or the tight blouse showing cleavage? Joanna decided on the slinky black top. It would go well with the pink French scarf that she liked to wear. Joanna glanced at the clock. Then in a moment of inspiration, she picked up her phone and speed-dialed Erika. Erika answered.

"Instead of going to the Wharf Restaurant, how about we have dinner at my place?" asked Joanna. "I can send out for Szechuan? ... Yes, I agree, bring a toothbrush."

Nye Beach

When Ethan and Mary returned to Bettie's, a parking space in the front had opened up and Ethan parked the Pilot. He looked at Mary in the passenger seat, still obviously shaken, staring straight ahead, deep in thought. Ethan shut off the engine.

"I need a few minutes alone," said Mary, still staring. "I'm going for a walk."

Mary opened the door and headed for the beach. Ethan watched her walk down the sidewalk towards the ocean.

After loading the remaining boxes, Ethan bought Mary a present in a nearby shop and had it gift wrapped. Outside, he waited ten more minutes and then headed towards the beach. He spotted Mary standing near the surf, watching the ocean. Walking up behind her, Ethan rested his hands on her shoulders and gently massaged. Mary sighed at his touch.

"Who are you?" asked an amazed Mary. "A complete stranger just tried to rob us and you gave him sixty thousand dollars."

"Are you worried about the money," said Ethan, "because—"

"No. It's not that," interrupted Mary.

"Are you afraid of me?" asked Ethan.

"Absolutely not," said Mary, shaking her head. "I just want to know why you did it."

Ethan leaned down and spoke into Mary's ear.

"A business's obligation to its stockholders is to maximize profits. When healthcare is a business, it means it must financially squeeze the most vulnerable people in society at their most vulnerable moments. People have the right to live. They shouldn't have to die or be impoverished because their job doesn't make as much money as the next person, or they can't work. He obviously needed the money more than us."

"I'm so proud of you," gushed Mary between tears.

She turned around to face Ethan and gazed curiously into his eyes.

"I've never had a man in my life that I could feel that way about," said Mary.

"I'm not that great," said Ethan, lightly stroking the outside of her shoulders.

Mary sighed. "Keep that up and we'll find out on the beach right now, whether that's true or not."

Ethan smiled devilishly into Mary's eyes.

"You know," said Ethan, "Nye Beach has been voted three times the best place to kiss on the Oregon Coast."

"Then cowboy, what the fuck are you waiting for?" said Mary, grinning.

"Nothing, I...uh..."

"Too much talking," said Mary, and grabbing Ethan, she kissed him.

Chapter 5

A Tale of Three Bedrooms

Fred Meyer Grocery Store,
Newport, Oregon

Ethan stopped the grocery cart and pointed at the shelf.

"Mary, could you hand me a bottle of General Tso sauce?" requested Ethan.

Mary turned towards the third shelf. Lined up together were four different brands. She reached for one.

"Is this the brand you want?" she asked.

Ethan moved closer to Mary and rested his hands on her hips, so he could have a closer look over her shoulder.

Mary sighed as his breath warmed her ear.

"No, not that one," he said as his fingers gently walked down her hips. "The one next to it."

Mary moved her hand to the next bottle.

"This one?" she grinned.

Ethan thought a second as his hands pulled her gently against him.

No," said Ethan. "I think the next one will do."

Mary reached for the bottle as she subtly massaged her bottom against his lower region, and it was Ethan's turn to sigh.

"Yes. That one."

He leaned down and kissed her neck as she handed the bottle over her shoulder to him.

"Thank you," said Ethan.

Mary turned around.

"I never knew grocery shopping could be so much fun," giggled Mary.

She looked at their cart full of groceries, clothes for Ethan, toiletries, and two suitcases.

"Is there anything else you think that we might need before we head to the house?" asked Mary.

"Just one thing," said Ethan. "Since we're not as young as we used to be..."

He rolled the cart to the next aisle and stopped in front of a shelf. Ethan looked around until he found what he was looking for. Kneeling down, he selected a box from the bottom shelf and handed it up to Mary. Mary read the box.

Astroglide

"Oh, you are definitely my hero," giggled Mary.

Marina District, San Diego

Erika pulled into a guest spot and parked. From her convertible, she scrutinized the old red brick warehouse, which had been converted into apartments and studios.

"Nice building," said Erika. "Great view of the marina."

She took a deep breath.

"Wonderful breeze."

Erika looked at the address Joanna had given her and then

upward at the third floor. On the roof, she could see small trees, plants, red and purple bougainvillea crawling up trellises.

Pushing a button on her BMW convertible's dashboard, Erika raised the top. As she got out, she slung her overnight bag over her shoulder and picked up a bouquet of flowers. At the side of the building protruded a small covered porch with a four-step stairway. When Erika reached the door, she pressed a buzzer. The buzzer buzzed back and the door clicked open. Erika walked to an old freight elevator inside and pressed three.

As the elevator slowly moved upwards, Erika suddenly wondered if she was doing the right thing. After all, she had just met Joanna. Her mind raced. Yes, Joanna was beautiful and they had chemistry... Suddenly, the elevator stopped and the doors opened. In front of her stood Joanna, wearing a short pink nightie.

Joanna smiled. "Are you hungry?" she asked lifting her arms as she ran her hands through her hair so Erika could get a good view.

"Famished," replied Erika, as she took Joanna's hand.

Lizard Valley Retirement Village, San Diego

Clara sat in the garden of her retirement community home and watched the sun sink slowly towards the horizon through distant red clouds while she fumed. On a small folding tray table beside her, stood a bottle of Stolichnaya Vodka and a crystal glass. She took a sip. Compared to other vodkas, it wasn't very good, but the taste of it did bring back memories. Good memories that had been tarnished and blackened when she found out the man who now called himself Ethan Jones had used her for three months while he patiently waited for her to slip up.

"Oh. He was a clever one," she whispered aloud. "He never asked me about Demetri or the business. He just made love, waited, and carefully listened. Then he took advantage of my trust."

Clara took another sip. She felt a little tipsy. In Southern California, she had grown unaccustomed to hard liquor, and instead had gotten used to drinking chardonnay. She remembered how Daniel loved German Riesling and how she would always have several bottles in the hotel refrigerator chilling for him. She remembered his kiss on her naked shoulders, his fingers twisting her nipples, his thrust, the fire that exploded within her, and she moaned. She missed him. She had never loved anyone else since him.

For years, Clara had imagined Daniel returning to her. He would tell her that he loved her. Ask her to forgive him. She would and they would run away and live the rest of their lives together. Clara took another sip as years of lonely resentment welled up inside her and she viciously threw the glass as hard as she could against a patio wall. The glass shattered.

"Just like my life," she said shaking her head. "Why did he have to be an operative and betray me like he did? Why couldn't he just love me like I loved him?"

Clara cried. She had wished him dead for years so she could rationalize why he hadn't returned to her. Now that she knew differently, it required her to do something. Something she didn't want to think about any further.

Her phone rang and wiping away her tears she answered it.

"Hi Clara, this is Rita," said the voice on the other end. "You ok? I heard some glass break."

"Just had a slight accident," grumbled Clara.

"Hey, listen, the girls are coming over next door," announced Rita "You want to join us and play dominos? I have lots and lots of chardonnay."

"Sure," replied Clara. "I could use a diversion."

475 Spass Drive

The address for the vacation house was easy to find, and when Ethan and Mary arrived on the secluded street, they were greeted by a patient and grateful Rex Arturus. His earlier reservation had been canceled and when he had tried to charge the couple's credit card for the late-cancelation fee, he found that it had been maxed out and wouldn't go through. Trying to find someone to rent a four-hundred-dollar-a-night house for three nights at the last minute was almost impossible. But then his nieces had miraculously found a solution. Rex made a mental note to thank them for their help in some special way.

After everyone introduced themselves, Rex showed them around. The house stood on top of a rocky cliff, with a long stairway that led down to the beach below. Inside, a stainless-steel kitchen gleamed, along with an oversized fireplace that dominated the small but roomy house. From the living room, an expansive view of the Pacific beckoned.

"This is wonderful," sighed Mary, looking out over the vast blue of the ocean in front of her. "Now, where's the bedroom?"

Rex showed them up a stairway to a bedroom with an even more unobstructed view of the ocean. Mary ignored the view and, sitting on the bed, she bounced and patted the space next to her.

"Ethan," invited Mary, "give it a try."

Ethan sat next to Mary and bounced a little.

"You're going to have to do better than that," warned Mary.

Smiling, Ethan bounced so hard that Mary, giggling, fell backwards onto the bed with Ethan on top of her. Ethan looked over at an amused Rex, still standing by the door.

"This will do," he said. "You take cash?"

Rex laughed. He liked watching children play.

"Of course."

Ethan paid Rex, and afterwards Rex helped Ethan and Mary bring their stuff in. Rex left, and while Ethan put away the groceries, Mary unpacked their clothes in the bedroom and hung them so they wouldn't wrinkle. After building a fire, Ethan went to work in the kitchen. One by one, he laid out the ingredients to cook a romantic Chinese dinner for Mary. He set a wok on the stove with a little sesame oil inside and finally, he had everything ready to make his special Ethan Krieger version of Mongolian beef. All he needed to do was chop and then stir.

Ethan heard Mary float into the kitchen behind him. He turned around. Glowing in front of him, Mary wore a blue silk robe and suddenly Ethan stood at another crossroad.

"I thought maybe we could fix a little dinner before..."

Mary put her finger to his lips to quiet him while she slowly shook her head.

"You've primed the pump enough," said Mary softly. "I'm all wound up and taut as a guitar string waiting to be played. So, play me."

Ethan looked down.

"Maybe first a little wine?"

With her other hand, Mary opened her robe to reveal a skimpy purple baby doll negligee. Her erect nipples beckoned through the fabric like energetic little rockets, and Ethan took a deep breath.

"I should probably just pick you up and carry you to the bedroom now," said Ethan, nodding.

Mary grinned and nodded happily back.

Leaning down, Ethan picked Mary up into his arms and while they kissed, he headed upstairs to the bedroom where ...they bounced.

Chapter 6

Encores

A very satisfied Mary curled into Ethan's chest and sighed. Though she had been married twice, for the first time in her life, she felt like someone had actually taken the time to make love to her. Before, it had only been sex, and usually one-sided at that. However, in two short days, Ethan had showed he valued Mary as more than just a pair of tits and a vagina, and in bed he had expressed that respect by taking his time and asking her what she liked.

Using his hand, Ethan combed Mary's hair from her face.

"We're good friends now, aren't we?" asked Ethan.

"Well duhh!" said Mary. "I have your DNA swimming around inside of me."

"Then, can I ask you a question?" said Ethan.

"Sure," giggled Mary as she rubbed his naked chest.

"Why'd you change your name?" asked Ethan.

Confused by the question, she stopped rubbing.

"I got married," replied Mary.

"No. That's not what I meant," said Ethan. "Why do you go by Mary, instead of Nona?"

Mary suddenly sat up and turned towards Ethan.

"How long have you known?" she asked, looking down at him

"Since the first moment I saw you at the side of the car when you picked me up," said Ethan.

"But how?" asked an astonished Mary. "It's been..."

"...fifty-two years since I last saw you at graduation," finished Ethan.

He smiled. "Some women have faces that you never forget."

"I can't believe you remember," said Mary. "I've changed so much in fifty years. Sometimes, I can't even recognize myself in the mirror."

"You're still the prettiest girl in school," said Ethan, smiling.

Mary's heart overflowed.

"So, why'd you change it?" asked Ethan.

"My second marriage changed my last name to Katz," said Mary, "and my husband liked my middle name more than my first name, so I went by Mary. After our divorce, I just went with what was familiar."

"Which do you prefer?" asked Ethan.

"Nona," she replied.

"So do I," grinned Ethan. He suddenly grimaced.

"Is your reflux bothering you again?" asked Nona.

Ethan nodded as he rolled onto his side. Nona jumped off the bed and found his messenger bag. Popping a lozenge, she brought it to Ethan and he eagerly sucked on it while Nona ran her fingers through the side of his hair to soothe him. A few minutes later, he was better.

"These attacks seem to happen a lot," observed Nona. "Maybe we should see a doctor."

"No doctor," said Ethan. "They won't be able to tell me any more than what I already know."

He smiled.

"You hungry?" asked Ethan.

"Hungry like food?" said Nona. "Or hungry for more, like do I want to get on top and ride the big bad bulldog again until he's ready to behave?"

"I was thinking food first," said an amused Ethan. "Then afterwards maybe you can make the bulldog *behave* again."

Nona giggled and put on her robe. Ethan joined her and they headed downstairs to the kitchen. The ingredients for Ethan's dinner were still laid out on the center island, ready to go. Pulling the flank steak from the refrigerator, Ethan, after he unwrapped it, laid the meat on a cutting board in front of Mary.

"First, we need to cut this into thin slices," said Ethan.

Nona pulled a butcher knife from a block and quickly chopped off a piece.

"Like that?" she asked.

"No," replied Ethan. "You need to slice it at an angle in order to make the meat more tender."

Nona tried again, and acted like it totally dumbfounded her. Ethan shook his head.

"I guess you'll just have to show me," said Nona coyly.

Ethan stood behind Nona and taking her hands, he guided them as they sliced off a piece of meat at an angle. While he helped her, Nona stroked her ass slowly up and down the long ridge she felt growing under Ethan's robe.

"I still don't think I have the hang of this," teased Nona. "Could you show me again?"

Ethan dutifully guided Nona's hands again while Nona kept stroking him. Then reaching down with her left hand, Nona pulled the back of her robe upward.

"One more time," pleaded Nona, "and I think I'll get it."

Holding Nona around the waist, Ethan untied his robe while Mary bent forward over the stainless-steel counter rack and offered herself to him.

Suddenly a quivering moan escaped from her lips as she inhaled a deep breath.

"Oh yes," said Nona, smiling. "I definitely got it."

Twenty minutes later, Nona and Ethan, happily naked on the couch, surveyed the mess they had just made of the kitchen. Ethan's proposed dinner lay strewn in a trail across the floor into the living room.

"It's early enough that we can still order out," said Ethan. "You like Szechuan?"

Marina District, San Diego

"Right there!" moaned Erika, clutching the rails of the headboard behind her. "Right therrrrrrrre!"

Suddenly her body contracted wildly.

"Yes! Yes! Yes!" she shouted, as Joanna's fingers and tongue performed wondrous feats of magic.

Several minutes later, Joanna lay snuggled in Erika's arms on the bed. Using a pair of chopsticks, Erika plucked a shrimp from a takeout box and held it up to Joanna's lips.

"You were right," sighed Erika. "This really is good Szechuan."

Using her tongue, Joanna grasped the shrimp from the chopsticks and sucked it into her mouth while Erika watched.

From Joanna's bed, they had a magnificent view of the marina and its forest of sailboat masts.

"This is a nice place you have here," said Erika, looking around. "I like what you've done with it."

"I own the building," said Joanna with pride as she picked up some chopsticks.

"The whole building?"

Joanna nodded and plucked some noodles from a box and held them up for Erika, who eagerly sucked them into her mouth.

"When my father died, he left me some money," said Joanna. "When I saw this old warehouse building, I imagined what I could do with it and bought it. Then I leveraged my investment and renovated it. The bottom two floors are apartments that pay for the renovation loan and taxes. The third floor and roof belong strictly to me, and a management agent runs the building for me."

"It looks like you have lots of room here," said Erika, looking around.

"I do," said Joanna, smiling.

"I saw glimpses of the roof on the way in," said Erika. "Can we go up there?"

"Sure," replied Joanna, "why don't we have breakfast on the roof tomorrow morning?"

"I like the way you think," said Erika, as her chopsticks slowly worked their way between Joanna's legs.

Chapter 7

Going Rogue

June 4th
San Diego

Except for the bathroom and bedroom area, everything including the kitchen, dining room and Joanna's studio were part of a vast open-concept design. Six-foot tall windows had been installed, as well as skylights on the twenty-foot high ceiling. Together they gave the space a bright, airy, welcoming atmosphere.

On the side of the building, Joanna had her own private entrance. To take care of the building's energy needs, she had installed solar panels on half of the roof. She devoted the other half of the roof to her garden, a vast array of tropical plants that cherished the San Diego sun.

When Erika walked onto the roof the next morning, she was amazed.

"This is beautiful," she gushed. "But how do you keep it all watered?"

Joanna pointed to a thousand-gallon tank on a ten-foot high metal platform at the corner of the roof.

"All the rainwater that falls on the building is collected in the gutters and pumped into that tank. The tank, in turn, gravity-feeds into a drip watering system. There are sensors in the soil to turn the watering system on and off, so that the plants don't get flooded."

Erika turned to Joanna and looked into her auburn eyes while she ran her fingers through her hair. She wanted to tell Joanna that her heart sang from the moment she met her. But she didn't want to seem too anxious.

"Let's go fix some breakfast," said Erika.

"After breakfast, will you let me paint you?" asked Joanna.

A surprised Erika smiled.

"I just need to check something on my computer first, but sure, yeah, I'll pose for you," she said.

"What did you have in mind?" asked Erika. "Maybe something by the window with the sun shining on me?"

"Actually, I was thinking in the nude on the antique loveseat," said Erika. "You have a beautiful body. I think the world should see it."

Erika silently studied Joanna while Joanna wondered for a moment if she had offended her. Erika inhaled deeply and looked at Joanna in way that Joanna knew exactly what she thought and felt. A rush of adrenaline coursed through both women.

"I know we only just met, but..." Erika sighed.

Joanna reached out and pulled Erika to her.

"I feel the same way."

A breeze from the ocean blew Erika's hair over her shoulder as she kissed Joanna.

Newport, Oregon

When Nona woke the next day, she noticed Ethan, wearing only his robe, at the window, staring into the seemingly infinite blue of the Pacific. He looked sad and Nona wondered what he was thinking about.

"How did this happen?" she quietly wondered to herself. "How could I fall in love with someone I haven't seen in over fifty years in just three days? Probably, because he cares more about me than himself." And then she wondered in a whisper, "if he cares more about me than himself, he must love me too?"

Nona suddenly became warm and tingly at the thought.

Ethan, sensing Nona had woken, turned, and walked to the bed. Sitting on the edge, he leaned down to kiss her.

"Did you sleep well?" he asked.

"Un-huh," grinned Nona between kisses.

"I fixed breakfast for you," said Ethan, pointing with his thumb over his shoulder.

Nona looked across the room at the tray of food on the dresser and giggled.

"So, get your robe on, and go to the bathroom," said Ethan. "And when you get back, I'll feed you."

Nona kissed Ethan one last time, and hopping off the bed, she headed for the bathroom. Returning a few minutes later she found that while she was gone, Ethan had fluffed up several pillows so she could sit up against the headboard. After making sure Nona was comfortable, Ethan brought over the breakfast-in-bed table and set it in front of her. Opening the lid covering the plate, Nona discovered an omelet and whole wheat toast waiting for her.

Staring at her breakfast, Nona felt like crying. No one had ever brought her breakfast in bed. Ethan sat on the edge of the bed, puzzled.

"What's the matter?" he asked. "if you don't like omelets, I can fix something else."

Nona reached out to kiss him.

"No, no," she said between kisses. "it's all just so wonderful."

"Good," said Ethan, smiling.

"Do you want some of this?" asked Nona as she took a bite of toast. "I don't think I can eat all of it."

Ethan shook his head.

"My stomach is a little queasy this morning," he said, rubbing his midsection. "Must have been the Szechuan last night."

Ethan nodded towards the ocean.

"It's going to be a beautiful day today," he said. "Do you want to go for a walk on the beach after you get cleaned up?"

"Will you take a shower with me and scrub my back?" asked Nona.

Ethan smiled and nodded.

"Deal," said Nona, grinning.

Marina District, San Diego

Erika had laid on her side in the nude for almost three hours. Joanna had given her several breaks, but each time, she covered the canvas before Erika's curiosity could sneak a peek.

Suddenly, they heard the freight elevator descending. Erika looked at Joanna.

"Are you expecting somebody?" asked Erika.

Joanna shook her head and covered the painting.

"Nobody should be able to get in, unless I buzz them in," said an anxious Joanna.

Grabbing her clothes from a nearby chair, Erika quickly put them on. The freight elevator stopped at the bottom. They heard people get on, and then the elevator started upwards.

Running to Joanna, Erika stood beside her. The elevator stopped and the door opened. Two muscular men in suits and a five-foot-two woman with short black hair wearing a dark pant suit emerged.

"You really should get a better security system," said the woman. Reaching inside her jacket she showed her badge, followed by the other two men.

"Uh-oh," said Erika.

Joanna turned to Erika.

"Do you know why they're here?"

"Maybe?" said Erika hesitantly.

"I need to talk to you alone, Ms. Barton," said the woman. "Is there somewhere private we can talk?"

Erika turned towards Joanna.

"Is it ok if we go to the roof?"

Joanna pointed at the two men. "I don't want to be left alone with them. Can you take them with you?" she asked.

"Yes, we can do that," said the woman.

Erika showed the agents to the stairway leading to the roof.

"This is nice," admired the woman, looking around as they emerged into the San Diego sunlight. She turned to the males accompanying her.

"Could you fellows give us some room?" she asked. The two men moved to the far corner of the roof and took a seat on the edge while the agent and Erika sat at a patio table.

"I didn't catch who you three were with?" said Erika.

The woman pulled out her identification again for Erika to examine.

"My name is René Scipio." She pointed with her thumb over her shoulder at the two men. "And those two big bags of testosterone are with Homeland Security. I call them Thing 1 and Thing 2."

"Aren't you a little outside your jurisdiction?" said Erika, studying René's credentials.

"A little," said René. That's why I'm coordinating with Thing 1 and 2."

She pulled out her phone and held it up in front of Erika.

"You know this man?

Erika looked at the image and shook her head.

"Nope, never seen him before," said Erika. "Who is he?"

"His name is Ethan Krieger. He's the man you've been checking on for your grandmother." said René. "You know him as Ethan Jones. Are you sure you haven't seen him?"

Erika, about to deny what she had been doing, quickly concluded that they already knew everything and decided to cooperate.

"Ok, so I've been checking on him," she said. "What about it?"

"Ethan Krieger is one of ours and has gone rogue," said René. "He's been working with a master hacker named Fernando and together they're going to do something very destructive and highly detrimental to national security. We need your help in order to stop him."

"Why should I help you?" asked Erika, a little suspicious.

René leaned across the table.

"Because, if you help us, we'll leave him alone. I know your grandmother is interested in seeing him. I'll be generous and allow their romance to blossom again."

"What about local authorities?" asked Erika.

René waved a finger in the air.

"Don't worry about them. They won't interfere," said René with a smile.

"So, what do I have to do?" she asked.

"We need you to find a way into one of our operative's computer security systems," said René.

"You want me to hack one of your own operative's computer systems?" repeated an incredulous Erika. "Why?"

"He has a lot of classified information stored on his hard drives, along with all his contacts. Ethan Krieger, with Fernando's help, is going to try to break in, and steal the information," said René. "If our enemies find out what we're doing, it's going to compromise a lot of operations, and a lot of people are going to die. We want you to find his system's weaknesses, so we can prevent the break-in."

"This sounds funny," said Erika. "Why aren't your own people working on this?"

"It had been determined by the head of our agency that it would be best handled by an outside source," replied René. "That way, if something happens, we keep our operative's confidence, and with no footprints, we have plausible denial. Also, we don't want other parts of the agency knowing we've been gathering intelligence in this particular way."

Erika stood and walked to the edge of the garden while she gathered her thoughts. She turned to René.

"Why don't you just arrest Krieger?" she finally asked.

"We know generally where he is, thanks to you," said René. "But he's a really good ghost when he is on the run. Bottom line is, he knows our operative's security weakness and can pass it on at any time to someone else. We need to know what that weakness is."

Given, her concern for her grandmother's happiness, Erika didn't see that she had any choice.

"Ok. I'm in," said Erika, nodding. "Who's our target? Who do I have to hack?"

"Jimmy Bob Swindle," said René smiling, "and the Supernatural Seed of the Lord Prosperity Ministry."

"You have got to be fucking kidding me!" exclaimed a stunned Erika, leaning downward towards René. "He's an operative of yours?"

"Why do you think he has so many planes?" said René. "Being a televangelist with an overseas congregation is the perfect cover to do a lot of things."

"Are all televangelists who have congregations overseas CIA operatives?" asked an astonished Erika.

René hummed and smiled.

Twenty minutes after they left, the three agents and Erika walked down the stairs together. Joanna didn't like the look of them. She hoped they would leave, and she really hoped that Erika wasn't in any trouble.

Erika walked to Joanna.

"Everything ok?" asked Joanna.

"Everything's fine," assured Erika. "I just need to go with these people and do something for them. I'll be back in your arms in a couple of days."

"You sure?" asked Joanna.

Erika stroked Joanna's cheek with her hand.

"As sure as I can be about anything in the world," said Erika.

She looked towards Joanna's easel.

"Can I see the painting before I go?"

Joanna shook her head.

"No. I'm going to hang it in the bedroom," said Joanna with a smile, "so you have some incentive to return."

Erika kissed Joanna.

"I am so in love with you," she whispered in her ear. And she left with René.

Newport, Oregon

Outside, the morning fog slowly cleared while the sun peeked through in patches as Ethan and Nona walked down the long fifty-foot stairway to the beach. When they approached the bottom, Nona reached for Ethan's hand, but Ethan instead stretched his arm around Nona's waist as they walked.

Nona leaned against him and purred.

"I love hearing your name," said Ethan as they walked. "Nona. It has such a melodic ring to it."

Nona turned and kissed him for the compliment.

"So why did you allow your husband to bully you into using your middle name?" he asked. "You always seemed so fearless in school."

She shook her head as if trying to rid herself of regrets.

"I was in my late forties, divorced and worried that there was never going to be someone in my life again," said Nona. "I just wanted to please him."

Nona stopped. Her face angrily clouded over.

"But then, he divorced me ten years later and married a deaconess in the evangelical church we attended," vented Nona. "I was never religious and I went to services every Sunday only because of that fucker. Turns out the moral hypocrite was having an affair with Betty Sue Ferrari for over seven years. Now I know why he was so intent about going to church every Sunday and why he stayed after services to help with the communion plates! He really just wanted to ride a Ferrari! Turns out everyone in the church knew he was fooling around except me. How's that for Christian fellowship?"

"When he broke the news to me, he told me that she understood his spiritual needs," said an exasperated Nona. "Can you believe that? His God damn spiritual needs! What he should have said was that she was twenty years younger and not going through menopause like me!"

Ethan squeezed Nona sympathetically around her waist and they began walking again.

"I heard you married Kenny Peters just after graduation," said Ethan.

Nona grimaced.

"I had to," lamented Nona. "I was pregnant."

"So, you have kids?" asked Ethan.

"No," replied Nona. "The pregnancy miscarried at four months and took with it my ability to ever have children again. Kenny didn't want to take care of a child that wasn't his own, so we never adopted."

"I'm sorry," said Ethan.

Nona continued.

"Kenny went to law school and eventually became an attorney. I became a dental hygienist, because we needed to have a source of income while he went to school. Fifteen years later, Kenny went to jail and lost his license for evidence and witness tampering. We were never really a close or a happy couple together and I suspected he had a bimbo or two on the side, so I used the opportunity to divorce him. Ten years later, I met Phillip. At the time, I knew I shouldn't marry him, but I was lonely."

Nona turned to Ethan and ran her fingers through the hair on the side of his head.

"Ethan," asked Nona. "What did you do in the military?"

Ethan smiled a little while he stared at the Pacific.

"You're a smart woman and I think you know already."

"Did it involve killing people?" asked Nona.

Ethan massaged her waist as they walked, but didn't say anything, giving Nona her answer.

"How did that happen?" asked Nona.

"After graduation, my draft number came up," said Ethan. "My father, an 82nd Airborne veteran from WWII, didn't want me to go to Viet Nam, so he advised me to join the military, so I could choose something less dangerous than being a ground pounder. Ironically, at the military depot in St. Louis, I was approached by two men who had seen my test scores and wanted to know if I would like to work in intelligence. While I was in the military, I was recruited to do other things after my folks died and my family connections became scarce. After leaving the military, I did freelance work and retired completely five years ago. Since then, I've been quietly working in my greenhouse, growing orchids."

"Was it an exciting life?" asked Nona.

"Exciting, ...interesting, but extremely lonely," replied Ethan. "The main lesson I learned was that you could be just as lonely in Paris as you could on the Bering Sea in Alaska."

"So, there was never anyone special in your life?" asked Nona.

"I learned not to love," said Ethan. "It was a luxury that could get you or someone else killed."

He looked down at Nona.

"But that might be changing."

They stopped. A flock of sea birds circled the shoreline. Suddenly, one dived steeply into the water and came up to the surface with a fish. Soon all the birds were diving. Then, as if on cue, they all flew off together and circled the beach again, hunting and feasting in an endless dance. Ethan and Nona strolled on.

"Though I was good at what I did, knowing what I know now," reflected Ethan, "if I had to do it again, I would do it all differently."

Nona became curious.

"What would you do differently?"

Nobody had ever asked Ethan any of these questions. They were things he thought but never expressed out loud. It felt good to have someone to tell them to.

"I feel like I've been selfish with my life," said Ethan sadly. "Because what I did was dangerous and highly secret, I never got involved with anyone, never had a family, and never committed myself to anything in the world, other than my work. I should've become a teacher or organizer, so I could work with people who needed help. I should've joined the peace corps or worked for an NGO and been one of those people taking care of refugees, alleviating suffering and reporting on it to the world. I know now that I can't save the world and a lot of people's lives are going to be short, hard, brief, and miserable. But I could've, for some of them at least, made the time they did have a little bit more comfortable."

Ethan shook his head.

"Look around us," he lamented. "We have so much *stuff* and we're not willing to share. Many people might look on my life as a success, but here at the end, I feel like I squandered my real potential."

"Then why did you?" asked Nona.

"I was lazy," said Ethan. "It was easier and seemed more exciting doing what I did, than the alternative."

Ethan turned to Nona.

"How about you?" he asked. "Knowing what you know now, would you do things differently."

"I would've been less concerned with being cool and popular," said Nona. "But more importantly, I wanted to become a doctor. I wanted to help people feel better. Maybe work with refugees overseas like you. I didn't want to spend my entire life cleaning teeth and handing the dentist drill bits."

"Why didn't you become a doctor?"

"Same reason as you," said Nona. "I was lazy and it was easier to keep doing what I was doing than the alternative."

Nona changed the subject.

"When we were in school, why didn't you ever ask me out?" said Nona.

Ethan took a deep breath while he gathered his thoughts and looked at Nona. He debated what to tell her. He wanted to tell her about wanting to ask her to the Wildey in ninth grade, but thought that would shift responsibility from himself.

"Pure adolescent cowardice," admitted Ethan. "Later I broke out with an awful case of acne and my self-image took a huge hit for the rest of high school," said Ethan. "I was sure no one would go out with someone with as much crud on my face as I had. Then, after graduation my draft number came up and I joined the military...."

Ethan stroked his cheek.

"My face cleared up and I lost any shyness that remained within me."

Nona grinned and giggled.

"Remaining shyness? No kidding? Really? It's hard to believe that you were ever shy."

They continued strolling while they enjoyed the morning breeze. But then something Nona had been a little concerned about bubbled to the surface.

"Ethan, I've watched you shell out a lot of cash in the last few days," said Nona. "How are we doing money-wise?"

"Don't worry,' said Ethan. "I have half a quarter of a million remaining in my bag. And a great deal more in a secret offshore account if we need it."

"Good," said Nona. "We might have to make it last."

"I have more than enough to take care of us for a long time," said Ethan, holding Nona against him. "My work also paid very well."

Nona squeezed him a little tighter. A half hour later, she noticed Ethan looked a little tired. On the beach nearby lay a large driftwood log, and Nona coaxed Ethan to sit in the sand against it while he held her and she rested her head on his shoulder.

"Ethan," asked Mary as she looked out at the ocean. "Have you ever thought about what comes next?"

"Do you mean lunch?" joked Ethan, "or after you've stopped breathing."

"Breathing," replied Nona.

Ethan smiled a little.

"What person over fifty hasn't?"

"So, what do you think happens?" asked Nona.

Ethan inhaled a deep breath while he considered what to say.

"My version of the afterlife is a little different," said Ethan. "In my version heaven is not a place. It's a time."

Nona looked at Ethan.

"A time?"

"In it, you get to go back to a point in time in your life where you get a chance to experience other things," said Ethan.

"Like helping refugees."

"Yes, like helping refugees."

Ethan kissed Nona's forehead and changed the subject.

"So, what do you want to do with the rest of the day?" asked Ethan. "Your wish is my command, milady."

"Well, first I thought we could eat lunch along the waterfront," said Nona, snuggling in a little more. "Then after doing a bit more grocery shopping, I could fix you dinner this evening. Afterwards we could finish up by drinking wine, eating popcorn, and watching old movies until it's time for bed. Then we can snuggle each other to sleep. How does that sound?" asked Nona.

Ethan sighed and kissed her forehead again.

"Absolutely wonderful."

Chapter 8

To Be or Not to Be

June 5th
Newport, Oregon

When Nona woke the next day, she looked at the ceiling and stretched with pure joy. Each day with Ethan just kept getting better and better, and she had no reason to believe today would be any different. As she lay in bed, she thought about Ethan fifty years earlier in school, and wished that he had asked her out then so her life could've turned out differently than the disappointment it had been —that is, until she'd found Ethan three days earlier.

Nona heard water running in the bathroom, and deduced Ethan was taking a shower. Putting on her robe she walked to the window. Thick fog blanketed the beach and Nona wondered what they should do with the day.

Then something that she had been wondering about surfaced in her mind. Nona walked to Ethan's messenger bag and pulled out his reflux medicine. Taking note of the brand name, Nona went downstairs to the household computer. She turned it on, googled and then stared at the screen as she read.

Upstairs, Ethan stepped out of the shower and reached for a towel to dry himself off. An old tune popped into his head and he hummed along. His heart danced and he picked up the pace, so he could rejoin Nona in bed and feel her warmth against him.

Wrapping a towel around himself, Ethan opened the door. Nona stood at the window looking forlornly out at the ocean. In her hand she held a lozenge package. Ethan heard tears. Suddenly she turned and glared at him.

"You bastard," screamed Nona. "When were you going to tell me?"

"Tell you what?" asked Ethan.

She held up the lozenge package and angrily shook it at him.

"When were you going to tell me that these lozenges are not for reflux!" shouted Nona. "They're for pain or fun! I looked up the brand name. It's a high dosage of fentanyl! There are only two reasons you would have fentanyl. Either you're an addict or you're terminal."

Her voice trailed off while Nona stared at Ethan.

"Please...please...please tell me that you're an addict," begged Nona.

Ethan looked into Nona's pleading eyes and slowly shook his head.

Nona threw her arms into the air.

"Great!" exclaimed Nona as tears flew everywhere. "Just fucking great! I finally find the man of my dreams, I fall in love, and guess what, folks—he's fucking dying!"

Nona sat on the edge of the bed. Ethan sat next to Nona and put his arms around her as she cried into his shoulder.

"I'm so sorry," said Ethan through Nona's tears. "I wanted to tell you, but how does one tell someone they've loved for over fifty years that they're going to die?"

Nona looked up at Ethan and sniffled.

"You've loved me for over fifty years?"

"Ever since ninth grade," said Ethan, gazing into Nona's big brown eyes.

"You've never fallen in love with anyone else?"

Ethan shook his head.

"Nope. It's always been you. Not asking you out has haunted me all my life."

Nona reached up and lovingly stroked Ethan's cheek.

"How long do we have together?" she asked.

"I don't know exactly," said Ethan. "Two, three weeks, maybe as long as a month."

"Do you have enough pain medication?" asked Nona.

"Plenty," said Ethan.

A thought suddenly floated into Nona's mind.

"Wait, I have a question," she said. "I read online that fentanyl decreases sexual performance..."

"Oh yeah. Sorry about that," apologized Ethan. "I've only been bringing my C-minus game to bed."

"Holy shit!" exclaimed Nona. "That was only your C-minus game?"

Ethan nodded. Nona balled up her fist and whacked him hard on the arm.

"That's for not telling me," said Nona as Ethan recoiled from the pain.

"Duly noted," grimaced Ethan.

Nona hugged him tight.

"Ok," said Nona, burying herself against him. "If we only have a month together, we need to make some plans. First, I want you to tell me all about Operation Tyrannosaurus. Second, there's something we need to do afterwards in town."

Erika's Home in the Hills Above San Diego

René woke from the couch and sat up. Thing 1 and 2 were still sleeping on the couches in the living room downstairs. As she stretched, René looked at Erika across the room, studying three large screens, still working on the Jimmy Bob Swindle project, still trying to find his security weakness.

Erika took another sip of energy drink and scrolled down another page of code. She looked across the room at René, trying to get a hold on the morning.

"I don't know what the problem is," said Erika. "He has all sorts of security safeguards on his main ministry hard drive that I haven't been able to get past."

"Keep checking," yawned René. "Ethan Krieger and Fernando are very smart. They know something you're not seeing."

Erika stared at a screen for a second.

"Maybe I'm overthinking this," she wondered. She scrutinized René and then turned back to her screen.

Looking up at the screen above her, Erika then compared the computer code to the screen on her left.

"Wait a second," she muttered to herself.

She scrolled again.

"When I'm good," she excitedly said aloud. "I'm really good!"

René hurried over.

"What'd you find?"

Erika pointed at the top screen.

"If Mr. Krieger tries to go through the front door, it will be difficult," said Erika. "There are a lot of safeguards and encryption."

She pointed at the screen to her left.

"This is probably where he's going to hack Jimmy Bob Swindle."

"What am I looking at?" asked René, looking over Erika's shoulder.

"This is a server he keeps at home," said Erika. "It only has a five-digit password and, for convenience, it's linked with what I call a freeway connection to the main server at his ministry. The good Reverend Swindle is lazy about security at home. He logs in here and he's automatically logged in at the highest security level to the system as a whole."

"What about the five-digit code?" asked René.

Erika shook her head.

"Any good hacker can break five digits in ten minutes."

She smiled.

"Given the naivety behind his home security, I'd probably try J-E-S-U-S or S-U-S-E-J first."

"Will they see any of your scrutiny on their computers if they run a diagnostic?" asked René, putting on her jacket.

"Not a bit," said Erika, looking back over her shoulder. "I have my own special ghost algorithm that I use to cover my tracks. They won't even know I was trying to invade their system."

René noticed a red light flashing on Erika's laptop sitting on the table next to them.

"What's going on here?" she asked.

Erika picked up the laptop and set it in front of her. She double-tapped the flashing icon.

"Oh shit," said Erika. "Grandma's definitely not going to like this."

"What is it?" asked René.

Erika grinned.

"Our boy just got himself a marriage license."

Newport, Oregon

A long-polished mahogany bar lining one side of the Pink Elephant greeted Ethan and Nona as they walked in holding hands. On the far wall beckoned a stage, while in the center, numerous round tables spread out like mushrooms across the floor. It looked like any other elegant old wood bar, except that the color scheme centered on purple and ... a lot of leather bed implements.

As they entered, a lady outfitted in a purple striped shirt, leather fringed vest, cowboy chaps, and dark horn rim glasses greeted them. She had long bright Raggedy-Ann-red hair and, along the edge of her right ear hung ten small round earrings neatly in a row.

"Can I help you?" she asked.

"We're looking for Lizzie Borden," said Nona. "She works at the storage place. We were told she would probably be here."

The lady pointed her thumb over her shoulder at a door.

"She's out back having a smoke," said the lady. "Is there something I can help you with?"

Just then, Lizzie emerged from the back door. When she saw Ethan and Nona, she laughed hilariously.

"Gloria, these are the people from the storage place. You know, the ones your salesman Barry sold the car to," said Lizzie.

Gloria burst out laughing while she held out her hand to Nona.

"Hi, I'm Gloria Faith," she said. "Did you really have a prayer meeting in the showroom of my Honda dealership?"

Nona, not knowing how to react, nodded.

Gloria laughed so hard, she had to hold her ribs.

"Did you really tell Barry you wanted a car that you and him..." She pointed at Ethan. "...could drive to the Rapture in?"

"I hope I didn't get Barry into any trouble," said Nona. "I was only playing with him."

"No, no, not a bit. He managed to sell a car under interesting circumstances," said Gloria, holding up her hand. "It's good to know he's on his toes. Besides, right-wing, self-righteous hypocritical evangelicals bore the fuck out of me."

"So, what brings you to my place?" asked Gloria.

Nona looked up at Ethan. Ethan reached inside his coat pocket and pulled out an envelope.

"We're getting married," said Ethan, grinning. "We just got our license from the clerk's office at city hall around the corner and since we were in the neighborhood, we thought we would drop by and invite Lizzie. She's the closest we have to knowing someone in town."

"And," added Nona, "now that we've met you, you're invited too."

"You two are getting married?" said a pleased Gloria. "Where are you having the ceremony?"

"We were thinking maybe city hall," said Ethan.

"When?"

"Today."

"No, no, no!" exclaimed Gloria waving her hand wildly. "Two people as fun as you are getting married here tonight. No boring, sedate ceremony for you two. We're having a special drag queen review at eight. Let's get you married at seven. Then a reception. Then the show to help you two celebrate. Do you have a minister or justice of the peace yet?"

"Uh, no," said Nona.

"Don't worry about it," exclaimed Gloria. "Lizzie and I will take care of all the details. You two just invite your other guests."

Nona smiled up at Ethan.

"Ok?"

Ethan laughed and smiled back at Nona.

"Ok."

Somewhere Over Northern California

Erika glanced at her grandmother, sipping vodka in the first-class seat next to her on the Boeing 737 heading for Portland. The flight attendant stopped by.

"Ma'am, would you like another drink?" she asked.

Clara shook her head and the flight attendant left. Erika looked at her laptop on the fold-out table in front of her.

"Grandma, why are we going to Oregon? By the time we get to Newport, he's going to be married already. How's that going to help your case with him?"

"What's the name of this place he's getting married at?" asked Clara.

"According to their website," said Erika, "it's called the Pink Elephant Bar."

"Pink Elephant? What kind of place is that?" asked Clara.

"According to their website, it's a women's bar," replied Erika. "Looks like they're having a drag queen review after the wedding."

Erika watched her grandmother stare straight ahead and frown. She knew what she was thinking—*Sin! Sin! Sin!* Erika wondered what her grandmother would think if she knew that her favorite reverend was a government operative and that she had just saved his bacon. She chuckled to herself at the irony.

She scrolled her computer desktop page.

"His bride just bought a new car several days ago," said Erika. "A red Honda Pilot, dealer's license DLR 666 from Gloria Faith Honda."

She turned to Clara.

"So, Grandma. Why are we going to Oregon?" asked Erika again.

"It's complicated," said Clara. "Maybe I just need to hear him tell me face to face that he doesn't love me anymore."

"What good will that do?" asked Erika.

Clara patted her hand.

"Closure, my dear. You'll understand when you get older."

Erika didn't like her grandmother's condescension, but she also didn't want to argue, so she dropped the subject. Instead, she decided to concentrate on something a lot more pleasant. Closing her computer, she sighed and thought about Joanna.

Chapter 9

Elvis has Left the Building

Newport, Oregon

Hearing a car drive up, Ethan went to the curtain to peek out. A white GMC Yukon SUV parked in the driveway, and Fernando emerged from the driver's side, holding up a clothing bag. Before Fernando was even able to knock, Ethan opened the door.

"There's been a shooting at a food festival in California," exclaimed Ethan wildly at Fernando, "and I can't believe what these God damn pundits on POX News are saying!"

Turning, Ethan walked back to the television in the living room with Fernando following.

"If they had just allowed everyone to enter the festival with a weapon," said the pundit, "there wouldn't have been any loss of human life. People would have been able to defend themselves."

The panel looked around at each other and nodded.

Visibly agitated, Ethan shook his index finger at the television.

"Those gun-idiots!"

He turned to Fernando.

"Can you imagine what that would have been like?" exclaimed

Ethan. "Shots ring out and everyone draws a gun and starts shooting at someone else holding a gun. Even if they had the real shooter in their sights, an untrained amateur would hesitate and die! These people don't realize how much training it takes to be able to shoot someone without blinking first. And if they are able to shoot without hesitation and without training, they are psychopaths that I would never ever want as friends."

Ethan wagged his finger at Fernando.

"And shooting at a paper outline is not training—it's target practice! Do you know how long it took me before I was able to spend a bullet on a live person without thinking?"

Fernando smiled and laid his arm on Ethan's shoulder.

"My old friend," said Fernando, "that is because you are a human being and not a monster like these brain-dead clownish POX commentators. You need to start thinking of them as comedy. You know, like pro-wrestling. Take Prawn Rannity the Robot. Now, he is really hilarious in a tepid mechanical sort of way. Just think of them as macabre entertainment. None of the stuff they say is real or truthful, and they know it. They just say it for the shock effect, in order to make money. They are the barkers of sideshow freaks at a carnival."

Ethan inhaled a deep breath.

"I know," said Ethan. "I just wish they could appreciate life for all the wonder that it is. Instead of being so cynical and filled with hate."

They sat on the couch.

"It must be hard for you at this stage of your life to watch?" said Fernando, trying to calm Ethan.

Ethan looked at Fernando and nodded.

"Then let's talk about things filled with life," said Fernando, "like your upcoming marriage?"

He looked around.

"Where's your beautiful bride?"

"She's with Lizzie and Gloria, making all the arrangements," said Ethan. "She dropped me off and said for me to show up at the Pink Elephant after you arrived with the tux."

Fernando glanced at his watch.

"Then let's get you dressed and be on our way," he said with a big grin. "It's about time to get you married. Hope you like Armani."

Fernando held out a flash drive.

"What's this?" asked Ethan grasping it in his hand.

"An updated and better version of the Tyrannosaurus program," said Fernando with a smile.

Portland Airport

Erika and her grandmother departed the aircraft and made their way down the long concourse, through the security gate to the baggage claim area. Erika had brought only her rolling carry-on, but her grandmother had a larger suitcase that needed to be picked up. When they reached carousel six, a large man in a dark suit already had her luggage and stood by the door, holding up a small sign with her grandmother's name on it.

Clara walked to the man and spoke in Russian to him. He nodded and replied, "Da!"

Clara motioned for Erika to follow them and she hesitantly trailed them to the passenger pickup area outside, where another ominous large man with a long beard and a greased pointed mustache waited with a black Toyota SUV. After putting the luggage in the trunk, the man opened up the back doors and Clara and Erika got in. As they started to drive away, the man in the passenger seat turned and handed Clara a box. Clara opened the box and grabbing the Glock inside, she quickly thrust the weapon into her purse.

"Grandma," whispered a disturbed Erika. "Why the gun, and who are these two men? I thought you only wanted to talk!"

Clara patted her granddaughter's hand.

"And we are just going to talk," assured Clara. "The gun is just in case of trouble."

"What kind of trouble? What are you not telling me?" asked Erika, peering at Clara.

"Nothing, nothing," said Clara with a slight smile, still patting Erika's hand. "We're just going to talk."

Clara turned to the driver.

"How long to Newport?"

"Normally two and a half hours," said the man in a heavy accent. "But you arrive in rush hour, traffic murderous. Maybe plus one more hour."

Red flags flew everywhere for Erika. She didn't like the ghost they were chasing. She didn't like these two Russians. She didn't like the gun her grandma now her grandmother was obviously lying to her. Erika wished she had never told her grandmother about what she had found. She wished she had not come along and that she was still on the roof of Joanna's building, drinking wine and kissing the woman she was in love with. Erika, feeling momentarily trapped, decided to exit the situation at the first opportunity afforded her and go home. She turned towards her grandmother. The stony look on her face as she stared straight ahead scared Erika. She had always known Barton wasn't her real last name, but now she wondered who her grandmother really was.

The Pink Elephant Bar

When Ethan walked through the doorway of the Pink Elephant Bar, white flowers sprouted from seemingly everywhere and hung from all the leather toys on the wall. Purple ribbons and large bows lined the entryway leading to the stage while above, Christmas lights flashed on the ceiling. Gloria, in a white sequined cowboy outfit, met Ethan and Fernando at the door and looked him over, nodding in approval.

"Nice tux," said Gloria, grinning.

She held out her hand and led Ethan and Fernando towards the stage. Around seventy patrons sat in the audience. Among them,

Ethan spotted the Kit-Kat twins and Rex Arturus, Bettie Wage from the clothing shop, Barry Height, the Honda salesman, along with Artie Thompson, his failed assailant from several days before, with his arm around his wife Martha. Ethan stopped at Artie and his wife sitting on the aisle. His eyes examined Martha and he smiled. She looked frail as she smiled back. Ethan looked at Artie.

"You have a beautiful wife, Artie," commented Ethan and they continued walking.

At the edge of the stage, Gloria positioned Ethan and his best man, Fernando. Then looking around to see that everything was ready, Gloria signaled with her hand. The curtain on the stage suddenly opened and an Elvis impersonator from his leather non-overweight period leaped forward and sang "Burning Love" through a microphone while he gyrated wildly on stage.

As Elvis sang, Nona emerged through the front door, dressed in a short sexy red satin dress, bouncing lots of cleavage and waving a bouquet of pink roses, preceded by her maid of honor, Lizzie, who wore a sequined cowboy outfit that matched Gloria's.

Nona danced and skipped joyfully side to side down the aisle, greeting people, and arrived onstage to face her soon-to-be-husband just as the song finished, with Lizzie and Fernando taking flanking positions.

Like two little children, Ethan grinned down at Nona and Nona giggled upward at Ethan. Ethan reached out and grasping Nona's hand, they turned towards Elvis.

Elvis cocked his leg and shook it while his arms swung about.

"Dearly beloved," drawled Elvis, "we have gathered here today to join this man and woman in the hollllly state of matrimony."

"Do you, Ethan, uhh-huh-huh," crooned Elvis, "take Nona to be your lawfully-wedded wife till death do you part?"

"I do," said Ethan, as the "till death do you part" reverberated in his brain.

Elvis turned toward Nona and cocking his leg, swung it twice this time.

"Do you, Nona, uhh-huh-huh, take Ethan to be your lawfully-wedded husband till death do you part?"

"Yes, I do," said Nona. "Uhh-huh-huh."

"Who here has the rings?" asked Elvis.

Fernando produced two simple gold rings from his pocket. Ethan placed one on Nona's finger and, as Nona placed the other on Ethan's finger, Elvis recited, "I now pronounce you man and wife."

He looked at Nona and winked.

"Uhh-huh-huh. It's now legal to kiss your husband."

Nona leaped on Ethan and passionately kissed him, while seventy pairs of hands wonderfully clapped.

Fifty-five years of loneliness suddenly left Ethan and he grasped Nona, lifted her and spun her about on the stage, as she giggled and kissed and giggled some more.

Elvis sang a slow song and Ethan led Nona from the stage to dance. Other couples joined in and Nona looked up into Ethan's eyes.

"Now that we're man and wife, you trust me, don't you?" asked Nona.

"We didn't have to be man and wife for me to trust you," said Ethan, laughing a little.

"Good," said Nona," because I recruited some people to help us with Tyrannosaurus."

Ethan suddenly stopped dancing.

"What? Who?" He looked around. "We didn't need any help!"

Nona stroked Ethan's cheek.

"Ethan, my darling," said Nona, "you want to get this guy, don't you?"

"Well...uh...yeah."

"And you do want this operation to take this hypocritical televangelist to the cleaners and bankrupt his whole corrupt organization, don't you?"

"Well...uh...yeah."

"Ok. Then you're going to need some help," said Nona delightfully. "Who knows when you're going to suddenly keel over?"

"It's not going to happen like that," frowned Ethan.

"Well, nevertheless," said Nona, "you have a team to help you out. You are no longer the secret agent loner. You have back up now."

Nona looked around, and catching Lizzie and Gloria's eyes at the bar, she waved them over. Then finding the Kit-Kat twins, she waved them over as well. Seeing the women heading in Ethan's direction, Artie Thompson escorted his wife to a chair and, after she was seated, he crossed the room to join the others.

The group stood in front of Ethan and Nona, and Nona motioned towards them.

"This is your team," said Nona. "I've already explained everything to everyone."

"We all volunteered to help you get this guy," said Gloria.

"Besides," said Lizzie, flexing a large bicep inside her cowgirl outfit, "you're going to need a little muscle."

Ethan looked at the five people facing him and stopped at Artie.

"Artie," said Ethan. "You really should stay at home with your wife."

"Nope," said Artie, shaking his head. "I owe you. It's the least I can do."

"Don't forget about us," said Kit and Kat proudly in unison, as they waved to get Ethan's attention. "We're your backup singers."

They sang a few notes and grinned.

"What are your orders, secret agent man?" asked Gloria.

Ethan looked at Nona smiling up at him and then at the other five. Having this much support was something new in his life. Reluctant for a moment, he sighed, and decided he liked it. He didn't feel lonely anymore. He had friends.

"Ok, ok," said Ethan. "First let's enjoy the drag show. Afterwards, we'll gather and discuss what to do and we'll leave together in the morning."

Suddenly Fernando, who had been talking on his phone at the edge of the group, interrupted.

"Sorry Ethan," said Fernando, "but you're all going to have to skip the show."

"Why, what's happening?" asked Ethan.

"Clara Barton's on her way," replied Fernando.

"Oh shit!"

"Oh shit is right," said Fernando. "I've been keeping tabs on her just in case. Earlier today, before she left San Diego, she called a restaurant in Portland and ordered two stroganoff dinners to go."

"Let me guess," said Ethan, "the restaurant doesn't have stroganoff on the menu."

Fernando shook his head.

"What does that mean?" asked Artie.

"It means she's not alone," replied Ethan. "She's bringing two Russian heavies to the party."

He looked around at his crew.

"You people still want to participate in Tyrannosaurus? It might be dangerous. These are three really bad people coming our way," said Ethan. "I wouldn't fault anyone for backing out now."

Everyone looked at each other hesitantly, but then shook their heads.

"Sounds like fun," grinned Gloria. "When do we leave?"

"Clara is about an hour out," said Fernando. "So you need to leave as soon as possible."

He turned to Ethan.

"I took the liberty of having one of my men, Hector, pack up yours and Nona's stuff. It's in the car."

"Our motorcycles are outside," said Lizzie. "Gloria and I are ready to go now. All we need is our helmets."

Ethan turned to Kit and Kat.

"How about you two?" asked Ethan.

"We need to go home and pack," said Kat.

"How about I buy you new clothes and whatever else you need

along the way?" asked Ethan.

"That'll work," Kit said with a grin.

Fernando patted Artie on the shoulder.

"Kiss your wife goodnight," said Fernando, "and I'll make sure she gets home safe."

Artie looked at Ethan.

"You can trust him," said Ethan.

"Ok," said Artie, "good enough."

Artie turned.

"Come with me, Fernando," said Artie, "and I'll introduce you to my wife."

Fifteen minutes later, a red Honda Pilot with two cowgirls on large Harleys following drove south along Highway 101 into the night, while Ethan wondered if he was doing the right thing by including his new crew in what was now a dangerous operation.

Forty-Five Minutes Later

The black SUV drove slowly past the Pink Elephant in downtown Newport and then parked on a side street. Clara and Erika got out, followed by the two Russians. They stopped at the corner and Clara opened her purse to glance at the Glock. Then, taking a deep breath, she snarled, closed her purse and nodded for the heavies and Erika to follow her. When they opened the double glass doors to the bar, any sign that a wedding had just taken place had been removed and hidden.

"Excuse me," said Clara to a nearby lady drinking a beer, "we're here for the wedding."

The lady shrugged her shoulders.

"What wedding?"

"This is a bar," sarcastically added another lady sitting next to the beer drinker. She pointed. "If you want a wedding, there's a nice little church two blocks up."

"Who's the babe next to you?" she continued, smiling at Erika.

She winked and Clara had enough.

"Fuck this!" she grumbled loudly.

Clara reached into her purse, pulled out the Glock and pointing it at the ceiling she fired off three very loud, quick rounds to get everyone's attention. As she raised her arm to shield her eyes from the large chunks of debris falling on top of her, she heard a familiar symphony of metal against metal play around the room. When the plaster powder cleared her eyes, Clara looked up at sixty-six angry lesbians in cowboy outfits with sixty-six six-shooters trained on her and her companions.

Clara felt Erika lightly touch her arm.

"Grandma," she said cautiously, as she stared at the roomful of guns pointed at them. "I think it's time for us to leave."

Slowly, the four backed up and quietly exited the bar.

"What the fuck was that about?" shouted Erika on the sidewalk outside as they quickly walked back to the car.

Clara opened the door.

"Get in," said Clara.

"No!" shouted Erika, "Not until you tell me what's really going on! Either you tell me or I'll find my own way back to San Diego if I have to."

Clara looked at Erika and sighed. She knew it was time to tell her the truth.

"Erika, honey," said Clara, "he killed your father."

Meanwhile in Anaheim

René slid the flash drive into the side of her computer at her apartment. Opening the drive on her desktop, she clicked on the algorithm file that Erika had given her. Then, as she frantically tried everything she could to prevent it from happening, René helplessly watched as all the data on her computer was scrubbed irreversibly clean.

"That fucking bitch!" screamed René.

Part Two

Operation Tyrannosaurus

Chapter 10

Acid Test

Somewhere on Oregon Highway 20

Ethan stared down the dark two-lane road ahead of him, wondering about his new team. He didn't want any of them prematurely joining him in the afterlife; that is, if an afterlife actually existed. He didn't think anyone would get hurt, but still, he worried. Ethan glanced in the back seat. Artie and the Kit-Kat twins were asleep. Then he glanced at Nona sitting beside him.

"Nona," apologized Ethan, "I'm sorry I didn't have time to buy you an engagement ring. You deserve something really nice."

Nona chuckled.

"Ethan," she said, "did you know that women in the United States were convinced by an ad campaign in the late thirties and early forties that they should be given diamond engagement rings by their fiancés as a symbol of their love? Did you know that the figure of two to three months' salary for a ring was an arbitrary amount thought up by an advertising executive based on how much money the greedy diamond monopoly wanted to profit? Women were brainwashed to think that the larger the diamond, the more a man loved them."

"Hmmm," mulled Ethan. "I didn't know that."

Nona reached out and rubbed Ethan's hand.

"Any woman who cares about a man because of the size of the ring he gives her should be boiled in her own greed. I would much rather spend the money we'd save not buying a ring on other things," said Nona. "Like a down payment on a house, furniture, or a trip overseas. Big things that we would use or cherish."

Ethan looked at Nona smiling at him in the passenger seat, and realized that he may have doubts about an afterlife, but he definitely knew what heaven was. He loved Nona's practicality.

"Nona," asked Ethan. "Could you do something for me after I'm gone?"

"Anything, my love," said Nona without hesitating.

Ethan pointed to his messenger bag.

"In my bag you'll find a small notebook," said Ethan. "In it is an account number for a bank in Switzerland and all the passwords and everything that you'll need to access it online. After I'm gone, make sure Artie doesn't go broke taking care of his wife and Martha has all the medical care that she needs."

Ethan glanced at the Kit-Kat twins sleeping.

"And make sure Kit and Kat have money for as much college as they want."

Nona nodded, but changed the subject. She didn't want to be reminded of Ethan's imminent departure.

"Don't worry," replied Nona. "I'll take care of all of them."

A road sign stating that Corvallis was five miles away zipped past them.

Ethan thought for a moment.

"Radio Gloria and Lizzie behind us that we're going to stay the night in Corvallis."

Around the Corner from the Pink Elephant Bar

"Oh no, no, no!" shouted Erika, staring into Clara's eyes. "Grandma! You've got a lot of fucking explaining to do! What do you mean he killed my father?"

"Exactly that!" snarled Clara. "He killed your father! My son!"

"How? Why?" exclaimed Erika. "What the hell were you two involved with?"

Silent for a moment, Clara contemplated her granddaughter's angry face. Finally... "I know he shouldn't have been doing it, but he was laundering money through our import/export business."

"For who?"

Clara nodded at the two men.

"For the God damn Russian mob?" Erika shook her head. "I can't believe you got me involved with the Russian mob!" she exclaimed. "I'm not doing this anymore! I'm leaving!"

Erika started to turn, but Clara grabbed her and forcibly turned Erika back towards her.

"He killed your father! Your blood! He cold-bloodily put him on his knees, held a gun to the back of his head and blew his brains out!"

"I don't care!" shouted Erika. "I never knew my father!"

"This man is the reason you never got to know him," shouted Clara back. "I need you to help me find him."

"I don't care," growled Erika. "My father was a criminal and I'm not. I'm going back to San Diego. Find him yourself!"

Clara grabbed Erika's arm and pulled her to the back of the SUV.

"If you won't do it for your own blood," whispered Clara, "then do it for that artist girlfriend of yours."

Alarm raced across Erika's face. Erika couldn't believe what she had just heard from her grandmother.

"What do you mean by that?" said Erika, unable to hide the desperation in her voice.

Clara pointed in the direction of the two men at the front of the SUV.

"Other people are looking for him too," whispered Clara. "If these two men go back to their people and relay that you're not helping us find him, those people might take out their frustration on your pretty pink-haired girlfriend."

"They'd do that?"

Clara nodded her head.

"They'd do that and not even think twice," said Clara. "And they like to use acid."

Fear shrouded Erika as she stared at her grandmother. Feeling trapped, like she no longer had a choice, Erika looked into her grandmother's eyes and wondered who she really was. What happened to the kind, retired woman that she grew up with?

"Also, if you are thinking about warning her, don't!" advised Clara. "They'll find her and they'll hurt her worse. If I were you, I wouldn't even contact her!"

"Ok, ok," muttered Erika in a near panic "I'll help you find him."

As she walked away from Clara, Erika eyed the two large Russians waiting for them with contempt. Erika's father was Russian, but her mother was Ukrainian. She remembered very little about her father; he hadn't been around that much, and now she knew why Demetri had disappeared when she was very small. However, she had no sympathy for him. He was a criminal, and Erika still remembered, the loud arguments in the next room when he was around, furniture breaking, and her mother occasionally with black eyes and bruises on her face, before she committed suicide when Erika was only eight. She didn't care about her father, and she didn't care about the man who killed him. He'd probably done everyone a big fucking favor. But she did care deeply about Joanna.

Erika walked to the corner and looked up and down the street. On top of the traffic light at the intersection a block away, she saw a camera. Erika returned to the SUV and pulled her computer from her backpack. Ten minutes later, she scanned street footage while Clara looked over her shoulder from the back seat of the car.

"They left an hour before we arrived, heading south on Highway

101," said Erika. "There's seven of them now. Two men, and three women in the car and what looks like two cowgirls following on Harley hogs."

Clara looked at the road atlas.

"They must have backtracked on a side street at some point," said Clara, studying the map. "They're probably heading for Corvallis."

"Why do you say that?" asked Erika.

Clara nodded in the direction of the bar.

"Somehow they knew we were coming," said Clara. "This man is way too smart to allow himself to be outflanked and trapped on a slow road like Highway 101. If he drives to Corvallis, he can move quickly in four or five different directions. We probably passed them on the road on the way here."

She looked at Erika.

"We'll stop for the night in Corvallis and you can see if you can locate him from there, or find out which direction he is heading," said Clara.

She leaned forward and gave one of the men instructions in Russian and he started the car.

Sitting back in her seat, Erika silently raged as the car drove away, and hid how much she boiled over inside regarding her grandmother. She already knew which direction Clara's prey were heading, probably south to Anaheim, towards her idol Jimmy Bob Swindle. But all things considered, Erika decided she didn't have to tell her grandmother everything.

Chapter 11

Quietly and Quickly

June 6th
The Hills Above Anaheim, California

The southern Californian early morning sun crept slowly across Jimmy Bob Swindle's face through a crack in the curtains as he lay happily sprawled in bed between two sleeping hookers. His bloodshot eyes gradually opened to the warm light of daybreak. Glancing right at Peter, and then left at Paula, he sighed.

"They were worth every cent," he told himself with a grin. When Peter's twelve inches of slick rapture entered him from behind while he fornicated Paula doggy style, Jimmy Bob's forty-five-year-old cocaine-lubricated soul suddenly felt a choir of angels sing on high and the bounty of the Lord euphorically squirt from him into Paula.

"Hallelujah!" rejoiced Jimmy Bob. "Praise the Lord and the good fortune he has bestowed upon my prosperity ministry. Hallelujah!"

Suddenly, the door burst open and his wife Cyndy Lyn staggered in wearing a bathrobe. She glared at Jimmy Bob from the end of the bed. Without her voluminous pink wig and four coats of cheap makeup, short, plump Cyndy Lyn looked pale and needy. Between her hands she held a loaded gun.

"You bastard!" shouted Cyndy Lyn, pointing the gun at him. "Why aren't I ever enough for you?"

He could tell by her slurred words and the way she walked, that his wife was drunk again. Jimmy Bob held up his hands.

"Please, Cyndy Lyn, don't!" he shouted.

"Watch ye therefore: for ye know not when *the mistress* of the house *cometh!*" screamed Cyndy Lyn, as her shaking hand wildly fired six shots.

The smoke cleared and Jimmy Bob, with his ears ringing, stared at the two, bleeding bodies on the bed next to him. Reaching down, he poked them for signs of life. Paula groaned. Picking up a pillow Jimmy Bob held it firmly with two hands against Paula's face.

"Really, Cyndy Lyn!" growled a frustrated Jimmy Bob staring at his wife, as Paula momentarily struggled but then stopped. "Sometimes you are such a bitch! Look at this mess you've made! There's blood everywhere!"

Jimmy Bob leaned over Paula, careful not to get any of her blood on him, and reaching for his cell phone, he pressed a button.

"René, please get up here right now," he requested. "Cyndy Lyn's done it again!"

6 a.m. Hotel Rancho 66, Corvallis, Oregon

Ethan's nose tickled. He opened his eyes and looked up. On the bed, peering down at him, sat Kit and Kat. Kit's hand—at least he thought she was Kit—held a feather.

"Are you really dying?" asked Kat, studying him curiously. "We've never been around a dead man walking before."

"Nope, never," said Kit as they both shook their heads.

Ethan rubbed the sleep from his eyes with his fingers.

"We're all dying," he answered. "The only difference is how long it takes for us to get there. I'm just getting there sooner than you two."

"Well said," acknowledged Kat, turning towards her sister.

"Yes, very well said," responded Kit, nodding her head in unison with Kat.

Ethan chuckled and smiled up at the twins. They intrigued him.

"So, why did you two decide to join Nona and I on this mission?" he asked curiously.

They smiled.

"We're young..." said Kit.

"... and impetuous," added Kat.

"And this sounded adventurous..."

"... and fun."

"Besides..." said Kit.

".... it was time to leave our boyfriends," finished Kat.

"Boyfriends?" asked Ethan curiously.

"We think that they figured out that when we four went out on dates together..." said Kit.

"... Kit and I were exchanging clothes in the lady's room," finished Kat.

"It's really too bad because..." said Kat.

"... sex with Dean and Jerry..."

Kit looked at Kat.

"... Jerry and Dean..."

"... was really good when they didn't know we were constantly..."

"... switching back and forth between them."

"When they know, it takes all the fun out of it," said Kit.

"So out with the old, in with the new," said Kit and Kat in unison.

"Sounds like you two know what you want," said Ethan, chuckling.

"Absolutely," said Kit.

"Positively," added Kat.

"Do you know where my wife is?" asked Ethan, as he glanced at the clock.

Kit pointed.

"She's taking a shower," said Kat.

"Said something about you being so tired last night, that she didn't get any of the customary honeymoon nookie..." said Kit.

"... and that she wanted us to feed you..."

"... so you had enough energy to give her a good bebop before we hit the road."

Ethan scrunched up his face.

"My wife said bebop?"

"Yup," said Kat.

"And with a whole lot of emphasis too," added Kit.

"Well then," grinned Ethan, "bebop it is. So, what'd you get me for breakfast?"

Kat opened a bag and pulling out two sandwiches, she held them out for Ethan.

"We have two McDonald's Sausage McMuffins for you," said Kit.

"Delicious, but not healthy at all," said Kat. "In fact, very bad for you."

"But hey," said Kit, "that's one of the advantages of dying."

Kat cocked her head and smiled.

"These can't hurt you anymore."

7 a.m. (An Hour Later)

"Yes, honey! Yes! Harder! Harder!" shouted a women's voice. "Deeper! Deeper! Yes! Yes! Harder! Harder! Right there, honey!"

Meanwhile, a bed squeaked, creaked, and collided loudly against the wall. *Bam! Creak! Bam! Creak! Bam!*

Clara rolled over in bed and scrunched the pillow over her head, trying to block out the noise from next door.

"Fucking kids," she swore.

The hotel door opened and Erika walked in, carrying a bag from the McDonald's across the street. She looked at her grandmother on the bed.

"What's wrong?" she asked.

"It's those damn kids next door," muttered Clara. "I've been trying to sleep and, for the last hour, they've been doing that!"

Erika perked up her ears.

Bam! Creak! Bam! Creak! Bam!

"Harder! Harder! Harder! Fuck me—you beautiful stallion! Hi yo silverrrrr...!"

"You want me to go talk with them?" asked Erika.

"Would you?" said a grateful Clara. "That would be wonderful. I'd like to get a little more sleep."

Erika set the bag on a side table and left the room. Once outside, she knocked on the door of the room next to them. She heard a quick flurry of whispers and someone peeked out through the curtain. The door opened and Erika found herself face to face with Ethan Jones and his new wife Nona in their bathrobes.

"Can we help you?" asked Ethan.

Stunned, Erika stared at them in silence for several long moments. Then she giggled.

"You two need to quietly and quickly..." whispered Erika.

She rounded her hand and thrust the index finger of her other hand in and out like a piston before her hands exploded figuratively into the air.

"...then leave immediately!" said Erika. "Clara Barton is in the next room. I'll do my best to give you a two-hour head start."

When Erika reentered her grandmother's hotel room, she smiled. Without the racket next door, Clara had pleasantly gone back to sleep.

Chapter 12

A Four Car Train

Starbucks, Eugene, Oregon

While Ethan and Nona went to Starbucks to pick up drinks, Kit, Kat, Artie, Lizzie, and Gloria drove down the street in the SUV to pick up pizza for lunch. Inside Starbucks, at least a dozen orders were ahead of theirs, so after they told the cashier what they wanted, Ethan and Nona prepared for a long wait at the end of the counter while the overworked barista performed her caffeine magic. Nona slipped her arm around Ethan and lightly kissed his neck.

"I've never had anyone make love to me on the floor while they had a cocked gun in their hand," giggled Nona. "It's a good thing we parked the car and motorcycles behind the building."

Ethan nuzzled Nona's neck.

"Would you like to go to the bathroom?"

Nona looked at Ethan a little puzzled.

"Why would I want to go to the bathroom?"

"So I could strip off your pants and underwear and lift you up, so you can wrap your sexy legs around my waist," said Ethan slyly.

Nona, suddenly panting, grabbed Ethan's hand and led him to an empty restroom by the imported coffee racks. Then, making sure no one was watching, she quickly pulled Ethan inside and made sure the door was locked.

~

When the rest of their party showed up thirty minutes later, Ethan and Nona sat at an outside table under an umbrella, kissing and giggling, while they playfully teased each other.

Gloria eyed them suspiciously for a few seconds.

"Wait a minute," she said, "I know that look."

Ethan grinned.

Gloria looked around and then back at Ethan and Nona.

"Oh. My. God! You ransacked each other in the Starbucks bathroom? You two mangy old mutts!"

Nona grinned.

Lizzie looked in the direction of the door and nudged Gloria with her elbow.

"You wanna go...uh...place an order?"

Gloria smiled and taking her hand, took Lizzie inside.

Artie, Kit, and Kat sat across from Ethan and Nona at the table.

"Ethan, we have some bad news for you and Nona," said Artie. "While we were in the 7-11, the police put out a bulletin on TV about you. They said you were a terminally-ill cancer patient suffering from dementia and that you were a danger to yourself."

Ethan shook his head in disgust.

"I may be terminal," scoffed Ethan, as he kissed Nona, "but I certainly don't have dementia."

"By the way," asked Ethan, looking at Artie, "who are you?"

Artie stared at Ethan for a few long moments and then everyone broke down laughing.

"Very funny, Ethan," commented Artie as Ethan grinned at him. "Very funny."

"It gets worse," said Kit.

"Much worse," added Kat.

Artie pointed at Ethan and Nona.

"Someone recognized you at the Fred Meyers in Newport," said Artie. "The cashier who rang up your stuff gave them a description of Nona and said you were both behaving very strangely."

"Ho-ly shit," grumbled Nona loudly, "we were having fun enjoying each other's company. What's wrong with people? If you don't act like a couple of old fogies, they think you're acting strangely."

Nona threw her arms in the air.

"Quick! Somebody get me a rocking chair before I do something dangerous like go dancing!"

"Oh, I don't know," said Ethan, lifting an eyebrow, "a rocking chair sounds like a whole lot of fun to me."

Nona thought a second.

"It does. Doesn't it?" said Nona as she let her imagination fly.

"Before you two strays get overstimulated again, we have a plan," interrupted Artie.

"We're listening," said Nona.

"How about we lay low in Klamath Falls for a couple days..." said Kit.

"...you know, until this bulletin blows over in the public's mind," said Kat.

"While we're in Klamath Falls, we can fit you with disguises, and rehearse for Tyrannosaurus," said Artie.

"So, what do you think?" asked Kat.

"Think you two could spend four or five secluded days in a hotel suite with a hot tub and room service?" added Kit.

"I don't know," said Nona gazing at Ethan. "Sounds challenging? You and me naked in bed for four days. Top-bottom, bottom-top, sideways. Think you can manage?"

Ethan turned towards Kit, Kat, and Artie and smiled.

"I think we might be able to muddle through."

Fifteen minutes later, Lizzie and Gloria walked out of the Starbucks front door, grinning and holding hands.

"What did we miss?" asked Gloria.

"We're all going to Klamath Falls," said Artie.

"Great," said Lizzie. "But we're still eating Pizza at Hendricks Park first, aren't we?"

"Of course," said Ethan while he felt up Nona's leg underneath the table.

After the group feasted on pizza at Hendricks Park, they headed for Klamath Falls. Kit and Kat drove, while Artie sat in the car seat third row and Ethan and Nona cuddled and then slept in the backseat, unseen by passing cars. From Oregon Highway 99, they merged onto I-5 South and, three miles further, they exited onto Oregon 58 towards Klamath Falls. Three hours later, they arrived at the Lemmert Hotel, a fifteen-story monolith that towered over the city with a magnificent view of the lake to the north. Ethan gave Gloria a wad of cash and she went inside and rented the luxury suite on the top floor and three rooms on the floor just below it. Using his room keycard, Ethan and Nona snuck in using the side entrance and took the elevator to their room. Opening the door, Ethan, lifted his beautiful new wife, the prettiest girl in school, into his arms and smiling very broadly, carried her inside.

Earlier at 1 p.m. Starbucks in Corvallis

Erika scanned her computer screen on the table, while Clara sat beside her, watching intently.

"Ok," said Erika freezing the feed. "I found him."

Clara leaned forward to see as Erika pointed.

"This is a traffic camera at Eugene," said Erika. They're heading south on I-5."

Clara studied her road atlas.

"Good," she said. "We'll stop in Weed on I-5 until we pick up the trail again. Tomorrow we'll start our search a little earlier. I'll be a little more rested, without any kids keeping me from getting some sleep."

When her grandmother went outside to notify her two heavies to get ready, Erika let the digital feed run a little while longer. What she didn't tell her grandmother was that, if she had stuck around, she could've seen the Honda Pilot exit onto Oregon Highway 58 a few seconds later.

Three Hours Earlier, in the Barn at Jimmy Bob's Mansion

Extremely pissed described René's mood perfectly. When she'd been assigned to this job by her section leader, he'd informed her that Jimmy Bob Swindle had the potential to be an important asset to the agency and that her job consisted of watching over him and keeping him out of trouble. René never imagined cleaning up after his homicidal wife would be part of the job description. Her section leader, bound by instructions from his department head, who, unwilling to take the issue upstairs, told her to...well...uh...go with the flow, no matter what happened, because the potential information Jimmy Bob and his wife could possibly provide about North Euphorea, their nuclear program, and other closed-off parts of the world through his ministry could be a potential game-changer. However, despite the agency's instructions and assurances that René had a pass if the bodies were discovered, she still worried and took her own precautions.

Grumbling, René turned the key and listened to the backhoe chug to life. Earlier the entire staff of Jimmy Bob's mansion had been given the entire day off with pay to prevent prying eyes. Then, while Jimmy Bob and his wife conducted a prayer session in the chapel behind the house, to forgive each other's indiscretions, René was tasked with disposing of the bodies in the woods across the meadow, like she always did. Afterwards, she planned to begin the painstaking work of scrubbing down the crime scene and burning the furniture, and everything else that might have blood on it, behind the barn. René looked down at the two bodies wrapped in bed sheets and duct tape laying in the backhoe's bucket and shook her head in disgust as she drove.

Soon she arrived at the clearing in the woods where she had buried the other bodies and started digging. Stopping the backhoe for a moment, she wondered how many it had been in the last year and counted.

"Eight," she said aloud. "Yes, it has to be eight."

But then she wondered if she should also count the two collies and the monkey? She decided to stick with the strictly human-on-human trysts. It didn't bother her as much as imagining Lassie and Donkey Kong bouncing under the sheets with Jimmy Bob.

Digging two deep graves, René placed the bodies gently and reverently inside. Then, after saying a short prayer that ended, like it always did, with, "I'm sorry, you didn't deserve this," she pulled out a thick plastic bag containing the murder weapon with Jimmy Bob and Cyndy Lyn's fingerprints on it and tossed it into a grave. In case anyone ever discovered the remains, she wanted the finger to be stiffly pointed towards the right people.

"Thank God," she mumbled to herself, "I didn't have to give these two psychopathic religious morons my real last name when they assigned me to them."

As René drove the backhoe towards the barn, she stopped in back of the chapel. From past experience she knew exactly what was going on inside.

Jimmy Bob grasped Cyndy Lyn's hands into his as they stood facing each other at the front of the small chapel.

"I promise I will never fornicate with another wanton woman again, no matter how much they tempt me..." said Jimmy Bob.

"And licentious sodomites..." reminded Cyndy Lyn.

"And no licentious sodomites..." added Jimmy Bob.

"Don't forget promiscuous collies and philandering horny well-endowed monkeys," Cyndy Lyn further reminded him.

"Yes, yes... no promiscuous collies and philandering horny well-endowed monkeys," drawled an irritated Jimmy Bob.

"Ok," said Cyndy Lyn, adjusting her tall pink wig. "Then I promise I won't shoot anyone again and I forgive my sweet pea."

"Good," said Jimmy Bob sweetly. "Then I forgive my little honey melon for shooting those harlots."

Jimmy Bob looked up at Jesus on the cross staring down at them in judgement from the front of the chapel.

"Shall we ask for Jesus's forgiveness now?" asked Jimmy Bob.

Cyndy Lyn nodded her hungover head as they knelt on the carpet. Looking upward for salvation, they knit their hands together to pray for divine forgiveness.

"Jesus," said a solemn Jimmy Bob as they closed their eyes, "we pray..."

Just then, Jimmy Bob and Cyndy Lyn looked up at Jesus on the crucifix growling at them. Suddenly a backhoe burst through the wall behind Jesus with an enraged René at the controls.

"You want divine forgiveness!" shouted René maniacally. "I'll show you divine forgiveness!"

René brought the backhoe bucket down on top of Jimmy Bob.

Wham! Wham! Wham! Squish!

Terrified, Cyndy Lyn screamed and ran.

"Where are you going? Don't run! Don't run!" shouted René wildly, as she chased after her with the backhoe. "I thought you wanted to be forgiven?"

Wham! Wham! Wham! Squish!

"Forgive that! Assholes!" muttered René righteously.

René looked at the chapel for a moment while she fantasized and considered her options. Then finally, she muttered out loud "Nah," and drove the backhoe back to the barn.

7 p.m. The Lemmert Hotel Bar

"You sure?" asked Kit, subtly pointing towards a tall, muscular man entering the room.

"I'm absolutely sure," replied Kat with a sigh. "He's Dick Bangcock!"

Lizzie and Gloria looked towards the bar and then at Kit and Kat sitting across from them at the table.

"Who the hell is Dick Bangcock?" asked Lizzie.

Kat couldn't believe they had never heard of Dick Bangcock.

"Only the best-equipped male porn star..."

"...in the world!" finished Kit.

The twins spread their hands wide so Lizzie and Gloria could get the idea.

"And it must be..." said Kit.

Kat formed a very large O with her index finger and thumb the size of a coke can.

"...this big around."

"Wow," said Gloria, looking towards the bar again. "That's amazing. That is, if you're into that sort of thing."

"Oh, we're into that sort of thing," grinned Kit and Kat in unison. "Definitely all the way in."

"Well then," ordered Lizzie, "What are you waiting for? Go climb that...uh...mountain."

Tall, handsome, twenty-five-year-old Dick Bangcock, or as he was known outside the porn industry, Harold Namis, was about to order a drink and decide what he wanted to do with his vacation. Having filmed six sex scenes the day before, he needed a break to recoup and recharge his carnal batteries. Harold had just raised his hand to signal the bartender when he heard two melodic, sweet voices beside him and turned to see who they were.

"Hi handsome," said Kit.

"Can we buy you a drink?" asked Kat, smiling.

Harold stared at the two attractive young twins grinning lasciviously next to him. They were a fantasy come true for any normal healthy male, but he had concerns.

"That depends," he said. "Are you buying me a drink because you know I have a very large rocket and you want to fuck it, or for some other reason?"

"Hmmm," said Kit, looking at Kat. "That's a fair question."

"The first drink," said Kit, "is for some other reason because..."

"...just because you might have an extraordinary rocket..." said Kat.

"...it doesn't preclude you from being a total prick," finished Kit. "And..."

"...we don't fuck pricks," said Kit and Kat in unison. "We only fuck nice people."

Harold studied the pair for a moment and smiled.

"I'll have iced tea," said Harold with a sly chuckle. "It won't affect my performance in bed."

"Good to know," acknowledged Kit, happily nodding her head.

"Yes, very good," said Kat, nodding her head in lustful agreement.

She waved her hand.

"Bartender."

Ten minutes later, Kit and Kat were having a lively discussion with Harold, when Lizzie and Gloria approached.

"Friends of yours?" asked Harold as he studied them.

"They are," said Kat, looking at Lizzie and Gloria.

"Are they nice cowgirls?" asked Harold.

"Very nice, the best!" said Kit.

Kat draped her arm around Gloria's shoulder and smiled at her.

"You two feeling a little curious and experimental?"

Gloria nodded. "Uh, huh."

"Wondering if our new boyfriend would like to pull a four-car train?" asked Kit.

"Yup," admitted Lizzie, a little nervous.

Kat looked at Harold.

"What do you think?"

Harold smiled at the four ladies.

"Choo. Choo."

Meanwhile, Upstairs

Artie reached for his cellphone and speed dialed.

"Hi, honey," said Artie. "I really miss you too."

Chapter 13

Chairman Dim Ping-pong

Ethan walked slowly through the heavy, choking yellow mist, while he cautiously scrutinized his ominous rocky surroundings. Touching a nearby boulder he recoiled from the searing heat and the smell of sulphur. Walking further, he arrived at the entrance of a cave cut from the rock wall and stopped.

"Hello, Ethan," said an eerie voice from the black interior of the cave, "I've been waiting for you."

A shadowy figure stepped forward from the darkness.

"It's so good to finally meet you in person," he growled.

"Where am I?" asked Ethan.

"Search your soul, Ethan," said the figure, as it beckoned him onward with its finger. "You know exactly where you are and why you are here."

Ethan stared at the dark figure in silence.

"And if you still have a question about your fate," snarled the figure, "allow me to help you remember..."

Sunday, June 7th
3 a.m

Nona suddenly woke to Ethan groaning in bed next to her. His body shuddered in agony while his hands held his abdomen. Leaping out of bed, Nona ran to his messenger bag and pulled out a sheet of lozenges. Popping one she pushed it into his mouth. Ethan immediately began sucking, while Nona held him and ran her fingers through his sweaty hair. She pressed her wrist against his forehead. He felt like he was burning up.

Ethan looked up at Nona as he started to recover. It broke his heart to see her in pain. He wanted to do something to make her smile.

Several minutes later, it surprised Nona when Ethan's pain hadn't completely dissipated, like it had before. She popped another lozenge and, breaking it in half, she held it to Ethan's grateful lips, so he could take it into his mouth. He started to feel better almost immediately, and rested himself on Nona's chest as she rocked him against her.

In the morning, Ethan woke, still in Nona's arms. He looked up into her eyes and while she gazed downward at him with concern, he could see dried tear tracks on Nona's cheeks. Reaching upward he gently caressed her face with his hand.

"Thank you," said Ethan.

"It's getting worse, isn't it?" said Nona, trying to hide her sadness.

Ethan nodded.

"What can I do?" asked Nona.

"Keep me in the fight until the end," said Ethan. "Help me complete my final mission."

"I don't understand," said Nona, shaking her head. "Why can't you just walk away and forget about it? Why does this particular mission mean so much to you now?"

Ethan smiled at her.

"I know it doesn't make any sense, considering how much time I have left," said Ethan. "But I've got a lot to make up for in my life. When I close my eyes for the last time, I just want to know that I helped some people before I left this world, and atoned a little for the bad I've done."

"Ok, my love," nodded Nona, as she held him tight against her chest. "I just wanted to know why. I'll help you in any way I can."

Ethan, still a little shaky, sat up and stretched. Then turning to Nona he kissed her.

"Yesterday was wonderful," said Ethan, as he looked into Nona's eyes. "I feel better now, and... more energetic. How about I get the hot tub filled and ready to go, and you order up some breakfast from room service. I think I might be able to hold something down. Maybe some biscuits and gravy."

He smiled.

"We can eat while we play in the water."

"Now you're talking," said Nona, grinning.

The Diamond Cathedral, Anaheim California.
9 a.m.

Backstage, Jimmy Bob used the palm of his hand to shape his slicked-back coiffure one final time. Cresting like a black cockatoo's feathers, his hair made Jimmy Bob appear several inches taller than his five-foot-eight height. He turned to Cyndy Lyn.

"How do I look?"

She adjusted his tie.

"Perfect."

Then adjusting her breasts in the overly tight blue satin dress she wore Cyndy Lyn jiggled a little until she felt comfortable. To hide her plumpness, she wore a knee-length black knit frock over the top, while a red wig with a blue hummingbird adorned her scalp. Her lips gleamed bright pink and shone with tiny dots of glitter.

One of the stage crew fine-tuned the wireless connections around their ears and made sure their mics were working.

"Testing, one, two, three..."

He received a thumbs up from Jimmy Bob and Cyndy Lyn and faded into the background.

Then over their headsets, "Live in five ...four ...three ...two ...one..."

"And now," roared the baritone TV announcer, "live from the beautiful Diamond Cathedral in Anaheim, California, it's time for the Supernatural Seed of the Lord Prosperity Hour with Jimmy Bob Swindle and his gorgeous wife Cyndy Lyn.

"Brought to you today by the good people at Sure-Catch Undergarments. We catch what you can't... And Maxed-Out Loans. We have your back even when loan sharks won't risk it.

"Now, let's put our hands together for two ministers who have God and our Lord and Savior, Jesus Christ, on personal speed-dial, Jimmy Bob and Cyndy Lyn Swindle."

The curtain flew open and Jimmy Bob and Cyndy Lyn waved to the excited, clapping congregation, as the air in the cathedral filled with music from a fifty-person choir next to the stage...

Jesus loves you
–yes, he do!
Forgives your sins
This is –True! True! True!
Because you give and give and give
...a trip to heaven awaits for you.

So give some more...
Jesus loves you
More! More! More!
So he can forgive your sins
Credit cards accepted too!
Because he wants your love

–oh yes, he do!
–oh yes, yes, yes
–he really, really do!
Remember
Credit cards now accepted too!

While the choir sang and the organ played, Jimmy Bob and Cyndy Lyn, holding hands, strolled forward to a pulpit and several chairs at the front edge of the huge stage, while the two thousand people in the megachurch audience clapped in rhythm. Meanwhile on TV, millions of devotees watched worldwide, including a ruthless dictator in North Euphorea. As the music connected with the audience, Jimmy Bob and Cyndy Lyn pointed to individuals and shouted...

"Jesus loves you. Yes, yes, you bet he do, do, do!"

~

Erika shook her head as her grandmother watched Jimmy Bob on the seventy-five-inch 4K HDTV screen hanging on the hotel wall, which made the scene appear all the more surreal.

"I'm going for a long walk," said Erika, opening the door. "There's a grass shop a block away. Do you want me to pick up something for you? It might make what you're watching *make* sense."

Clara turned and stared at her granddaughter in stony silence for what seemed a long time and then...

"Grass is the devil's tobacco!"

"Whatever," said Erika dismissively, and she closed the door behind her.

Clara may not have wanted any grass, but Erika certainly did. She missed Joanna, and her grandmother had decided that they were going to stay in Weed, California until Erika uncovered a lead. Aside from the Pilot's exit onto Oregon Highway 58, which Erika wasn't going to tell her grandmother about, she had nothing, and desired to tell Clara less and less with each passing day. She needed a little grass to take the edge off her conscience, but finally decided against it because she wanted a clear head to think. On her phone, she received one worried text after another from Joanna. Erika decided it wasn't fair to worry her and simply texted...

–Am ok, please don't worry, be in your arms again soon.
–I love you too.

"Today's solo was performed by the beautiful Miss Janet Lee," announced Jimmy Bob. He waved his hand towards the choir.

"Janet, take another bow."

When Janet stepped forward and bowed, Cyndy Lyn suspiciously watched her. She didn't like the way Miss Lee subtly tempted Jimmy Bob by looking perfect in her flawless makeup. Miss Lee may deny that she wanted to take her husband away from her, but Cyndy Lyn knew a sex-crazed floozie when she saw one.

"There's a gun shop open on Sundays on the way home in Yorba Linda," remembered Cyndy Lyn, "and pretty Miss I-love-to-sing-for-the-Lord lives close by in Anaheim. I should take a midnight drive this week and arrange for the husband-stealing bitch to sing for the Lord in person!"

As René watched the service on a TV monitor backstage, she groaned to herself when she saw how Cyndy Lyn responded when Jimmy Bob gave Janet Lee a little attention, and she wondered how to keep a gun out of Cyndy Lyn's hands this time.

"After all, this is America," she reminded herself, "guns are as easy to get here, as beer for a teenager at a 7-11." But then René made a promise to herself: "If that maniac kills another person, invaluable to the CIA or not, I will fucking kill her myself."

~

"Remember this from 2 Corinthians 9:6-8," recited Cyndy Lyn from the pulpit. "Whoever sows sparingly will also reap sparingly, and whoever sows generously will also reap generously. Each of you should give what you have decided in your heart to give, not reluctantly or under compulsion, for God loves a cheerful giver."

Cyndy Lyn returned to her seat as Jimmy Bob walked to the pulpit.

"Thank you Cyndy Lyn for that inspirational reminder of why we are here today," said Jimmy Bob.

~

Clara picked up the remote and upped the volume so she could hear better.

~

"Today's sermon is 'Lust! How to thrust the ache of Say-tan from the depths of your loins,'" said Jimmy Bob.

"But first we are going to send the collection plates around for a special gift offering," he announced as he watched his ushers go to work. "As you all know, several weeks ago, I received a beautiful, perfect letter from the North Euphorean Dear Leader, Chairman Dim Ping-pong, who has been communicating with me about allowing missionaries into North Euphorea. The Dear Leader has invited me to meet with him this coming Sunday at his Stinkysong residence in Dongwang. Because of the time difference and the international dateline, the meeting will actually take place on Friday, West Coast time. To commemorate the moment, we are going to hold a special Friday evening Supernatural Seed service with special guest minister, the reverend Marion Morrison, at the same time I meet with the Dear Leader. We need funds to finance the trip and pay for the reverend's expenses, so please give generously. Every cent counts."

"And," he reminded everyone in the audience, "the collection plates now have chip readers, so you no longer have to swipe your cards. Just thrust it in. Enter the amount..." He sighed deeply. "...and enjoy the heavenly speed of your salvation transaction shooting forth."

"It couldn't get any more perfect," said Ethan while watching the TV screen. He looked down at Nona happily snuggled against him in the hot tub.

"Tyrannosaurus happens Friday," said Ethan. "We need to get everyone rehearsed and ready."

Chapter 14

Captain Kangaroo Loves You

Monday, June 8th
Lemmert Hotel

Over the weekend, Gloria rented the hotel conference room downstairs for two days, so the Tyrannosaurus team could rehearse on Monday and Tuesday. Ethan asked everyone to meet him there at eight Monday morning. When Ethan and Nona arrived, Gloria, Lizzie, and Artie were already in the room, drinking coffee and eating snacks supplied by the hotel staff. In the corner were stacked boxes of supplies they were going to need, that Artie had picked up on Saturday and Sunday after their arrival. It surprised Ethan when Kit and Kat strolled in with Harold sandwiched between them. Harold immediately reached out a hand to Ethan.

"Hi, I'm Harold."

Ethan warily shook hands with Harold and then looked at Kit and Kat.

"It's ok," said Kit. "Harold's a friend."

"A really good friend," said Kat.

"A really, really good friend," sighed the twins in harmony, "and he's decided he's going to help us."

Harold glanced across the room and winked at Gloria and Lizzie. Ethan looked at Gloria and Lizzie giggling and then back at Kit and Kat sighing on his arms.

"What the...?"

Ethan looked at Harold.

"I'm sure Kit and Kat have outlined our general plan to you. What are you bringing to the table to help us?"

Harold glanced at Kit and Kat and they let go of his arms. Reaching down, Harold unzipped his loose-fitting trousers and underwear and allowed them to fall to the ground.

"I'm bringing the salami to the potluck," said Harold.

"In the porn world, he's known as Dick Bangcock," said Kit, grinning.

"World's best-equipped private detective," said Kat with an even bigger grin.

Ethan's mind wandered as he stared at what emerged. He could understand Kit and Kat, but Lizzie and Gloria were hardcore lesbians. But then he decided, best not to ask.

"He can work with Artie," said Nona, rubbing her hand up and down Ethan's arm as she stared at the huge, growing appendage. "One shill is good, but two are better. And this makes it more interesting."

"It's a good idea," said Artie, looking downward. "It will give you more credibility for the finale."

"Ok, Harold, since the twins trust you, you're now part of the team," said Ethan, chuckling. "Pull your pants up and let's get started."

Ethan turned to Artie.

"Let's see what you found."

Artie led the group to the boxes in the corners and opened one.

"I bought these from a pastor at a local church after services yesterday," said Artie. "I gave him twice what new ones would cost. I told him we needed them for a funeral. So, for Gloria, and Lizzie, our enforcers..."

He pulled out a long floor-length dark red polyester robe with a big black cross on the chest. Artie held the robe up against Lizzie.

"Perfect," said Ethan, as the group nodded their heads.

Artie set the robe on a chair and opened another box.

"And for Nona, Kit, and Kat, our singers, I have the same robe in dark purple."

He held one against Nona, so everyone could see. Again, everyone nodded in agreement.

Artie handed the robe to Nona and opened another box.

"These were a little harder to get," said Artie, "but I unexpectedly found a bunch of new ones somebody had dropped off at a local Goodwill store on Friday."

He distributed tambourines to Nona, Kit, Kat, Lizzie, and Gloria, who immediately thumped them in the air and against their hips, bringing a smile to Ethan's face.

"Now, you and Nona are going to need disguises," said Artie, shuffling through a sack. "Nona was easy."

He pulled out a small box and tossed it to the twins. Nona, Gloria, and Lizzie peered at it over Kit's and Kat's shoulders for a moment.

"You three relax and discuss strategy," said Nona with a smile. "We'll be back in a little while." And the five women left the room as the men watched.

Artie turned to Ethan and held out a blond Captain-Kangaroo-style wig. Ethan took it from Artie's hand.

"Artie," said Ethan, examining it. "I can't wear this. I'll look ridiculous."

"But that's the point," grinned Artie. "People will be so busy looking at your hair, they won't notice your face."

"Artie's got a point," said Harold. "If you do this scene right, nobody's going to notice your face. They're only going to see the theatrics and magic around you."

Ethan and Artie looked at Harold for a moment, wondering if he was talking about...

"I majored in drama at UCLA," said Harold, knowing what they were wondering. "I only started doing porn to pay for my student loans."

As soon as Harold said *student loans,* Artie and Ethan knowingly grunted and nodded their heads.

"Student loans...porn...yeah, makes sense," they mumbled together. "Totally fucked anyway."

Suddenly Artie remembered something, and he turned to the pile of boxes. Pulling several aside, he found two long boxes at the bottom of the pile.

"As requested," said Artie, holding out his hands with pride after he had opened the boxes, "something very special for Lizzie and Gloria."

An Hour Later

Lizzie and Gloria stared at Ethan wearing his wig as they entered the room.

"See," said Artie, grinning. "They're not looking at your face."

"Good job," said Gloria. "I don't feel like I'm looking at Ethan at all."

Ethan, anxious to change the topic, asked, "Are you done with Nona?"

"Almost," said Lizzie and picking up a purple robe and a tambourine, she scampered into the hallway. A minute later she peeked back in.

"Ethan, turn around," requested Lizzie. "We want you to get the full effect."

Ethan turned. A few seconds later, he heard the door open and people walk in.

"You may look now," said Nona's melodic voice.

Ethan turned around and Nona immediately burst into laughter. Ethan didn't notice her laughing. He could only see Nona. Her grayish white hair had been dyed scarlet red and cut six inches shorter, so it lay just over her shoulders, accenting her radiant brown eyes. Nona suddenly realized Ethan was gazing intently at her and stopped laughing.

"So, what do you think?" asked Nona, pirouetting in her robe, her new red hair flying.

Ethan slowly walked to her. They stared at each other for a few moments while he caressed the back of her neck with his hand. Then Ethan pulled Nona to him and kissed her.

After waiting for what they thought was a respectful amount of time, Kit and Kat approached the still kissing couple and tapped them on the shoulders.

"We need to start rehearsing you two," said Kit.

"We haven't got much time," finished Kat.

Chapter 15

Sounds Yummy

June 10th, Two Days Later

Clara woke early on Wednesday morning and wasn't able to go back to sleep. It had been almost three days since they had lost track of her prey and she was becoming increasingly impatient. Picking up their road atlas, she studied it for a while. Remembering that the last sighting they had of Ethan Jones he had been heading south on I-5, she looked at Corvallis on the map. Using the shortest route to I-5, her finger traced a road and stopped. She studied the roads around that section of the highway for a second and wondered.

Clara got up and woke her granddaughter in the next bed.

"What do you want?" asked a groggy Erika.

Clara held out the road atlas.

"Where exactly was that camera on I-5?" asked Clara.

Erika peered at the atlas. Then, with her finger, she tapped a point on the map and rolled over to try and go back to sleep. Clara studied the map again and the roads leading from it. A minute later she pushed Erika's shoulder.

"Wake up," ordered Clara. "We have work to do."

Erika sat up in bed and stretched.

"What work?"

"What was the name of the owner of the bar where those two were married?"

Perturbed at being woken up, Erika picked up her computer from a side table and yawning, began searching.

Several minutes later, "Gloria...uh...Gloria Faith."

"Gloria Faith," muttered Clara. "Why does that name sound familiar?"

Suddenly, she snapped her fingers.

"Wait a second. What was the name of the car dealership that sold his girlfriend a car?" asked Clara, looking over Erika's shoulder.

Erika searched again while Clara watched.

"Gloria Faith Honda," said Erika.

"Ok," said Clara. "Now look for any recent hotel registrations or credit card transactions for Gloria Faith."

Erika searched again and found some credit card transactions.

"She's presently at the Lemmert Hotel in Klamath Falls," said Erika. "She rented three rooms and the upper floor super-suite. Paid cash. However, she put incidentals on her own credit card."

"Holy shit," exclaimed Erika with an amazed chuckle.

"What?" asked Clara.

"On Saturday night she had a hell of a party in one of the rooms," said Erika. She pointed at the screen while she whistled. "Look at these incidentals for the last several days, lots of alcohol... food... and three boxes of super-sized Señor Giganto brand extra-sturdy condoms. The next day at Walmart she bought two decks of cards, a Scrabble game, and Twister.

"It also looks like they've been watching non-stop porn on pay-per-view every night too," added Erika. "They seem to really like Dick Bangcock, private detective porn."

"Animals," muttered Clara contemptuously.

Erika did a search for Dick Bangcock.

"Dick Bangcock," read Erika off the screen. "He's billed as the world's best-equipped private eye."

She whistled again.

"Says here his rocket is—"

"Yeah, I know," interrupted Clara.

"You do?" answered Erika.

"Uh, I must have read it somewhere in a magazine," responded Clara.

"What kind of magazines have you been reading, Grandmother?" asked Erika with a slight chuckle.

"Get dressed!" ordered Clara. "We're leaving,"

Two and a Half Hour Later
9 a.m.

Clara strode into the lobby of the Lemmert Hotel with the two Russian heavies, whom Erika, not wanting to know their names, had nicknamed Boris 1 and Boris 2. Erika followed close behind. Clara spotted a perky young woman in a blue blazer behind the clerk's desk.

"I'm looking for a friend of mine," said Clara, "Gloria Faith."

"Oh yes, Ms. Faith," said the girl with a huge smile. "I remember her."

"Which room is she in?" asked Clara.

"We're not supposed to talk about the guests with strangers," said the girl.

Clara reached inside her purse and, pulling out a hundred-dollar bill, she laid it on the counter in front of the girl. The clerk, looking side-to-side, took the money and stuffed it into her jacket pocket.

"She checked out early with her entire party, three hours ago, around 6 a.m.," said the girl.

Clara muttered an obscenity in Russian.

"But I know where they are heading," said the girl.

Clara reached into her purse and laid another bill on the counter.

"I heard one of the blonde girls talking about going to San Diego," said the clerk.

"Where in San Diego?" asked Clara.

"I don't know," said the clerk.

Clara laid another bill on the counter.

"Ma'am," said the clerk, staring at the bill. "I'm sorry, but past San Diego I really don't know."

Clara muttered another obscenity in Russian and taking back the final bill, turned towards her heavies and Erika.

"Ok, we're heading back to San Diego," said Clara.

As she watched Clara and her party walk away and out the front door, the desk clerk mused to herself... "Two hundred from the scary lady and two thousand from the nice man in the funny wig. Now I have enough money for tuition for the nurse's program at OIT."

Reaching into her purse, she pulled out her phone and tapped a text message to a throwaway phone number.

–San Diego bound

John Wayne Airport, Orange County
Noon

From the window of the VIP Lounge, Jimmy Bob watched his luggage being loaded as airport personnel fueled his Bombardier for the long flight to Dongwang. Even though the jet could hold enough fuel to make the six-thousand-mile trip, just to be on the safe side, they were landing in Anchorage to fuel up along the way.

Jimmy Bob preferred this particular plane to all the others in his small fleet. Purchased several years earlier from a Saudi Prince who needed the money, it held thirteen passengers, and each luxurious seat had its own screen that hooked into the plane's satellite TV receiver. When he flew on his Bombardier, Jimmy Bob felt like he traveled the world in the comfort he deserved, and he was never out of contact with his spiritual and financial empire.

"The Lord works in mysterious ways," said Jimmy Bob aloud, as he gazed out the window, while thinking about his upcoming meeting with the Dim Ping-pong. In his letter, the Dear Leader had mentioned expanding Christian spiritual opportunities in North Euphorea, but Jimmy Bob knew this meeting wasn't about the spiritual angle. Given North Euphorea's economic problems, it probably had more to do with the prosperity message he preached; with which he was more than happy to help the North Euphorean leader.

The letter requested that he keep his party as small as possible for security purposes, so Jimmy Bob brought only his personal assistant, Thomas Truthahn. It was obvious to Jimmy Bob that the Dear Leader wanted their first meeting to be as intimate as possible, without news media present, and prying eyes and ears.

Jimmy Bob was also grateful that the Dear Leader had specified no wives in his invitation. In the past several months, Cyndy Lyn's homicidal jealousy and insecurity seemed to be escalating and because she wasn't coming along he didn't have to worry about what she would do if his host's wife smiled at him.

Sooner or later, Jimmy Bob knew Cyndy Lyn's extracurricular homicidal activities were going to be discovered, and that would be the end of his ministry. His *silent partner* had even suggested terminating the problem before it got out of control. But Jimmy Bob really did love his wife, four coats of make-up and all, and vetoed those ideas. At least for now.

"Besides," he reminded himself, "it won't be long before I'm so rich, I can buy my own country and shield my wife from any prosecution."

Meanwhile, sitting three seats away, short, balding, diminutive Harvey Atwater, Jimmy Bob's business manager, contemplated his iPad, while trying to make all the numbers in Jimmy Bob's financial empire work together. Using weekly donations and outside financing, the church had built and now operated the large "Glory-to-God" shopping mall, next door to the cathedral, the "Salvation" grocery chain in the L.A area, the "Prosperity" chain of twenty convenience stores, in addition to a string of "Death to Satan" bowling alleys, which, oddly enough, seemed to appeal to local biker gangs.

The mall, supermarkets, and convenience stores were heavily patronized by the local religious community, despite the high prices, and cash flowed from them like a waterfall. Harvey would be happy with what he had in front of him, except for one thing: their *silent partner*. The identity of which he suspected but dared not speak out loud.

Building for the mall had begun in 2007. But when the great recession hit in 2008, the church suddenly found itself with a financing problem, and was faced with either abandoning the mall project, or finding alternative financing. Jimmy Bob, miraculously, through prayer, came up with a fountain of cash funneled through an offshore bank that he'd had the ministry secretly set up in the Grand Payment Islands. Everything seemed fine until the project was finished and underway; then the *silent partner* suddenly demanded a five percent return on their money every month come rain or shine.

As long as the economy did well and grew, donations kept rolling in, and the church's cash-flow flourished, Harvey could keep making the monthly deposits to the silent partner's account in the church's Grand Payment Islands bank. But Harvey wondered at times how much longer he could keep juggling Jimmy Bob's financial world, which seemed to be built on a foundation of shifting sand. Lately however, whenever he approached Jimmy Bob about his concerns, Jimmy Bob assured Harvey that soon, he wouldn't have anything to worry about. Privately, Harvey wondered if his assurances had anything to do with this trip to Dongwang. Which, if it did, prompted Harvey to consider his own personal exit strategy. He smiled as he day-dreamed of a house on a quiet surf-caressed beach in Costa Rica, under an assumed name, financed by the five million dollars that he had diverted to a secret Panamanian bank account he had set up for himself in case of an emergency.

Refueling had finally finished and the pilots climbed aboard the aircraft to make final preparations. After instructing Thomas to go ahead of him to the aircraft, Jimmy Bob turned to Harvey, standing beside him.

"You're in charge while I'm gone," said Jimmy Bob, shaking hands. "Oh, and keep an eye on Cyndy Lyn while I'm away. And don't worry—I think all our money problems are about to disappear."

As he watched Jimmy Bob walk to the plane, Harvey suddenly grasped his forehead feeling as if he eaten too much ice cream, and had brain-freeze.

Biloxi, Mississippi, Twenty Years Earlier

Cracking the door open a tiny bit, Cyndy Lyn watched as her obese father climbed on top of Robbi Sue, to take charge of their moment in bed. It had been two years since her mother's death and Cyndy Lyn had just turned eighteen. Four years before her mother had died, when Cyndy Lyn developed breasts, the Reverend Noah Elijah Feelgood began coming to her bedroom at night to pray, and then after prayers, he would make her feel very, very good. One night, during one of these perverse prayer meetings, Cyndy Lyn decided to put the poison in mother's tea, so she could have her father's love all to herself. But when her father had stopped coming to her bedroom in the last several weeks, she realized the truth; this younger, sixteen-year-old, brazen sex-crazed hussy from his bible study class was trying to steal his love from her. Her father belonged to Cyndy Lyn, and her alone. It was with that singular homicidal thought in mind that she dissolved ten times her father's regular dosage of heart medication into his tomato juice when he wasn't looking and dug a hole in the garage reserved for the slut spreading her legs beneath him.

While her father pumped and sweated downward on Robbi Sue in the southern mid-day heat, Cyndy Lyn watched as he turned bright crimson red, knowing that it wouldn't be long before he succumbed and belonged to her forever. Suddenly his heart exploded like an atom bomb in his chest and the Reverend Noah Elijah Feelgood immediately didn't feel so good. His arms gave out and he fell, *smack*, on top of Robbi Sue. Struggling to get his weight and girth off of her, Cyndy Lyn watched with delight as Robbi Sue slowly smothered under the weight of her father's blubber, saving her the trouble of using the crowbar that she had found in the basement. Finally, when all movement had stopped, she walked into the bedroom with a measuring tape to make sure the hole she had dug was the right length.

Glancing at the clock on the wall, Cyndy Lyn realized that she had to hurry; she had a date with her dreamy new boyfriend Jimmy Bob Swindle in two hours. As she measured Robbi Sue a thought occurred to her. Jimmy Bob had just graduated seminary school in May and was searching for a ministry and her father had just provided an opening. True he was only twenty-four, but she knew enough of the church deacon's secrets to be persuasive.

"When god closes a door, he opens a window," she thought aloud. "...and Jimmy Bob is the perfect partner to spread the word of our lord and savior with. Praise Jesus!"

~

Janet Lee undressed in her bedroom and put on her robe. Remembering something, she sat at her desk by the window, and wrote a reminder to herself regarding groceries on her to-do list. Then, standing, Janet walked to the bathroom and closed the door behind her. After turning on the shower, she adjusted the faucets. Satisfied with the water temperature, Janet took off her robe and entered the steamy shower. As she wet her short blonde hair and enjoyed the hot water flowing down her body, Janet's mind drifted to an attractive new woman in the choir. After the service on Friday, Janet thought, perhaps she would ask if the woman wanted to meet for coffee and afterwards maybe... then suddenly, behind her, the bathroom door quietly opened and an ominous shadow threatened in the background through the semi-opaque shower curtain. Janet heard a noise on the other side of the curtain and turned just in time to hear a gun with a silencer.

Thwap! Thwap! Thwap!

I-5 California

Frustrated and tired, Clara knew her plan wasn't progressing as she envisioned. Originally, she imagined she would find her former lover, Ethan, as he was now known, and he would fall down on his knees, begging for her forgiveness. She would kiss him one last time and then put a bullet in his brain. Erika would be angry and upset, but eventually she would come around to see the logic in it, and forgive her. However, instead, Clara found herself on a long and fruitless chase and, by the way Erika looked at her, Clara wondered if her granddaughter would ever feel the same about her grandmother again.

They had been on I-5 all day, and Erika had been unable to discover anything new while they drove, so Clara directed Boris 1 to exit at Valencia, just north of Los Angeles, and get them rooms for two days at the Holiday Inn Express.

After finding their room assignments, Clara decided she wanted a bath. Meanwhile, Erika opened the mini-bar and poured two drinks of whiskey. In the bathroom, she handed one to Clara, and sat on the toilet sipping the other.

"Did you check the databases for hotel reservations?" asked Clara laying back in the tub.

"Yes," responded Erika. "There's nothing on the grid. He obviously knows you're following him now and is taking precautions. Have you thought that maybe he planted that information with the desk clerk in Klamath Falls?"

"That has occurred to me," said Clara, taking a long sip.

Erika hesitated for a moment, but then decided to say what was on her mind.

"Grandma," asked Erika. "Why can't we forget about all this and go home? We both have good lives. Why can't we go back to the way we were and just live our lives?"

Clara took another long sip of her whiskey.

"You never did fully embrace the Russian side of your blood," said Clara, staring at her granddaughter. "You've always been more like your Ukrainian mother. You need to become stronger and less of a sniveler. This hunt will teach you to be less of a weakling."

Erika felt like a dagger had been struck through her heart. Setting her drink on the counter, she stood and without saying a word, she left. In the bar across the street, she promised herself that from now on, she would stick very close to her grandmother, and become stronger.

Anaheim

Janet screamed as Cyndy Lyn tumbled, bleeding into the tub, pulling the shower curtain, rings and all, down with her. A large knife slipped from her lifeless hand, as the shower continued its relentless spray of warm water against Janet's tall, slim body and Cyndy Lyn's contorted torso. A steady stream of cheap makeup dribbled colorfully from Cyndy Lyn's face, diluting her bright red blood as it spiraled down the drain.

Backed up against the tile wall, Janet, naked and scared, stood frozen, unable to move. Slowly, her shock-filled eyes moved from Cyndy Lyn below her, upward to the door, where René stood, holding a gun with a silencer. René unscrewed the silencer and, lowering the gun into her shoulder holster, she walked to the tub. Kneeling down, René picked up the knife and looked up at Janet, who was still glued to the wall.

"This was meant for you," said René. "Because the apartments here are so close, I think she was going to use a knife instead of her usual MO, a gun, to keep the noise level down. Ever since the service on Sunday, I've been tracking her, waiting for her to make her move."

René smiled at Janet.

"Don't worry, beautiful, you're safe now."

René tossed the knife to the side of the bathroom and stood. Looking around, she pulled a large towel from a nearby rack and held it up towards Janet. Janet stared at Cyndy Lyn below her for a moment, and then, stepping over her body she allowed René to wrap the towel around her. She *appreciated* the way René snugly fit the towel along her sumptuous curves and afterwards, went out of her way to flatten the creases with her fingers and palm. Then, holding her hand, René led Janet from the bathroom into the bedroom and sat with her on the edge of the bed.

"Shouldn't we call the police?" asked Janet as she admired René.

"No," responded René.

"Why not?"

"It's complicated."

"How complicated?" asked Janet.

"CIA complicated," replied René.

"Oh shit!"

"Yes. A whole lot of oh shit!" sighed René.

"Why did she want to kill me?" asked Janet, obviously still a little shaken, but thanks to René's kindness, quickly recovering.

"She's a psychopath," replied René, looking towards the bathroom. "She probably thought you were after her husband."

Janet shook her head in disbelief.

"She thought I was after Jimmy Bob?" blurted an amused Janet. "Not hardly. He's not even the right gender for me!"

"You're a lesbian?" said René, looking into Janet's big blue eyes.

"And I think you are too," replied Janet, gazing back into René's lovely brown eyes.

"How do you know?" asked René.

"Maybe it's the sensuous way your fingers are slowly crawling up and down my leg," said Janet as she looked downward.

"You know," added Janet, smiling coyly, "they say rescue sex is the best."

"I've heard that too," said René grinning, as she started to lean towards Janet. But Janet stopped her just before their lips met.

"Before you have your secret agent way with me, could you please turn off the shower?" requested Janet. "And close the bathroom door. It would make me feel a lot more comfortable if I knew Cyndy Lyn wasn't staring at us.

"And," she added, "on the way back, take off your clothes."

René smiled and stood. As she walked towards the bathroom, she laid her shoulder holster and gun on the table and unbuttoned her blouse. After she had turned off the shower and closed the door, she returned to the bedroom and, in front of Janet, took off her clothes.

"Now, one last thing," said Janet. "Put your shoulder holster and gun back on, Double O-7. Then come to bed and reap your heavenly reward."

As René fit her shoulder holster back on her upper torso around her breasts, she made sure her pistol was not cocked and the safety securely on.

~

Two hours later, as Janet lay happily curled into her new lover's bosom, she glanced towards the bathroom.

"What about the body?" asked Janet.

"Not a problem," shrugged René. "I have someplace special to deposit her. But I might need your help while it's still dark, carrying her to my car."

Janet ran her finger between the soft pillowy curves of René's breasts.

"Anything for my hero."

"We also need to discuss us."

"Us?" said a surprised Janet. "You move quickly."

"I have to," said René. "In a few days, the agency is going to want to burn any connection with Jimmy Bob and his ministry. Given their usual procedure, I'll probably be put on an extended administrative vacation somewhere until things cool off. I was wondering if you might want to go with me and get naked for a while?"

Janet gently kissed René's breasts.

"With you, anywhere," she said as her hand wandered. "Where were you thinking of taking us?"

René took a deep breath as Janet lingered on a nipple.

"Flagstaff," moaned René. "Jimmy Bob has a beautiful secluded chalet a mile outside of town that he never uses. He owns it through a shell company, so nobody will think about looking for us there."

"Sounds yummy," said Janet kissing René. "When do we leave?"

Chapter 16

What Goes Around...

June 11th
Ventura, California

Marion Morrison sat in his office at the church, intently studying the pictures on his desk of him on top of one of the teenage girls from his purity class. Big droplets of sweat rolled down the side of his fat face as he studied the pictures.

Across the room, Fernando pointed his cigar.

"The fourth picture is the best. You can clearly see your face, the girl's face and your dick inside of her," said Fernando, smiling. "You set some kind of record on that one. It only took you what ...maybe six or seven seconds. Not even long enough for her to get in a good moan."

The reverend stared at Fernando, while thoughts raced through his panicked mind about losing his ministry, his standing in the community, and his beloved wife and kids.

"If you like," said Fernando, "I also have pictures of you with other members of your purity class.

"And recordings. Lots of recordings," added Fernando. "Does

'Please, Barbara Jean, suck the evil spirit of Satan from my big hairy balls' sound familiar?"

The reverend looked up at the ceiling, and closing his eyes, he sighed deeply. Then, as tears rolled down his face, he silently prayed.

Fernando let a few moments pass, so the reverend could feel the full gravity of what was happening to him. Then after Fernando felt like the direness of Reverend Morrison's situation had sunk in, the time had arrived for him to give the good reverend a taste of sugar. He walked across the room and, sitting next to Marion, he patted him on the shoulder.

"Now, I guarantee I won't release the pictures or recordings to the news media," said Fernando, "and all you have to do to make that happen is..."

He held up his thumb and index finger and squeezed them together.

"...one itsy-bitsy little favor."

The Diamond Cathedral
Anaheim, California

Harvey Atwater had just gone over details for the special Friday evening service when his cell phone buzzed. After looking at the caller ID, he answered it.

"Marion, I was just going over details for the service tomorrow night," said Harvey. "You're sick. I'm sorry to hear that. Your older brother can fill in. What's his name? Pat Dopeland. I think I've heard of him. Is he as good as you? Much better. A lot more charismatic. A personal-prosperity minister and an ultra-big fan of Jimmy Bob. Great! What does he need? Just an introduction and ...? He's that good. Great! I look forward to meeting him... Same schedule as you. Have him here at six."

Harvey set his phone on the table and googled Pat Dopeland on his computer. "Wow," said Harvey as he scanned the website that

Fernando had set up regarding the fictional Reverend Dopeland. "We got last-minute lucky on this one."

~

Fernando walked to the rented SUV in the parking lot of the Purity of his Glorious Word Christian Church, where Hector waited to drive them to their hotel in Anaheim. As Fernando sat in the front seat on the passenger side, he handed Hector a large-capacity flash drive.

"After Ethan and his team do their thing tomorrow night, make sure this is sent anonymously to the news media as soon as the service is over," he said.

"I only said *I* wouldn't send it," he added with a grin. "However, I said not a word to that piece of shit about you."

"With pleasure, Jefe," said Hector, smiling at the flash drive. "With pleasure."

Hector stuffed the flash drive in his vest pocket and pushed the button to start the car.

"While we're in Anaheim, do you want to visit with your granddaughter?" asked Hector as they drove away.

"Yeah, I'd love to see René," said Fernando. "But not until Saturday. After the service is over."

Palace Hotel
Anaheim, California

Ethan and his team stayed in Klamath Falls until Wednesday. During the day, they rehearsed for Operation Tyrannosaurus. At night, Ethan and Nona stayed in their suite, ordering room service and enjoying each other's company. Kit, Kat, Harold, Gloria, and Lizzie partied, while Artie kept a low profile and took care of the team's supplies and logistics. Every night, he called his wife. He missed her, and wanted to be with her, but felt that he owed Ethan not only for his generosity, but his mercy. Knowing what he now knew, he realized how lucky he was to even be alive.

On Wednesday, the team left for Anaheim at 6 a.m.. Before they left, Ethan got to know the front desk clerk, and contributed to her tuition fund, which ensured that Clara would get the wrong information if she showed up at the hotel. Since the desk clerk didn't know where they were actually heading, she didn't have to lie, just repeat the information that she had been given. More convincing that way.

Harold had his own SUV, so Kit and Kat rode with him, while Artie and Nona stayed with Ethan in the Pilot. The first day they traveled 400 miles of the 700-mile trip to Anaheim, and stayed in a small secluded hotel just off I-5, southwest of Modesto.

Artie and Nona drove while Ethan slept most of the way in the back seat. Pale, and a little more gaunt every day, it was becoming obvious to everyone that the former secret agent's life was soon coming to an end. However, in Anaheim, the team knew that Ethan had one last furious burst of energy left to burn. They just had to get him to the Diamond Cathedral and support him when he needed help, so that the light within him could burst forth one last time before it faded for good.

By the time the team reached the Palace Hotel in Anaheim in the late afternoon on Thursday, the group had jelled to the point that Operation Tyrannosaurus had become about more than one person trying to do one final bit of good. It was about a team enjoying the good within each other, and Ethan and Nona were the undisputed leaders.

Chapter 17

Felicity

North Euphorea

Jimmy Bob's flight took off from John Wayne International at noon on Wednesday, and though the flight lasted only fourteen hours, due to the time difference and the international dateline, it didn't land at Dongwang Hunglo International Airport until around six in the evening the next day, Thursday. When they landed, aside from a few military planes, Jimmy Bob noticed that no commercial or even private planes were visible on the runways or tarmac.

The tower directed the pilot to take Death to the Imperialists exit A from the runway and then proceed via All Glory to the Dear Leader taxiway, until they reached People's Heavenly Gate number six. Along the way, Jimmy Bob observed that everywhere he looked, the airport seemed immaculately clean and unused, and except for a few people mopping the floors, almost devoid of human beings.

When the jet arrived at People's Gate number six, they were met by a wide red carpet, lined with five heavily-armed soldiers on each side, at the position of attention, wearing green camouflage uniforms. At the end of the red carpet, an officious-looking pretty young

Euphorean woman wearing a black shirt, skirt, and jacket with a brown satchel looped over her arm stood next to a late-model black Mercedes limo.

Jimmy Bob exited the plane, followed by his assistant Thomas Truthahn, and was met by the woman halfway down the red carpet. She reached out her hand to Jimmy Bob.

"Reverend Swindle, on behalf of the Dear Leader, I welcome you to the Democratic People's Republic of Euphorea," she said, shaking Jimmy Bob's hand. "My name is Mee Yu-pee. During your stay in the People's Republic, I will be your guide everywhere you go. Anything you want, I have been instructed to provide for you."

Jimmy Bob noticed she had unbuttoned the top button of her blouse and the material seemed nicely full. Mee Yu-pee noticed him noticing.

"Anything?" asked Jimmy Bob with a smile.

Mee Yu-pee hesitated a moment and then smiled. She knew exactly what Jimmy Bob had on his mind, and what the Dear Leader required of her in his service. Mee Yu-pee licked her lips invitingly.

"Yes, anything," she repeated.

Jimmy Bob smiled again.

"Good to know. I think the Dear Leader and I are going to get along just fine."

Suddenly, Jimmy Bob heard banging. His eyes looked in the direction of the upper level concourse enclosure behind the Mercedes. The janitor working on the concourse stopped hitting the glass when Jimmy Bob's eyes met his. Dropping his mop, he pulled out a gun and, pressing it to his temple, the janitor pulled the trigger. Blood splattered everywhere on the glass and the man dropped to the floor.

Mee Yu-pee and the soldiers quickly grabbed Jimmy Bob and Thomas and shoved them into the backseat of the limo. Burning rubber, the limo sped off.

Meanwhile, inside the limo, Mee Yu-pee got on the radio.

"It happened again! Clean up on Concourse Aisle B," she said in Euphorean.

"Find out where he got the gun," she added, "and round up his counter-revolutionary family if he has any."

"What just happened?" asked a stunned Jimmy Bob, frantically wanting answers. "What was that about?"

Mee Yu-pee smiled.

"In our workers' paradise, some deranged people cannot handle the wondrous joy and love the Dear Leader provides them. His affection is too much for them to absorb."

"Do things like that happen often?" asked Thomas, taking deep breaths in an attempt to control his breathing.

"Some mentally disturbed people are just never going to be satisfied, no matter how much happiness you provide them," explained Mee Yu-pee. "However, the Dear Leader loves every one of his innocent children and will continue to give them what they need."

"Right," replied Thomas, while Jimmy Bob elbowed him.

"How far is it to the Dear Leader's residence?" asked Jimmy Bob.

"First we have to go down *Victory over Capitalism' Road*," said Mee Yu-pee, "and then take a left on *Invaders Burn Horribly in Hell Boulevard*; finally, a right onto *Prosperity and Love Lane* to the residence." Mee Yu-pee thought for a few moments. "About half an hour."

Opening a box next to her on the seat, Mee Yu-pee changed the subject.

"The Dear Leader knew you would be hungry after your long flight, and knowing you were from the southern U.S., he provided you with a familiar snack for the drive to his residence."

Mee Yu-pee proudly held out a bucket of Kentucky Fried Chicken.

"Also," she added, "he wanted me to convey to you his heartfelt support of your sport collective." Holding up a clenched fist Mee Yu-pee loudly proclaimed, "Violent ghastly death to all opponents of the Crimson Tide!"

Jimmy Bob glanced at Thomas glancing at him, and held up his hand to wave off the chicken.

"Please," said Mee Yu-pee, gesturing at him with the bucket. "It would be best if I put in my report that you both ate at least two pieces before we arrive. It was flown in special, at great expense, from Singapore just for your visit."

Jimmy Bob reached for a leg and Thomas, giving into the stress, gobbled a thigh, a wing, and a breast.

"Will the Dear Leader be there to meet us when we arrive at the Stinkysong residence?" asked Jimmy Bob, munching the greasy chicken. He swallowed the tasty fowl, knowing he would suffer for his sin later on the toilet, while hoping Thomas had remembered to pack the Tums.

"It is officially known as Residence No. Seventy-Seven," corrected Mee Yu-pee. "And the Dear Leader wants to meet you alone after you have settled into your housing assignment."

Mee Yu-pee leaned forward and wiped Jimmy Bob's mouth with a napkin while he smiled.

"I was wondering," said Jimmy Bob, his stomach starting to rumble, "does the Dear Leader speak English?"

"Fantastic English," gushed Mee Yu-pee, holding out the bucket. "The Dear Leader is extremely fluent whenever he wants to make a *point.*"

~

Jimmy Bob's housing assignment at the Stinkysong residence stood directly across from the Dear Leader's residence. Only a round stone cul-de-sac in the road with a fountain in the center of it separated them. The luxurious three-bedroom house spanned over two thousand square feet and had everything Jimmy Bob could want—silk sheets, full bar, and even a hot tub; not to mention a still almost-full bucket of KFC sitting on the coffee table, waiting for seconds. Against the wall hung a sixty-inch high-definition TV, which had already been preset and received only two channels: Euphorean Central Television and the NBA channel. Jimmy Bob perused the English translation in the guidebook of the channel's content. Currently they were showing a movie called, *The Running Dogs of Capitalism Must Die a Gruesome Death.*

Synopsis: Courageous villagers hunt down evil U.S Navy pilot shot down over the glorious People's Republic and dismember the gangster before he is able to flee and bomb their innocent peasant village again.

Though it sounded like a North Euphorean classic, Jimmy Bob thought he might skip that one.

After Mee Yu-pee showed Jimmy Bob and Thomas the house and its amenities, she let him know that she would be back in an hour to escort him to a private meeting with the Dear Leader. Thomas, very tired from the flight, turned in for the night.

At nine fifteen, Jimmy Bob heard a knock. When he opened the door, he immediately noticed that Mee Yu-pee had changed into a traditional Euphorean red and green hanbok dress for the occasion.

"You look beautiful," said Jimmy Bob, admiring her dress. "Why'd you change?"

"You'll find out soon," said Mee Yu-pee, taking his hand. "Tonight, we visit the Dear Leader's inner-inner-inner sanctum. Only a chosen few are allowed in. It is a sign of *trust*," she giggled, "that he allows you access."

Mee Yu-pee walked Jimmy Bob across the street and into the residence of the Dear Leader. Not much different in style than their quarters, thought Jimmy Bob, except bigger, and carved into the far wall, an elevator.

They walked to the elevator and Mee Yu-pee pushed the button. The door opened and, after they entered, she pressed another button with the designation B6 on it, and the elevator descended.

"The inner-inner-inner sanctum of the Dear Leader is in the bunker below," explained Mee Yu-pee, "in case of a cowardly sneak attack by evil running dog capitalist forces."

The elevator stopped, and when the door opened, she led Jimmy Bob down a long hallway to a heavy iron door with an armed guard on each side.

Mee Yu-pee knocked and then motioned with her hand.

"From here, you go in alone," she said. "I'll be here when you return."

Jimmy Bob slowly opened the door and walked into a large dim room. Closing the door behind him the guards locked it. The sides were illuminated by a few lamps, but most of the light in the room came from a massive fireplace with several large La-Z-Boy recliners in front of it. As Jimmy Bob approached the fireplace, a figure arose from one of the chairs to face him.

Jimmy Bob stared.

"Oh my God!" he whispered to himself.

In front of the disbelieving Jimmy Bob, with the fireplace illuminating him from behind, stood Dim Ping-pong, wearing an extra-large hanbok dress, much like the one Mee Yu-pee wore. From the square of hair on top of his head protruded a big shiny bow made of blue ribbon.

Jimmy Bob peered at his host. "Are you...?'

"Female?"

"Yes."

"My body is male," said Dim Ping-pong, "but my spirit within has always been female. Is this a problem for you?"

A stunned Jimmy Bob lied and shook his head, but somehow, it didn't surprise him. There had always been something a little effeminate to him about Dim Ping-pong in his pictures.

"No. No. Not at all."

"Good," said the Dear Leader. "I'm glad you're not offended."

Dim Ping-pong motioned for Jimmy Bob to sit in one of the chairs in front of the fireplace and walked to a nearby bar.

"Would you like a drink?" he asked.

"Yes, please," said Jimmy Bob, "a double scotch."

His host poured him a double from a bottle of Johnny Walker Blue. Then, from below the bar, he pulled out a bucket of Kentucky Fried Chicken and a plate. Using a pair of tongs, Dim Ping-pong picked a leg from the bucket and held it up.

"How many pieces would you like with your drink?"

Jimmy Bob wondered what the Euphorean obsession was with him and KFC.

"Just one for now," said Jimmy Bob, trying to be polite.

Dim Ping-pong set the drink and chicken on the side table next to Jimmy Bob and then sat facing him.

"In this room I can embrace the real me," sighed Dim Ping-pong, as he cupped the ample breasts of his obese body through the dress. "While we're in here, please call me Felicity."

He smiled at Jimmy Bob.

"You know, you are much more handsome in person than your pictures," complimented the Dear Leader, patting him on the knee.

~

Jimmy Bob prodded Thomas on his shoulder and he opened his eyes.

"Get up," said Jimmy Bob. "We've been given exit visas to depart."

Thomas sat up in bed.

"Leaving? Already?" yawned Thomas. "But we just got here. What time is it?"

"Ten a.m.," said Jimmy Bob. "No time to take a shower. Mee Yupee will be here in twenty minutes to take us to the airport. So, hurry up and get dressed."

"But I thought...?"

"All our business has been concluded," said Jimmy Bob. "We're going to stop off at the house in Hawaii for a couple of days to celebrate, rest, and make some plans."

"What business did you conclude?" asked Thomas, as he stood up and put on his pants.

"I'll explain on the plane," said Jimmy Bob, grinning. "If we leave now, we can watch the special Friday service on TV."

"By the way," he added. "Mee Yu-pee is coming with us."

Chapter 18

Probable Cause

Yellow sulphur-laden fog surrounded Ethan as he stood at the cave's entrance and stared at the dark figure hovering just inside.

"I know what you're doing," growled the dark figure, "and I know why you are doing it. It won't work, you know. You've lived a life that has led you to me. Now you must reap what you sow."

"You think that I'm trying to buy my way into a good afterlife?" asked Ethan.

"Well, aren't you?" replied the voice.

Ethan shook his head.

"No. No matter what happens, I know I'll belong to you soon," said Ethan. "Nothing can change that."

"Then why go to all the trouble?" growled the voice. "Give up gracefully. Accept your fate."

"I have already," said Ethan. "My time on this earth is almost done. Finished. But..."

Ethan hesitated,

"But what?" growled the figure, wanting to know more.

"But..." Ethan thought for a moment and then blurted out what he

was thinking. "Haven't you ever wanted to just do something on a grand scale because it was simply the right thing to do?"

"Not for a while," said the dark figure as it slowly receded into the darkness. "Not for a while."

June 12th
Palace Hotel, Anaheim

Ethan woke before Nona and lay in bed, gazing at her sleeping face for over an hour, while he contemplated what he had to do to make Tyrannosaurus succeed that evening. A delicate balance needed to be struck in the evangelical fundamentalist imagination, and then the bridgehead expanded. Ethan knew that not only did he have to hit a home run in the Diamond Cathedral, but the ball had to soar from the building and take the audience with it on a flight into the next county.

The team had rehearsed and rehearsed, but still, Ethan, nervous, worried about their chances. In the past few days, though he tried not to show it, Ethan could feel himself physically weakening with each passing day as more and more of the medicine was needed to alleviate the pain. He knew the end was coming sooner than he had hoped. He could feel its icy grip and smell the sulphur fumes. The dark figure waited patiently for him, but Ethan was determined that before he left the warm confines of the earthly world, he would do something to make himself a little less worthy in the dark figure's eyes. So, Ethan steeled himself to what he had to do. One final burst of magic was all that he asked of himself, and then he would go quietly to his fate.

"That's all I ask," he prayed, as a tear emerged from the corner of his eye. "Please, if anyone's there. If anyone's listening...just one final burst of the old magic. That's all I ask."

Nona opened her eyes and smiled up at Ethan. Ethan wiped away his tears and snuggled her tight against his chest.

"How did you sleep?" asked Nona.

Ethan lied.

"Good," he said. "The best sleep I've had in weeks."

Nona gently rubbed Ethan's chest with her hand. She knew he was lying. She had watched him toss and turn during the night, but for his sake, she said nothing.

Nona knew the end was near as well. Not by what she could see or hear, but by the diminishing life force she felt within him whenever she held her *husband.* A word that, in the last eleven days, had new meaning for her. She loved Ethan in a way she had never experienced before, and she felt his adoration every day. So tonight, when he was under those stage lights being scrutinized by millions, Nona was determined that, with every single breath she had left in her body, her husband would accomplish the final mission of his life. Then afterwards, quietly, in the short time they had left, they would say goodbye to each other in their own special way.

"Are you ready—" asked Nona.

"For you to order us some breakfast while I get the hot tub ready?" interrupted Ethan." I feel like massaging your back while we eat."

Not what she was asking but... "You're reading my mind," responded Nona.

Room 666

Harold looked first at Kit on his left, smiling up at him, and then at Kat on his right, smiling at him too as he lay in bed snuggled like a Harold sandwich between the two young, blonde goddesses. Never happier in his life, he decided to go for broke.

"Kit-Kat, Kat-Kit, I love you. Will you two marry me?" he asked.

The two stunned women suddenly sat up in bed and turned around to stare at Harold.

"You're not kidding..." said Kit.

"Are you?" said Kat

Harold slowly shook his head.

"But why...?" asked Kat

"Why do you want to marry both of us?" asked Kit.

"You can't break up perfection," said Harold, smiling.

Kit and Kat giggled.

"What about your porn career?" asked Kat as she rubbed his chest.

"Would you still fuck other women?" asked Kit, sucking his ear.

"If you two say yes, I will give up porn," said Harold, "and I will be yours and yours alone."

"Are you ready to..." said Kat.

"Forsake all other women?" finished Kit.

Harold reach out and stroked Kit and Kat's cheeks.

"As Paul Newman once said, 'why would I ever want hamburger when I can have steak at home?'"

The twins giggled appreciatively.

"I don't know," said Kit, contemplating the future.

"What would you do for a living?" asked Kat.

"I've paid off my student loans and saved my porn money," said Harold. "I've got quite a nest egg."

"So maybe you could go back to school?" proposed Kat.

"And become a doctor?" commented Kit.

"Perhaps a proctologist?"

"Or maybe a gynecologist?"

Harold sat up in bed and looked at his two lovers in frustration.

"You girls are not taking me or my proposal seriously!"

"We're taking your fake wedding proposal..." said Kit.

"...very seriously," finished Kat.

"If it comes from the heart," exclaimed Harold, "it's not fake!"

Harold reached his arms around the two women and squeezed them to him while Kit and Kat mewed softly against him.

"I love you both. I can't do without either of you," sighed Harold.

"This is about commitment. From now on I'm willing to give myself exclusively to you two."

"We love you too," said Kit, enjoying Harold's warmth.

"We really, really do," emphasized Kat, as her hand tried to get Harold interested.

"But you can't marry both of us," said Kit, adding her hand to Kat's.

"No magistrate would ever perform the ceremony," explained Kat.

Harold had an epiphany as he lay back on the bed and sighed.

"I have an idea," he moaned lying in place.

"Tell us later," said Kit, climbing his face.

"Yes, later, later!" repeated Kat, his rocket gliding slowly

...into space.

"Three, two, one..." roared his tongue in a fit.

"Houston, we have ignition," moaned Kit.

An Hour Later

Nona lay back in the hot tub, mewing softly as Ethan kneaded her appreciative shoulders. Suddenly an anxious knock on their door.

"Ethan, Nona, open up," exclaimed Kit and Kit. "It's important."

Nona disengaged from Ethan and climbed out of the tub.

"You stay here," said Nona. "I'll see what they want."

Ethan watched Nona head to the closet and pull out a terry cloth robe from the closet. He liked to watch the little wiggle she had in her hips as she walked across the room.

"We're getting married!" squealed the twins as the door opened.

Confused, Nona scrunched up her face.

"To Dick Bangcock?"

"Actually, from now on..." said Kit,

"He's just going to be Harold Namis," added Kat.

"Don't tell me. Let me guess," said Nona. "The best-equipped husband in the world."

"Yes, exactly!" giggled Kit and Kat. "We need your help."

~

"Kit and Kat are getting married," said Nona, slipping back into the hot tub.

"So I heard," said Ethan with a chuckle.

"They want our help," said Nona. "Could you be cleaned up and ready at two?" she asked.

"Sure," replied Ethan. "For what?"

"I'll tell you at two," said Nona. "In the meantime, I want you to sit on the edge of the tub."

Ethan, not knowing what to expect, stood and sat on the edge of the tub. Nona leaned forward and as one hand massaged Ethan below, she kissed him.

"You've been so wonderfully accommodating in the last several days," said Nona, "and you've asked for nothing in return. I want you to lean back and enjoy this gift from me to you."

Ethan gazed into Nona's adoring warm brown eyes for a long moment. Finally, he smiled slightly.

"Ok."

~

At two o'clock, Ethan received a text message asking him to come downstairs to the hotel's conference room. When he walked into the conference room wearing his wig and his black minister suit, he noticed lots of purple flowers in stands at the front. Kit and Kat were wearing matching long white wedding dresses and Harold, an Armani tuxedo. Nona approached Ethan as he entered and handed him a book.

"What's this?" asked Ethan, examining the book.

"Wedding vows, Reverend Dopeland," said Nona. "Since this is a non-legal ceremony, you're the closest thing we have to a real minister. Besides it'll give you some practice for your role in Operation Tyrannosaurus tonight."

Nona leaned forward. "Don't worry about legalities. This ceremony is really about commitment," she whispered.

Ethan nodded his head and walked to the front of the room to take his place, while Kit and Kat scampered past him to the back of the room. When they were situated, Gloria tapped her iPhone and, as the wedding march played, the two happy grinning brides strolled forward towards their waiting, grinning groom.

When the pair arrived, Ethan situated Kit and Kat so that they faced Harold, and Gloria turned off the wedding march.

"Hallelujah," exclaimed Rev. Dopeland, holding his hands to the heavens. "Dearly beloved, we are all gathered here in the sight of Gawd, and our Lord and Savior, Jesus Christ, to join this man with these women. Let us pray."

Everyone bowed their heads.

"Oh Gawd, please bless the marital union of these three people before us today," prayed Reverend Dopeland, "and give them your grace, so that they may live out their lives in peace and harmony together. Also, dear Gawd, please watch over these two women and make sure Harold does not pleasure these poor twins into an early grave."

Kit and Kat giggled.

Reverend Dopeland turned to Harold.

"Repeat after me. 'I, Harold Namis, take thee, Kit and Kat Hugmeister, to be my lawfully-wedded wives, to have and to hold, from this day forward, for better, for worse, for richer, for poorer, in sickness and in health, to love and to cherish, till death do us part.'"

Harold repeated the vow and Reverend Dopeland turned to Kit and Kat.

"We, Kit and Kat Hugmeister, take thee, Harold Namis, to be our lawfully-wedded husband, to have and to hold, from this day forward, for better, for worse, for richer, for poorer, in sickness and in health, to love and to cherish, till death do us part."

Kit and Kat repeated the vow.

"Who here has the rings?" asked Reverend Dopeland.

Artie raised his hand and produced three rings. He handed two to Harold. Kit and Kat reached out their hands and Harold slipped a ring on both their fingers at the same time. Kit and Kat took the remaining ring and, holding it together, slipped it on Harold's finger.

"I now pronounce you man and wives," said Rev. Dopeland. He looked at Harold. "You may kiss your brides." Kit and Kat grinned and then, to symbolize that Harold belonged to both of them, they kissed him on the lips at the same time.

Afterwards, everyone gathered around to congratulate them.

"Does this mean," asked Gloria, "that Lizzie and I..."

"Sorry ladies," said Harold with his arms around his new wives. "But I'm only servicing these two goddesses from now on."

"Good work," said Nona, looking up at Ethan. "Great practice for tonight."

Ethan didn't reply and winced.

"Do you need to go to the room?" asked Nona.

Ethan nodded and they quickly excused themselves. They didn't need to say anything; everyone knew why they were leaving.

When they entered their room, Ethan collapsed on the bed, clutching his abdomen. Nona rushed to his messenger bag. Holding him tightly against her, Nona inserted two lozenges into Ethan's mouth while she cried and rocked him in her arms.

Somewhere Over the Pacific

Thomas poured two whiskey doubles and walked towards Jimmy Bob, who had been silently staring out the window of the Bombardier, deep in thought ever since it had taken off from Dongwang Hunglo International Airport hours earlier. Sitting across from

Jimmy Bob, Thomas held out a drink to him as he glanced at Mee Yu-pee, sleeping on the couch seat.

"Ok, boss," said Thomas, "what kind of business did you conclude with the Dear Leader? Why are we leaving so early?"

Jimmy Bob turned from the window, and taking the glass from Thomas, drank half of it in one long gulp.

"While we're on the way home, the Dear Leader will announce that, after talking with me, he has decided to allow Christian missionaries into North Euphorea at some point in the future," said Jimmy Bob.

"Terrific," said Thomas, sipping his drink. "That'll make you look great in the evangelical Christian community."

"It'll never happen," said Jimmy Bob, shaking his head. "We both know that. That's not why we came."

"Then, what did we get out of this trip?" asked Thomas.

"Around half a billion dollars in money laundering fees over the next year through our Grand Payment Islands bank," said Jimmy Bob. "Mee Yu-pee is our Dear Leader liaison."

Thomas stopped sipping his drink.

"Holy shit."

"*Holy* shit is right," said Jimmy Bob. "God has smiled on my ministry, and apparently, we came highly recommended by our silent financing partner, who I have to give a percentage to. Last night, while you were sleeping, the Dear Leader transferred an initial two billion dollars from secret overseas accounts to our bank. In a week, we're going to start shifting the money past the U.N. and U.S. sanctions. Our service fee is five percent. That means we initially get to keep a hundred million off the top, with a lot more to come if everything works out."

"That's a lot of money," whistled Thomas. "How were you able to persuade the Dear Leader so quickly?"

Jimmy Bob stared out the window while his mind remembered two enormous round mountains staring up at him each time Felicity bent over a table and pulled up her dress. Though he had experienced a lot of things in his life, Jimmy Bob wondered if he would ever get over the sound of Felicity squealing like a Georgia backwoods piggy in Deliverance, while, at her request, he fiercely slapped her hips.

"*Weeh! Weeh! Weeh!*"

But then Jimmy Bob thought about the amount of money involved, and he decided he could get used to it.

Anaheim Police Department
Late afternoon

It had been a slow day for Anaheim homicide detective Basil Mathbone. The DNA results were not back yet in the Robertson case, and the autopsy wasn't finished in the Hinn death. Earlier in the day, Basil had filed his report regarding the Copeland double murder. All evidence pointed to the couple's gay drug-dealing lovers. An arrest warrant had been issued for the fugitives. And the autopsy in the Swaggart case showed that he had faked his own death to avoid prosecution for fraud. They were still trying to determine whose body he had used in the fiery car crash and whether or not they should charge him with murder too.

Basil looked across his desk at Homicide Detective Cake, sitting at the desk facing his. Patricia had been his partner for almost ten years, and they were close. Both had attended each other's weddings and they were an elite team that had put their heads together to solve many of Anaheim's most prominent celebrity murders. At the moment, Patricia intensely studied her computer.

"Patty," said Detective Mathbone. "I'm thinking about going home early today and spending some quality time with Sharon. Could you cover for me?"

Patty unexpectedly shook her head no.

"I think we'd better call our spouses and let them know we'll be putting in some overtime and we're going to be late for supper tonight," said Patty. She waved Basil over to her computer.

"Come here," she said excitedly. "You really need to see this."

Basil walked to Patty's desk while she pointed at the computer screen.

"I received this email an hour ago," she said. "On it are listed eight missing person cases of prostitutes plus one more, along with the dates they went missing."

Patty pointed again. "Look at the plus one name at the bottom of the list."

Basil leaned forward to see.

"Holy shit," he exclaimed. "That's Cyndy Lyn Swindle! Have you called their house?"

"First thing I did," said Patty. "The household staff haven't seen her in three days. Not since the date on the list."

"What else did the email say?" asked Basil.

"Only a precise longitude and latitude," replied Patty. "I've already googled it. Guess where it's located?"

"Don't tell me," said Basil, thinking ahead. "On the Swindle estate."

"Bingo," replied Patty. "In the woods behind their house."

"There's one other thing," said Patty.

"What's that?" asked Basil.

"The email is anonymous and our tech people can't trace it," replied Patty.

"So, we better call our spouses and let them know we're going to be late for dinner," said Basil.

~

"You sure it's not a prank?" asked Lieutenant McQueen ten minutes later. "Because if we go barging into the Swindle estate and this is a prank, we're all going to be in a lot of trouble. We might even get sued. You know how sensitive these fundamentalist religious types are when they think they're being persecuted."

"Since we don't publish in the reports the missing person's illegal occupation," said Basil, "we're pretty sure that this is for real."

"Aside from Cyndy Lyn's name, eight people, eight hookers. It's way too coincidental to be anything but real," commented Patty. "Whoever sent this knew what the victims did for a living. We might be dealing with a serial killer."

Lieutenant McQueen thought for a moment and weighed the options. These were his two best detectives. He trusted them. It wasn't much of a decision.

"Ok," he said. "I'll get you a search warrant for only the woods, based on the list in the email and what we know about it. If you find probable cause in the woods, let me know, and I'll get you a search warrant for the house too."

7 p.m.

Two hours later, after serving the ministry's lawyer with a search warrant, homicide detectives Patricia Cake and Basil Mathbone walked across the meadow behind the mansion, to the woods just beyond. Five minutes later, Lieutenant McQueen received several pictures in a text. The first contained an image of a dead Cyndy Lyn holding a gun, sitting underneath a tree. In the second, eight small white crosses were staked out neatly in the soil behind her. On the ground in front of each cross lay a bouquet of flowers cut from the Swindle garden.

Lieutenant McQueen showed the pictures to the detective sitting in his office.

"Now, this is the dictionary definition of probable cause," he said with a grin.

Chapter 19

The Church of the Holy Chastisement

The Anaheim Palace Hotel

Ethan sat in his hotel room, wearing his blond wig, black suit, shirt, and tie. Taking into consideration traffic, it was time to leave. He and Nona headed downstairs to the parking lot below the towering twenty-story Anaheim Palace Hotel, where his team gathered for the final time after they had packed the car.

"Everybody remember their escape plan?" asked Ethan. "Nona and myself in the Pilot. Artie, Kit, and Kat with Harold, and Lizzie and Gloria on their hogs. Scatter, and take the back roads home. If anybody questions you, you were recruited and paid by me to perform in a theater improv production. Nothing more. But really, I don't think anyone will ever come after you. They'll focus on me and soon ...well...you all know the story on that one."

"If everything goes as planned, I won't have time afterwards to say goodbye," said Ethan, "so I'll say my goodbyes now."

Ethan's voice choked with emotion.

"I don't think I've ever served with a finer more dedicated group of people. Thank you," said Ethan, looking into his friend's faces, "... and I wish each and every one of you a long and very happy life."

Artie and Harold approached and shook Ethan's hand.

"You ok?" asked Artie, noticing that Ethan's hand shook a little. "You going to be able to do this?"

"Just get me to the church on time," joked Ethan.

The women couldn't restrain themselves and in one big group hug, they enveloped Ethan as Nona watched, knowing she would have her own moment with her husband later.

Nona drove to the Diamond Cathedral located five miles away by freeway while, in the passenger seat, Ethan reviewed in his mind what lay ahead of him.

"Disneyland and the Diamond Cathedral in the same town," said Ethan as they passed a sign. He chuckled. "How's that for irony?"

Suddenly, the Diamond Cathedral came into view and Nona exited the freeway.

"It's beautiful," said Ethan, admiring the structure.

A sign pointed to the back entrance. When Nona turned the corner, Ethan couldn't believe what he saw. Besides the lone guard, twenty women on loud idling Harley hogs were waiting for them at the gate.

Stopping at the small guardhouse, Nona pointed to Ethan.

"This is the Reverend Pat Dopeland," said Nona. "The car behind us and all the motorcycles are with the Church of the Holy Chastisement to participate in the service today."

The guard looked at Ethan.

"Is the reverend ok?" drawled the guard. "He doesn't look too good. Kind of pale."

"Just a slight touch of the flu," said Nona. "He'll be ok. You know how it is," she said. "The show must go on."

The guard nodded and looked over the entourage for a moment.

"Follow the yellow arrows on the pavement," he said. "You'll find a row of parking spaces reserved for your party by the rear entrance doors. I'll call Mr. Atwater and let him know you're on your way."

The guard opened the gate and waved them in.

As soon as they drove inside, Ethan was about to say something, but Nona spoke first.

"You needed help," said Nona, "and they were more than happy to volunteer. Don't worry about them being ready. They rehearsed at night with Lizzie and Gloria over the internet while you slept.

"And," she added, "they all have robes. Albeit, in a rainbow of colors."

Ethan gazed at Nona as emotions welled up inside of him. He didn't know how he could love her more.

"Thank you," said Ethan, as simply and concisely as his feelings would allow him.

After parking the car, Nona leaned over and kissed him. "You're welcome Reverend *Dopey*."

Then, reaching up, Nona pulled the wig off Ethan's head. "You're not going to need this today," she said. "By the time someone figures out you're the guy from the police bulletin, we'll be gone."

Ethan smiled and got out of the Pilot. Harvey Atwater met Ethan and Nona's entourage at the double-door back entrance and he seemed surprised to see so many in the party.

"Hello Reverend," said Harvey, looking over the group in motorcycle leather. "I'm a little... well, I was only expecting six people."

Reverend Dopeland glanced at the group.

"These are members of the choir from my ministry," drawled Reverend Dopeland's voice, quivering with joy. "When they heard I was going to be praissssing the word of our Lord and Savior at the beautiful Diamond Cathedral today, they all wanted to come. How could I not allow them to participate in this once-in-a-lifetime opportunity to purify their eternal souls in this sacred house of Gawd?"

Harvey felt flattered by the reverend's description of the Diamond Cathedral.

"That's a good point, Reverend," said Harvey proudly. "Come on in and I'll show you around."

The entourage followed Harvey down a long hallway. He

directed Reverend Dopeland's choir to a large room where they could change. When they entered the room, the regular members of the choir were a little startled by the large amount of lesbian cowgirl leather in front of them, but quickly calmed when a woman from the entourage asked if someone from the choir could help with her makeup. Since all the members of the regular choir were devout followers of Saint Mary Kay, they were very happy to be of assistance, and soon the air filled with the scents of blush, blue eye shadow, and cheap perfume that resonated like a can of Walmart off-brand air freshener.

Meanwhile, Harvey showed Reverend Dopeland and Nona to a room next to the stage. On the door hung a large star with a golden cross in the middle. He motioned towards several chairs next to their room, and a woman standing nearby.

"When you're ready, she will do your makeup for you," said Harvey. "After she finishes, the stage techs will fit you with your wireless mics."

Harvey looked at his watch.

"Forty minutes until showtime," he said. "You ready, Reverend?"

"As ready as a Georgia hound dog in a tick contest," exclaimed Reverend Dopeland.

Harvey had no idea what the Reverend meant by that, but went along with it anyway.

"Ok," said Harvey. "I'll leave you to it. I'll be back just before the show begins and watch as you're introduced by the announcer. If you need anything before then..." Harvey pointed down the hall. "My office is the first one on the left."

"Thank you, brother," drawled Reverend Dopeland, vigorously shaking his hand. "You've been most gracious and helpful. I'll make sure everybody in the audience tonight has a closer relationship to our Lord and Savior, Jessssuuuus, after we root out the evil of Say-tan!"

"I'm sure they will," acknowledged Harvey with a big smile, and he turned to leave. On the way back to his office, Harvey thought about how lucky they were to be able to have Reverend Dopeland fill in at the last minute.

When they entered the dressing room, Nona slid her purple robe on over her harem pants and loose shirt while she watched Ethan take another lozenge from his pocket. With each lozenge he sucked, Nona felt a little twinge of pain in her own soul. Walking to Ethan, she adjusted his tie while he popped the lozenge into his mouth.

"Be careful with those things," said Nona. "Or you'll end up going onstage tonight stoned."

Ethan smiled.

"Given our audience," said Ethan, as he hugged her to him, "I think I need to be stoned."

He looked down into Nona's expressive brown eyes.

"No matter what happens tonight," said Ethan. "Just remember how much I love you."

Nona melted against Ethan's chest while she nodded.

~

When the makeup artist finished, Ethan glanced at the clock on the wall and did some quick mental calculations.

"Quarter till seven. Perfect," said Ethan as he kissed Nona and walked down the hallway. Harvey was just leaving his office when Ethan ran into him.

"Mr. Atwater," said Reverend Dopeland frantically. "I need a quick favor."

Harvey glanced at the clock on the wall.

"What can I help you with?" asked Harvey.

"I promised my brother that I would email him a copy of my sermon tonight before I went on and I completely forgot to do it," said Reverend Dopeland. "I need to send it to him lickety-split so he can follow along during the service. Could you please help me?"

"Sure," said Harvey, motioning. "Come on in."

He unlocked his office and, sitting behind the computer on his desk, he entered his password. Using the mouse, he brought up his email application and then stood and motioned for Reverend Dopeland to sit.

Reverend Dopeland pulled a flash drive from his pocket and inserted it into the side of the computer. When the flash drive showed up on the desktop, he opened it.

"Just a moment, Reverend," said Harvey. "Before you drag that to the desktop I need to check it for viruses."

Harvey leaned down and using the mouse, he opened the file and examined it for a moment.

"Good," said Harvey. "It's just a Word file. I don't need to scan it."

Harvey straightened up and walked to the door while Reverend Dopeland dragged the file to the desktop and attached it to an email. Slowly, he entered his brother's email address, a few words on the subject line, and pressed send. A minute later, he pulled the flash drive from its slot and slipped it into his pocket. He started to get up, but then he stopped.

"Say, Harvey," said Reverend Dopeland, pointing at the computer desktop on the screen. "This background wallpaper you're using. Where's this picture from? It's beautiful."

~

Nona parted the curtains on the stage slightly and peeked out. Her mind had been focused not on the performance to come, but on Ethan's health, and she needed a distraction. She looked up and then downward, and saw that both the balconies and the ground floor of the Diamond Cathedral were packed. Oddly enough, sitting at the far end of the first row she noticed an interesting man in surfer baggies, a Hawaiian shirt and sandals munching what looked like a bag of caramel corn. Everyone else in the church seemed to be wearing casual evening clothes, except for a handsome man and a beautiful woman sitting in the center of the front row. Both wore black pinstripe suits and long dark overcoats. The first thought that entered Nona's mind was *government.* Suddenly she was glad she had thought ahead and had taken her own precautions.

6:55 p.m. California Time

An hour earlier, North Euphorean time, the Dear Leader, Dim Ping-pong, had announced to a few members of the foreign press that as a result of his meeting and talks with the Reverend Swindle, he might, possibly, in the future, consider allowing foreign missionaries from Reverend Swindle's church to enter North Euphorea. The Dear Leader mentioned nothing about when, nor where they would be allowed to enter, or what they would be allowed to do. Also, nothing regarding missionaries was allowed to be announced to the Euphorean public on state news, on the noontime broadcast or any other future broadcast.

Now in his inner-inner sanctum, the Dear Leader took off his political clothes and mulled over what dress he would wear. Felicity decided on a purple hanbok and a bright red *communist* bow for her square block of hair. Then, switching on the satellite TV, she tried to make up her mind whether she should watch a recording of a recent NBA playoff game on ESPN with hot sweaty basketball players, or the special Friday broadcast of Jimmy Bob Swindle's Supernatural Seed of the Lord Prosperity Hour. Felicity selected the Prosperity Hour and decided she would watch until it became boring. Then straight to the NBA. Her mind drifted and she wondered if dreamy Dennis Peckerman would ever visit her again. If ever there was someone properly named she thought, ...it was him.

Jimmy Bob glanced at his watch when his plane landed in Hawaii and concluded he couldn't make it to his house on time.

He looked at Thomas in the seat by the bar.

"Let the pilots know to keep the generator running after they park the aircraft," said Jimmy Bob. "I'm going to watch the broadcast from here.

"And if you would," he added, "I'd appreciate it if you could watch the broadcast from the lounge. I want to talk with Mee Yu-pee alone."

Thomas headed in the direction of the cockpit and Jimmy Bob turned to Mee Yu-pee, who seeing the look in his eyes, had already unbuttoned the top button on her blouse.

"Care for a drink?" asked Jimmy Bob.

~

Clara fluffed up two pillows and lay back against the headboard on her bed. Turning on the TV, she found the channel she was searching for. She looked at Erika sitting beside her on the next bed.

"Aren't you going to say something sarcastic or snarky?" asked Clara.

"No, Grandma," replied Erika, staring straight ahead at the TV. "You're right. I need to get stronger. I'm not going to snivel or be weak anymore."

~

Harvey wandered, searching, across the Cathedral stage.

"Has anyone here seen Cyndy Lyn?" he asked.

Harvey looked around and finally gave up, shaking his head. He really didn't care if she showed up for the service or not. Because of her nonstop carping and interference, she wasn't popular with the broadcast crew or the choir.

"To hell with her," he said.

He walked to Reverend Dopeland, who had lined up his colorful choir behind him.

"You ready?" he asked.

"We're ready as a flea on a hotplate," drawled Reverend Dopeland.

"Ok," said Harvey getting that one. "The announcer will open the service and introduce you. Then it's up to you."

"Are you going to stay and watch?" asked Reverend Dopeland.

"I usually watch from my office on the computer," said Harvey.

"Tonight, could you watch from just offstage?" requested Reverend Dopeland. "I'd like to get your up-close personal perspective, so that you may critique my ministry afterwards."

Harvey shrugged.

"Sure, I can do that."

Harvey left to take up a position in the wings, while Ethan gathered his team in a circle.

"Ok, everyone, all we need is half an hour," said Ethan. "Just stay with me for half an hour.

"You got it!" said Gloria. "Work some magic, Ethan."

He looked at the faces around him.

"Everyone, thank you for all your help," said Ethan. "This is going to help a lot of people, and it'll be something you can take pride in for the rest of your lives."

"Break a leg," exclaimed one of the ladies.

"Twenty seconds," was announced over their headsets, and everyone returned to their positions.

Nona leaned up and kissed Ethan.

"Remember how much I love you too," she said with a big smile.

Then, over their headsets, the final countdown. "Live in five... four... three... two... one..."

"And now," roared the baritone TV announcer, "live from the beautiful Diamond Cathedral in Anaheim, California, it's time for a special broadcast of the Supernatural Seed of the Lord Prosperity Hour with special guest Reverend Pat Dopeland, minister to the Church of the Holy Chastisement. Brought to you tonight by the good people at True Flow Catheters. Give'm a test drive. You won't regret it... And Time-Out brand non-flammable embalming fluid. Don't allow your loved one's funeral to be spoiled by fire. Ask for only the best!"

"So, let's put our hands together for our special guest minister who puts the rev in reverend and the crying back in Christ. The Reverend Patrick Dopeland!"

The curtain flew open and the Reverend Patrick Dopeland strolled forward dramatically, bouncing a tambourine above his head to the rhythm of the choir behind him, singing a slightly altered version of "Onward Christian Soldiers" while the audience applauded.

Onward Christian donors
Marching to the bank
Give your cash to Jesus
So, he you can thank
Christ the royal creditor
Wants you all to rend
So, he can thank you
With a holy dividend!

On the second verse, the Reverend Dopeland reached out his tambourine to urge the audience to clap in unison with music. The people in the audience were hesitant at first, but then both choirs urged them on, and they joyfully clapped in rhythm with the music.

Hell's foundations quiver
When you've paid for sin
Brothers lift your credit cards
So, your prosperity wins
At the sign of an ATM
Let your fingers fly
On, then Christian donors
Raise the collection plate high

As the choir ended the song, Reverend Dopeland raised his hands to the heavens and shouted, "Praise Jesus!" while the audience's hands rumbled their approval.

"Praise Jesus! Praise Jesus! Praise Jesus!"

~

The camera panned into a closeup of Reverend Dopeland while Clara stared at the TV. Suddenly she turned to Erika.

"Quick! Get your stuff! We're leaving now!"

~

Reverend Dopeland tossed his tambourine to a choir member and turned to the congregation.

"Hellooooo, Anaheim! Praise the Lord! Praise Jessssus!" he shouted. "I am the Reverend Patrick Dopeland of the Church of the Holy Chastisement."

Loud applause.

He motioned behind him.

"And these fine ladies are the Holy Chastised singers."

More loud applause.

Reverend Dopeland raised up his arms and reached out to the two thousand in the audience.

"Anaheim, are you ready to be saved?" he shouted.

"Yes!" the audience replied.

"I can't hearrrrr you!" shouted Reverend Dopeland, throwing his arms upward. "Are you ready to be saved?"

"Yes!" shouted the audience.

"Say it so our Gawd in heaven can hear you!" shouted Reverend Dopeland, reaching for the sky. "Are you ready to be saved?"

"Yes!" thundered the audience.

~

Jimmy Bob stared at the sixty-inch TV in his plane, while Mee Yupee cuddled next to him sipping whiskey.

"This guy is good," he said aloud. "Maybe too damn good! My flock might learn to like him better than me."

He made a mental note not to invite him on the broadcast again.

"My sermon today," boomed Reverend Dopeland's voice to the congregation, "is about whether giving is enough to gain the prosperity Gawd offers?"

"I quote the basis of our creed from 2 Corinthians 9, verses 6-8," drawled Reverend Dopeland as he walked across the stage "Whoever sows sparingly will also reap sparingly, and whoever sows generously will also reap generously. Each of you should give what you have decided in your heart to give, not reluctantly or under compulsion, for Gawd loves a cheerful giver."

"But is being a cheerful giver enough to obtain Gawd's grace?" questioned Reverend Dopeland dramatically. "Does all Gawd want from his children is for them to give, give, give hand over fist to the church. Is that really enough?"

He paused and looked out over the vast congregation ready to pose a question. He waved his hand towards the audience.

"Have any of you ever wondered why you give, give, give and nothing happens?" quizzed the Reverend. "Why you're still mired in the unhappiness that surrounds you? Or why you're still in financial trouble? Or why your spouse is still cheating on you? Or why you're still having constant overpowering impure thoughts about your step-brother, or step-mother?"

Reverend Dopeland pointed toward the congregation and while his hand swept the room, guilty looks spread across the whole of the congregation.

"Have any of you actually ever taken the time and wondered on that thought?" he shouted.

Reverend Dopeland looked at a stranger in the front row and pointed.

"Well, have you?" he exclaimed.

The man shook his head, as did many others unconsciously in the cathedral.

"I can tell you," exclaimed Reverend Dopeland, marching across the stage and pointing. "I can tell you why. But first you must be willing to listen!

"Are you ready to listen?" shouted Reverend Dopeland, waving his hand.

"Yes," shouted the anxious congregation back at him.

"You don't sound like it!" shouted the Reverend back at them.

"Tell us what we need to know," screamed someone in the rear of the cathedral.

Reverend Dopeland paused.

"Giving to the Lord by itself will not get you prosperity," boomed Reverend Dopeland. "Unless you're already in a state of grace."

"To be in a state of grace," he continued, "you must first rid yourself of sin. You must drive the lust and temptations of Say-tan from your soul. You must rid yourself of Say-tan's evil influence before you are worthy of the prosperity that Gawd is willing to bestow upon you if you do."

Reverend Dopeland smiled devilishly.

"You're probably asking yourself, how do I rid Say-tan from my soul? How do I make this evil demon want to leave? Brothers and sisters, the answer is easy—pain!"

"In Revelation 3:19, it states, 'Those whom I love, I reprove and discipline,' while in Hebrews 12:10, it tells us that 'he disciplines us for our good, so that we may share his holiness, and thus be in a state of grace.'"

"And how are we to be disciplined, so that we may share his holiness?" asked Reverend Dopeland, pointing at the balcony.

"Two Samuel 7:14 has the answer to that question, 'For I shall correct him with the rod of men!'"

Reverend Dopeland turned and waved dramatically towards the choir.

"Behold," he boomed with a flourish of his hand. "The rods of men!"

Gloria and Lizzie stepped forward, swinging two large wooden paddles in the air above them with, 'By the grace of God,' stenciled down the length of their stinging power.

The audience gasped in awe as the holy instruments of love flashed upon the two thirty-foot jumbo TV screens flanking the stage.

"Brothers and sisters!" cried out Reverend Dopeland suddenly, holding his hands to his face while closing his eyes.

"The spirit of the Lord is moving, flowing... coursing through my body," announced Reverend Dopeland dramatically. "The Lord is telling me that someone in the audience is possessed by Say-tan's evil."

Suspicious eyes in the Diamond Cathedral looked right and then left.

"This man takes the Lord's name in vain daily," announced Reverend Dopeland.

Many righteous people breathed a sigh of relief while others...

Reverend Dopeland opened his eyes and pointed sternly at Artie, sitting at the end of the second row.

"Sinner. Do you want to experience the grace of Gawd?"

Artie stood and raised his hands to his face.

"God damn it! I do! I do!" he shouted joyfully.

"Then come forth onto the stage," commanded Reverend Dopeland. "So that we may make you worthy of Gawd's love."

Artie quickly ran onto the stage and stood beside Reverend Dopeland.

Reverend Dopeland held a microphone to Artie.

"Sinner. What's your name?" asked Reverend Dopeland.

"George Carlin," replied Artie.

"George," asked Reverend Dopeland, "how often do you take the Lord's name in vain?"

George covered his face with his hands and sobbed.

"Every God-damn day," exclaimed George as tears rolled down his cheeks. "I can't help myself. Every cock-sucking Jesus mother-fucking Mary God-damn day!"

The congregation gasped.

"George," boomed Reverend Dopeland, "do you want to expel Say-tan from your life"

"Yes!"

"Do you want to share in Gawd's holiness?"

"Yes!"

"Do you want to reap the prosperity that will come from expelling the sin of Say-tan from your body?"

"Yes! Yes! Yes!" screamed George waving his arms above him.

"Then bend over and prepare your soul to be chastised, so that you may expel Say-tan!" commanded Reverend Dopeland.

Lizzie and Gloria approached with their paddles held high for the Lord. George bent over and Lizzie very dramatically gave him a good whacking while the choir behind them sang...

Oh God Oh
Spank me down below
Oh, my Lord
Spank me there some more
More, and more, and more,
Give me more...
–Spare the rod and spoil the soul
Ousting Say-tan is our goal...
We love our Lord so very, very much...
Allow our loins to feel his touch...

"I feel the power of the Lord moving through me," exclaimed George, as Gloria gave him a final whack.

"Say-tan begone," shouted Reverend Dopeland, dramatically

holding up a hand. "Say-tan begone and trouble this young man no more!"

Lizzie gave him one more good whack and George collapsed onto the floor, prostrating himself. Reverend Dopeland helped George to his feet.

"Young man, are you finally free of Say-tan?" boomed Reverend Dopeland's voice.

George inhaled a deep refreshing breath.

"I am! I am!" exclaimed George.

"How do you feel?" asked Reverend Dopeland.

"I feel swell!" shouted George, hopping up and down with his arms raised in triumph.

"Praise the Lord! He's feeling swell! Praise Jesssssus!" shouted Reverend Dopeland. "It's a miracle! Gawd bless you! You are now worthy of the Lord's gift of prosperity!"

The congregation applauded wildly while shouts of "praise the Lord," and "show us more," reverberated through the air in the cathedral.

"Goodbye, Ethan, thank you for saving Martha and me," whispered Artie as a choir member escorted him backstage. "See you on the other side."

Overcome with emotion for a moment, Reverend Dopeland suddenly turned back towards the audience.

"Brothers and sisters," announced Reverend Dopeland, as he closed his eyes and raised his hands fiercely into the air. "The spirit of the Lord is flowing... coursing within me again. The Lord is revealing to me that there is another person in the audience possessed by Say-tan's evil."

Again, suspicious eyes in the cathedral looked right and then left.

"This individual is seriously intertwined in pornography's evil grip," boomed Reverend Dopeland's voice.

Hundreds in the multitude silently hummed to themselves, trying to disappear.

"He is in pain," exclaimed Reverend Dopeland. "Say-tan has a vice grip on him down beloooow! He needs our help to free his testicles from SIN, so that he may be savvvvvved!"

Reverend Dopeland opened his eyes wide and pointed a shaking finger at Harold sitting in the middle of the fifth row.

"Sinner, come forth," commanded Reverend Dopeland, "If you want your soul to expel Say-tan and be cleansed of the evils of pornography!"

Harold, a good actor, wearing a red, white, and blue fringed cowboy costume that snapped together along the outside seams, gulped as an expression of panic raced across his face. Standing, he shuffled down the row and leaped onto the stage, as two thousand pairs of eyes in the cathedral stared and millions on TV wondered.

Reverend Dopeland held a mic to Harold.

"Sinner, what is your name?" asked Reverend Dopeland.

Tears flowed as Harold leaned into the mic.

"I am known as Dick Bangcock," choked Harold while tears flowed. "The best-equipped male star in the porn industry."

The audience in the cathedral gasped and millions across the airwaves suddenly became righteously curious.

"And how many craven lust-filled women have you sinfully satisfied in the porn industry," asked Reverend Dopeland.

"I don't exactly," sobbed Harold. "Maybe a thousand."

"Dick!" boomed Reverend Dopeland, "do you want to thrust Say-tan from your loins?"

"Yes!"

"Do you want to feel Gawd's holy plan grip your testicles?"

"Yes!"

"Do you want to reap the prosperity that will come from expelling the sin of porn from your penis?"

"Yes!"

"Do you want to feel the holy relief of salvation squirt joyfully from your body?"

"Yes! Yes! Yes!" screamed Dick. "Praise the Lord! Show me the Way!! I need God's love massaging my nether regions!"

"Then bend over and prepare thy soul to be disciplined!" commanded Reverend Dopeland. "So that we might chastise the evil sin of Say-tan from your body!"

~

In North Euphorea, Felicity was suddenly anything but bored and, while she watched with intense interest, her hand slowly slipped beneath her dress.

"Maybe I will let missionaries into North Euphorea after all," she mused aloud. "They seem like fun."

~

As Lizzie and Gloria approached with their paddles, Dick bent over and ripped apart the snaps on his cowboy costume. The costume fell to the floor, revealing that he wore nothing but a huge jock strap underneath, with a dinosaur sized bulge in the front. The congregation gasped in awe. Reverend Dopeland turned to the audience, while the choir continued to relentlessly sing and clap.

Oh God Oh
Spank him down below...
Oh God Oh
Spank him down below...
Oh God Oh
Spank him down below...
Spank him! Spank him! Spank him!
Oh God Oh...

"Is there a volunteer in the audience who would like to help chastise the sin from this well-equipped porn star's loins?" shouted Reverend Dopeland.

Suddenly, twenty-one women and four men stampeded to the

stage, crowding each other, to get in line. Reverend Dopeland pointed at the first two women in line and the rest disappointedly walked back to their seats and their irritated spouses.

Two plump women with way too much Mary Kay makeup ran up the stairs to the stage and grabbed the paddles from Lizzie and Gloria. Anxiously, they lined up, one on each side of Dick, ready to whack away while the choir sang...

> Oh God Oh
> Spank me down below
> Oh, my Lord
> Spank me there some more
> More, and more, and more,
> Give me more...
> Spare the rod and spoil the soul
> Ousting Say-tan is our goal...
> We love our Lord so very, very much
> Allow our loins to feel his touch...

The one on the left excitedly whacked Dick, while she giggled insanely. He winced.

"Oh Jesus! Sweet Jesus! That's it! Right there!" he shouted. "Spank Say-tan from my overgrown horny loins!"

The one on the right whacked Dick with equal zealous fervor.

"Yes, baby. I can feel Say-tan ready to shoot right out of me," he cried out. "Spank me some more! Suck my penis away from Satan's evil grasp!"

Kit cocked her head, so that she could see underneath her husband as she sang. She whispered to Kat standing next to her. "Our husband has an erection. This is about to get messy."

Both women gleefully whacked, and whacked, and whacked until finally...

"Say-tan begone," shouted Reverend Dopeland, slapping Harold's forehead again and again. "Begone! Begone! Begone!

Begone, you malevolent crotch demon! Torment his gonads no more!"

Dick suddenly straightened up with an expression of pure rapture on his face.

"Hallelujah!" screamed Dick, jumping up and down, holding his arms aloft in righteous victory, while the two disappointed women looked on. "Say-tan has left my body. I no longer feel like doing pornos anymore! I only want to fornicate and experience a blowjob within the bounds of holy matrimony."

"Praise the Lord," shouted Reverend Dopeland at the top of his lungs. "—It's a heavenly miracle! He now only wants a blowjob *after* he's married!"

"Hallelujah, if he'll marry me," shouted a female voice in the audience, "I'll give him a righteous blow job the second he says 'I do.'"

"The hell you say!" shouted another female voice waving a fist. "Married or not, the hell with Satan, I'll fuck him onstage right now!"

Meanwhile, a torrent of house keys and underwear rained down on the stage, while Kit and Kat frowned.

The choir joyfully with gusto continued to sing...

Oh God Oh
Spank me down below
Oh, my Lord
Spank me there some more
More, and more, and more,
Give me more...
Spare the rod and spoil the soul
Ousting Say-tan is our goal...
We love our Lord so very, very much
Allow our loins to feel the power of his touch...

...as Kit and Kat escorted their aroused husband offstage... to an empty dressing room to begin their honeymoon.

Officer Dumpfy of the Anaheim Police Department paid the cashier and picked up his precious box of two dozen Krispy Kreme doughnuts. After work, a bunch of his fellow officers were coming over to his house to watch the Lakers-Warriors NBA playoff game, , and nothing went better with cheap beer and Cheetos than Krispy Kreme doughnuts. His partner, Officer Shultz, met him at the door.

"Hey, we have to go," said Officer Shultz.

"Why? What's up?" asked Dumpfy.

"The switchboard at the station has been lighting up," said Shultz, as they got into the squad car.

"You know that guy in the missing person bulletin with dementia?"

"Yeah."

"Well, he's at the Diamond Cathedral posing as a minister and he's doing some weird things on stage. The station's sending us over to pick him up."

"What sort of weird things is he doing?" asked Officer Dumpfy.

"He's spanking members of the congregation," replied Shultz as they drove off.

"What's so unusual about that?" asked Dumpfy. "Don't all evangelical Christians deep down really want to be spanked?"

Oh God Oh
Spank me down below...
Oh God Oh
Spank me down below...
Oh God Oh
Spank me down below...

"The spirit of the Lord is moving within me again," announced Reverend Dopeland as he closed his eyes once more. "This feeling is extremely powerful. The Lord is revealing to me that there are still many, many troubled people in this congregation possessed by Saytan's evil."

Again, suspicious hair-trigger eyes swung right and then left in the cathedral.

"These individuals have been having impure thoughts about their babysitter, their next-door neighbor, their secretary, their stepmother, the plumber, the pizza delivery guy... the pool boy at the country club!" boomed Reverend Dopeland's voice. "And someone is even thinking about their pet poodle!"

He opened his eyes and stared manically out over the congregation. The terrified audience of two thousand men and women stared guiltily back at him, waiting on a razor's edge. Their tension rising, boiling, ready to erupt. Reverend Dopeland snapped his fingers and raised his hand to his temple.

"God is telling me more!" he exclaimed in a fervor. "These people have gone past impure thoughts and are actually mentally fornicating with the person sitting in front of them!"

Hundreds of curious people suddenly turned around in their seats.

Reverend Dopeland put his hand to his forehead.

"God is telling me who these sinners are. I have their names in my head, on my tongue, ready to be revealed!"

Reverend Dopeland's hands waved across the room and he circled his index finger to point ...but before it reached a target, a distraught wife picked up a hymnal from the seat pocket in front of her and furiously beat her husband with it.

"You bastard!" she screamed, as the man tried to fend her off. "I knew it! I just knew you were fucking our poodle, Fifi! She's been looking so happy lately!"

The fight triggered the entire tightly-wound congregation into a critical mass of pent-up angry suspicion bent on unleashing years of repressed fury, vengeance, and religious riot, as bibles, hymnals, purses, balled up fists, and loud voices exploded everywhere. Suddenly, everything that wasn't tied down was being used to whack Say-tan from suspected offending spouses.

Reverend Dopeland stopped prophesying as the choir watched the cathedral quickly devolve into a war zone.

Officers Dumpfy and Shultz observed the mayhem from the wings.

"Shouldn't we do something about this?" asked Officer Shultz with a mouth full of doughnut.

"Naw," said Officer Dumpfy. "Looks like they're having a religious experience. You know how they'll complain if we interfere with their first amendment rights."

He looked across the stage.

"But we should at least apprehend the good reverend."

Nona spotted the uniformed police officers moving towards Ethan holding handcuffs.

"Protect the quarterback!" shouted Nona to the choir. "Protect the quarterback!"

Instantly, the entourage crowded around Ethan and Nona. Then, from the center of the group, someone pitched packages of lit firecrackers onto the stage, along with fireworks that billowed colored smoke and crackled. Suddenly, the sprinkler system went off and the fire alarm blared and flashed throughout the hall. Anxiety erupted in the cathedral and the mob of women pushed forward towards the officers in an organized panic, with Nona and Ethan in the middle during the downpour. The officers found themselves jammed up against a wall, unable to move or apprehend the good Reverend Dopeland, while he and his wife escaped out the back door.

As the firecrackers exploded onstage, down the hall, a very satisfied Kit, Kat and Harold, upon hearing the alarm, opened the door of the dressing room and looked around, wondering what they had missed.

Kit and Kat looked up at their wonderful new husband and smiled.

"Shall we go home?" sighed Kit and Kat in perfect harmony.

...Meanwhile, 2,500 miles away in Hawaii, a very upset Jimmy Bob Swindle wondered what the fuck had just happened to his church?

Chapter 20

Chomp! Chomp! Chomp!

Saturday June 14th, 10 a.m.
CIA Headquarters, Langley Virginia

Matthew Sherlock, director of the Central Intelligence Agency, conferred with half a dozen of his department heads while they watched three sixty-inch TV monitors at the end of the conference room at Langley. The first showed a review of Dim Ping-pong's news conference a day earlier in Dongwang regarding the Reverend Jimmy Bob Swindle, and the second the riot at the Diamond Cathedral the night before, set off by one of their former agents, while the third broadcast showed live L.A. local news regarding the discovery of the nine bodies found overnight on the Jimmy Bob Swindle estate.

"Holy shit," said Matthew shaking his head. "This is a fucking mess."

He looked around at his department heads.

"Ok, what do we do now? I'm open to suggestions, people."

Before anyone could speak, the deputy director entered the room and whispered something into the director's ear.

Matthew turned to his deputy.

"What the fuck?" he exclaimed. "You're kidding."

The deputy shook his head and handed Matthew a file.

"We just received this."

Matthew scanned through the pages in the file for a few minutes and then looked up at his deputy.

"Get René Scipio on the phone now!"

Eleven Hours Earlier, in Anaheim

Clara's black SUV entered the parking lot at the back entrance to the Diamond Cathedral, just as the fire trucks were leaving. Followed by Boris 1 and 2 and Erika, she found a distraught Harvey Atwater sitting on the edge of the stage, staring blankly into the distance. Burn marks from the fireworks pocked and scarred the carpeting on the stage and everything seemed wet. Chairs and pews were overturned, hymnals and bibles were scattered everywhere. Paper littered the floor. The fire trucks didn't turn out to be necessary, but paramedics had to be called in to clean up the numerous minor cuts and scrapes meted out by vengeful, repressed partners. No one knew what had happened to Mr. Weinstein. Last time someone saw him, his wife chased him out the front entrance with a baseball bat that she had found somewhere. In the front parking lot, the police were still untangling the five car wrecks initiated by frantic, fleeing male spouses.

Erika pointed to the wall as they approached Harvey.

"Is that blood?" she asked.

"Probably," said Harvey.

Harvey looked up and when he saw Clara, he immediately stood.

"Ms. Barton," stammered Harvey nervously. "So good to see you."

"What happened here?" asked Clara, looking around.

"Reverend Patrick Dopeland is what happened here," said Harvey, shaking his head. "By the time he was done with them, the congregation was so riled up, they were settling old martial grudges with fistfights in the aisles. We pulled one eighty-year old man off his eighty-year old neighbor, whom he suspected of fornicating with his sixty-year old wife."

"Was he?" asked Erika.

"Apparently he was," answered Harvey. "For over thirty years."

"The reverend's real name, at least the name he is going by now, is Ethan Jones," said Clara.

"I wonder why he was posing as a minister," said Harvey curiously. "He seemed a little strange. Maybe he was crazy."

"This man is not crazy, nor does he do irrational things," said Erika impatiently, tired of the conversation. "If he was posing as a minister, it wasn't for fun. There was something he wanted to accomplish."

Erika looked around at the carnage. "My guess is that this was a diversion to distract you from what he was really doing."

"Very good," said Clara, impressed with her granddaughter's logic. "What would you do next?"

Erika motioned towards Harvey.

"If we want to find out why he posed as a minister, Mr. Atwater here needs to walk us through everything the good reverend did while he was here."

"I agree," said Clara.

"Harvey, would you?" she requested.

"For you, Ms. Barton," said Harvey, "of course."

Starting at the back door, Harvey guided everyone step by step through the building and showed them exactly what Reverend Dopeland did, from the time he arrived, until the service began.

"And then he walked out on stage," said Harvey. "I really don't know what else I can tell you."

"Think Harvey," said Erika. "Was there anything else he did? Maybe something small."

"Well," said Harvey, thinking for a few moments, "he did want to send an email to his brother with his sermon attached to it."

Erika lightly slapped her forehead.

"Show us the computer he used," groaned Erika.

Harvey led everyone to his office.

"What happened first?" asked Erika.

Harvey sat behind his desk.

"First, I sat and entered my password," said Harvey as he typed in his password and pressed return, "and then ..." Harvey stopped and stared at the screen. "Oh darn!"

Erika frowned and waved her grandmother over. On the screen was a picture of a Tyrannosaurus. Below it read...

Chomp! Chomp! Chomp!
Motherfucker!

René Scipio's Apartment, June 14th, 7:05 a.m. PST

René rolled out of bed and slipped on her silk robe. Walking to the balcony on the other side of the bedroom, she opened the door to smell the air. Her life had been transformed overnight. She had freed herself from the toxic atmosphere of Jimmy Bob and Cyndy Lyn Swindle, and she was in love. Gazing at Janet in bed, watching her, René smiled. She was about to rejoin her when her cell phone buzzed.

"Hello," she said. "This is René. Can I help you?"

"Code in," requested the voice on the other end.

"Sunny," responded René, confirming her identity.

"Nimble," said the voice on the other end. "René. This is Matthew Sherlock. Do you know who I am?"

"Yes, Director. What can I do for you?" asked René, very surprised that he had called her, since she was only a field agent.

"I just wanted to call and personally congratulate you," said the director. "The operation was a complete success. Why didn't you tell us about Tyrannosaurus?"

René hesitated for a moment. She didn't know what the director was referring to, but decided to play along.

"No one but those participating had a need-to-know," said René. "And if things went south, we wanted the agency to have plausible denial of the operation."

"Good initiative and thinking," said the director. "The entire operation was a masterpiece of ingenuity. Your uncle told us about the way you coordinated with Ethan Krieger to insert your Uncle Fernando's virus onto the ministry computer server, while he distracted their people by posing as a minister. Pure genius. It only took the virus thirty minutes in their system to strip away every cent from the church's Grand Payment Islands bank accounts and get their records. We now know every one of the Dear Leader's secret bank accounts overseas and the Justice Department has been busy this morning coordinating with various governments to freeze those assets."

"How much money were we able to freeze?" asked René.

"Counting the billion dollars that mysteriously showed up in the Widow and Orphan Trust Fund in the CIA Credit Union, over fifteen billion dollars so far. We think that it's the Dear Leader's entire overseas reserve. That should put a hell of a dent in his nuclear program."

"Who thought it up?" asked the director.

"It was a group effort," said René, improvising.

"Well, it was a mighty fine example of what can happen when great minds put their heads together," complimented the director. "Terrific teamwork.

"Also," added the director, "distracting the news media from the real story yesterday by revealing his wife's homicidal tendencies was pure genius. I'm not going to ask who put the three bullets into Cyndy Lyn Swindle, because I'm sure that she deserved it and the gun that killed her has been thoroughly cleansed in the system."

"I'm sure you're right on that one," said René.

"Ok, I won't keep you," said the director. "I just wanted to call and congratulate you and your team. We haven't been able to locate Ethan Krieger, so if you run across him, tell him thank you from the agency and give him our best wishes. We understand from your uncle he is on death's door, and he came out of retirement to do this one last operation for the agency."

"Oh, and one last thing," said the director. "You know of course that we're going to have to burn your connection to the Swindles. So, take a long vacation and we'll contact you in two months regarding your promotion and new station."

"Promotion, sir?"

"Yes, promotion," said the director. "We need more three-dimensional thinkers like you in the field.

"Have a good vacation, René," said the director. "I look forward to seeing you when you get back."

René ended the call on her cell and set the phone on the dresser. She now realized why her uncle had wanted her to approach Erika, and made a quick mental note to call him later to find out what else she needed to know.

"Sounded like a good call," said Janet, looking up at René from the bed.

René smiled at Janet sweetly.

"Let's go to Flagstaff."

Part Three

The Road Home

Chapter 21

Whatever a Man Sows...

Somewhere on the Interstate

Their escape from the Diamond Cathedral had been fast and easy, and after Ethan merged the Honda Pilot onto I-15 just north of Anaheim, Nona watched her husband for a long time, noticing every subtle change in his behavior and appearance. Having just seen Ethan's star burn bright in the Diamond Cathedral, she now watched as he faded away in front of her like a balloon that had just been untied and its air slowly dwindling away. His movements had less conviction and his speech became hesitant. Behind the steering wheel, Ethan stared into the distance, as if he saw a different road than the highway they were on. Just then, a sign appeared, announcing a rest stop in a mile.

"Do you mind?" asked Ethan. "I'm feeling a little..."

"No, of course not," replied Nona, rubbing the outside of his shoulder. "When you get back from the restroom, I'll drive. Ok?"

Ethan nodded and exited the highway. He parked along the side, so they wouldn't have to back out in case they ran into cops and needed to make a quick departure.

As Ethan got out of the Pilot, he had only walked a few steps when he suddenly covered his mouth and ran for the men's room. Inside, he leaned over a toilet, and his stomach let go. Unable to eat much lately, he retched.

Ten minutes later, a worried Nona walked to the entrance of the men's room and listened. She didn't hear anything.

"Ethan, you belong to me," said the dark figure inside the cave. "It's time to meet your fate."

Ethan shook his head.

"No. Not yet," said Ethan. "I have to make it to the Wildey."

"What's so important about the Wildey?"

"You wouldn't understand," said Ethan.

"You might be surprised," said the dark figure.

Ethan felt a wet paper towel caressing his forehead. Opening his eyes, he gazed up into Nona's agonized face. Looking around he noticed that he lay on his side on the restroom floor.

"What...?" muttered Ethan, sitting up with help from Nona.

"After a while, I got worried," said a frantic Nona. "I found you here, on the floor. What happened?

"I must have passed out," said Ethan, smiling into her big brown eyes. He stroked Nona's cheek with his fingers. "I'm better now."

With Nona's help, Ethan stood and they went outside. As they walked to the Pilot, Nona noticed that a black SUV had parked twenty meters behind them. The windows were tinted and she couldn't see inside. A woman in a long black coat got out of the passenger side and watched as Nona opened the car door for Ethan. Nona looked directly at the lady. She stood just out of the light and Nona couldn't make out her face in the dark. Nona waved. The woman waved back. Relieved, Nona jumped into the driver's seat and drove away. In her rearview mirror, the SUV didn't move, and the woman still stood next to the car, looking in their direction.

While Nona glanced into the mirror, Ethan had punched an address into the GPS.

"Where are we heading?" asked Nona, looking at the map appearing on the dashboard screen.

She didn't receive an answer. In a few short seconds, Ethan, exhausted, had relaxed into his seat and had already fallen asleep. Nona looked at the map and saw a street address located around a mile outside of Flagstaff, Arizona.

"Hmmm, 66 Cougar Mountain Road," she said. "I wonder how he came up with that address?"

She smiled at her sleeping husband.

"Don't worry, my love," she promised. "I'll get you home."

Jimmy Bob's Hawaiian Estate

Hallelujah! Hallelujah! Hallelujah! Hallelujah! sang Jimmy Bob's ringtone. He rolled over in bed and picking up his cellphone from the nightstand, he squinted through hungover eyes at the caller ID—

Clara Barton

"Oh shit," muttered Jimmy Bob, as he pushed the button to refuse the call from his silent partner. The last thing he felt like doing was taking a call from the boss of the local Russian mafia. Ever since the Anaheim police had found his wife and eight other bodies, he had been more concerned about the squad car stationed outside his Hawaiian estate gate making sure he didn't go anywhere. Already *distraught* over the death of his wife, the Los Angeles news outlets suddenly reported that Jimmy Bob's fingerprints had been found on some of the guns interred with the victims. His first thoughts when he heard the news were—*that bitch René!* He had fooled the CIA into thinking he was going to help them obtain information, in order to get their protection. He now intended to blame them for the bodies. He would tell the public that it was obviously an effort by the agency to foil his evangelical missions to North Euphorea, and people would believe him. After all, he was Jimmy Bob Swindle and thanks to the internet and the movies, people nowadays would believe just about any conspiracy theory involving the government.

Still a little drunk from the night before, he looked across the bed at Mee Yu-pee sleeping. But then his phone sang again. *Hallelujah! Hallelujah! Hallelujah!* Again, Jimmy Bob squinted at the caller ID.

Harvey Atwater

Jimmy Bob had been trying to get a hold of Harvey ever since he had heard the news, but his phone had been turned off. He quickly answered the call.

"Why haven't you been answering your phone when I call?" shouted Clara on the other end.

"... uh... well... uh..."

"And where the fuck is my money?" she demanded.

Jimmy Bob held the phone away from his ear.

"Please not so loud, Clara," pleaded Jimmy Bob from hangover hell. "I'm a little under the weather."

"I don't give a flying fuck if you're in the middle of a God damn typhoon," shouted Clara. "Again! Where the fuck is my money!"

"What the hell are you talking about?" asked Jimmy Bob. "It's in the Grand Payment Islands bank."

"No, it's not!" shouted Clara. "That preacher you had subbing for you introduced a virus into your computer system which cleaned out all our accounts at your bank. You owe me and my associates two hundred and fifty million dollars, and we're holding you personally responsible."

Jimmy Bob did some quick thinking.

"Clara, I know how we can quickly make this right," he assured her. "Put Harvey on the phone, so I can make the arrangements."

In the background Jimmy Bob heard voices and then Harvey came on the phone.

"Yes, boss."

"Harvey," he said, "this is Jimmy Bob. I'm expecting two billion in transfers to the bank soon from our new client. When they arrive, transfer two hundred and fifty million to Clara's account."

"I would if I could," said Harvey. "But that money has come and gone too."

"All of it?"

"All of it!" said Harvey with emphasis. "I've been in my office all night trying to find out where all the money went, and I haven't been able to trace it. Do you want me to put Clara back on the phone?"

Jimmy Bob abruptly ended the call.

"He ended the call on me!" yelped a panicked Harvey. "Why would he do that?"

Clara grabbed the phone from Harvey and threw it violently against the wall.

"I'll tell you why!" shouted Clara, glaring at Harvey. "Because he doesn't have two hundred and fifty fucking million dollars!"

Harvey gulped while Clara pointed at him and then motioned to Boris 1.

"He's the fool who allowed that bogus preacher into the ministry computer system. Take him outside and shoot him," she ordered.

Erika blocked the door.

"Please, Grandmother, no," pleaded Erika loudly, "I think Harvey can still be of some use to us. He might even be able to help me get you your money back. If he isn't helpful, you can always shoot him later."

Erika turned towards Harvey.

"Harvey, you'll help me, won't you?" asked Erika.

Harvey quickly nodded.

"Now, Harvey," asked Erika sweetly. "Was there anything else this man did on the computer that maybe you have forgotten about? Maybe something you didn't think was important?"

Harvey thought hard for a moment.

"Well," he said, "there was one very small thing he was interested in that I may not have mentioned."

During his conversation with Clara, Mee Yu-pee had woken up and lay provocatively naked on top of the bed covers, watching Jimmy Bob after he hung up.

"That didn't sound good," she commented.

Desperate, Jimmy Bob looked down at Mee Yu-pee.

"Do you think the Dear Leader can help me out with a little more money?" begged Jimmy Bob. "I really need his help."

Mee Yu-pee stood, and strolling to Jimmy Bob, she ran her finger sensuously up and down the bridge of his nose.

"I know the Dear Leader likes you," purred Mee Yu-pee. "He'd probably be willing to help some more. Why don't you take a shower and while you're cleaning up, I'll get on the satellite phone and find out how much he is willing to help you?"

"Thank you, baby," said a greatly relieved Jimmy Bob, kissing Mee Yu-pee. "I appreciate all the help the Dear Leader can give me."

Jimmy Bob headed for the bathroom to take a long, relaxing shower. A half hour later, he returned, dressed himself, and went looking for Mee Yu-pee. He found her in the living room wearing a flowered Hawaiian sarong with an orchid in her hair that she had plucked from his garden.

"Good news," announced Mee Yu-pee, handing Jimmy Bob a drink, "the Dear Leader said for you not to worry. He is willing to help you achieve peace of mind."

Relieved, Jimmy Bob took a long drink of his whiskey while he admired Mee Yu-pee's dress.

"Say Mee Yu-pee," said Jimmy Bob, "how about you and I..."

Jimmy Bob never finished the sentence. The world around him spun into darkness and he fell unconscious onto the couch. A little while later, he woke just in time to feel himself dangling in midair, choking from a noose around his neck while his hands were tied behind him. Looking down Jimmy Bob saw Mee Yu-pee smiling upward at him.

"My real name is Dim Poo-ping," said the former Mee Yu-pee. "You really didn't think my older brother would send that much money to your church without someone close to him to keep an eye on you. Did you?"

Dim Poo-ping watched Jimmy Bob turned purple. As his feet thrashed in the air, Dim Poo-ping wondered if Jimmy Bob actually believed in God, or whether it was all just an act, before conceding to herself it really didn't matter; he would find out for himself soon enough.

"Oh my," she frowned as he stopped struggling, "it seems poor Jimmy Bob was highly distraught and couldn't live without his dear wife in his life."

Dim Poo-ping checked his pulse and untied his hands.

"But then, on the other hand," she mused as she strolled to the sliding patio door and opened it to leave. "Maybe Jimmy Bob couldn't live with the shame that he had just lost fifteen-FUCKING-billion dollars of the Dear Leader's money."

CIA Headquarters, Langley Virginia

Director Sherlock signed off on the budget request and handed it to his secretary.

"Anything else?" he asked.

"Yes," said Hattie. "The deputy director is waiting outside. Says he has something else interesting to show you from California."

Given what the deputy director had presented him with earlier in the day, the director immediately became excited.

"Send him in."

Half a minute later, the deputy director strolled in with a big smile on his face, carrying a file.

"Now what do you have for me?" asked the director

The deputy director handed the file to the director.

"Do you remember Susanna Rybkanowski, AKA Clara Barton?" he asked as he sat down.

"Of course, I do," said the director, opening the file. "It was Ethan Krieger who brought her and her organization down. She turned and we bled her dry for information. Afterwards, we allowed her to retire to San Diego on lifetime probation after extracting a guilty plea from her."

"Well, someone should have watched her more closely," said the deputy director. "We received further insights from the information Fernando has been passing on to us all day. Turns out Clara is the boss of the Russian mafia in the San Diego area and has been using the Supernatural Seed of the Lord Prosperity Ministry and its associated businesses to launder money for years. According to what we have, they practically owned the mall, and the supermarkets etc. Ethan's team cleaned them out of around two hundred and fifty million dollars."

"Holy shit," said the director. "I wish Ethan were here, so I could congratulate him on a job well done."

"Holy shit is exactly what that church is going to think when the parishioners find out they have been a front for the Russian mob," said the deputy director.

"Ok, I've heard enough," said the director. "You get the paperwork together and I'll call the attorney general, so they know to send the marshals after Ms. Rybkanowski."

"You know they'll stick her in super-max for violating her lifetime probation," said the deputy director with a smile.

"Ain't it a shame," said the director, chuckling.

But then he thought of something.

"Make sure you call René as soon as you leave my office and give her a heads up about Clara," advised the director.

"Wait, I almost forgot," said the deputy director almost gleefully. "We've reached the bonus round and I have more."

"More?"

"Yes," he said. "The police just found Jimmy Bob Swindle dead in Hawaii. He hung himself from the rafters at his home. Local authorities think it was a suicide over his wife."

"What do you think?" asked the director.

"If you ask me," said the deputy director, "I think he was lynched for losing the Dear Leader fifteen billion dollars."

"Whatever a man sows, that he will also reap," said the director. "Galatians 6, verse 7."

Chapter 22

Painkillers

Stopping only to get gas, Nona drove through the night, while Ethan slept. When they arrived at the GPS address, a golden ornate, heavy metal gate and fence greeted them just as the Saturday morning sun rose in the valley beyond. The gate was chained and locked and from the road Nona couldn't see the house. She looked at Ethan sleeping in the passenger seat, and not wanting to disturb him, Nona reached into his messenger bag and carefully pulled out his Glock. Then, walking to the gate, Nona, holding the gun with two hands, pointed at the lock and pulled the trigger. The lock exploded and left Nona's ears ringing. As she turned to check on Ethan, Nona poked her finger in her ear and twisted, trying to rid herself of the ringing. Relieved that he was still sleeping, she took all the evidence of her breaking and entering and tossed it out of sight behind a nearby bush. Then, after opening the gate, she climbed back into the car, drove in and closed the gate behind her.

The road to the house stretched around a hundred meters. A grove of pine trees shielding the house from the road cleared away halfway to the house. The large two-story chalet sat on the side of a hill, overlooking the valley below. The bottom floor, contained the garage door and in order to enter the house, one had to go up a flight of stairs on the side of the balcony area.

Parking the car in front, Nona got out and walked up the stairs to a door at the side of the spacious balcony. She thought for a moment and looked around while she wondered where they might hide a spare key. Her attention was drawn to an unusually large crucifix next to the door. Nona pulled it from the wall. In a cloth pocket on the back of the cross, she found a key.

Inside the chalet, Nona strolled admiring the stainless-steel kitchen and the luxurious living room furnishings. On a side table she noticed a picture. Nona picked it up and chuckled when she saw a wedding photo of Jimmy Bob and Cyndy Lyn Swindle.

Somewhere on I-40

Clara glanced at Harvey cowering in the back seat next to Boris 2 as they drove along I-40. The unforgiving vengeful part of her soul wanted Boris 1 to drive the SUV off a secluded exit and have Boris 2 splatter Harvey's brains across the desert.

"After all," she reminded herself, "he was the stupid fucker that allowed Ethan into their computer system in the first place. The moron deserved to die!"

However, the rational side of her agreed with her granddaughter that he might still be of some use to them if they had any hope at all of recovering her two hundred and fifty million dollars.

"Besides," she reminded herself, "like Erika said, I can always kill him later."

Clara stared at the cacti in the desert and wondered why Ethan had done it. Was it a deliberate act against her? Or was his real target Jimmy Bob's hypocritical church, and he didn't know anything regarding her involvement? She preferred to think Ethan didn't know, because in her heart of hearts she still loved the asshole. But, that aside, it wouldn't prevent her from doing whatever she had to do to get her money returned to her and avenge her son.

Clara glanced at her granddaughter, sitting on the other side of Harvey, tapping on her computer. Erika was finally giving her something to be proud of. She wasn't being weak anymore. At least she had that.

Jimmy Bob's Flagstaff Chalet

Sitting in the car, Ethan's face shimmered pale, gaunt and ghostly. Dark circles ringed his eyes. While he slept, he groaned and his head swayed, as if he were reliving a long-ago unpleasant memory. Nona debated whether she should wake him, but decided that if this was the end, she could make him more comfortable inside.

"Wakey, wakey, handsome," said Nona, nudging Ethan's shoulder.

Ethan opened his eyes and winced.

Nona held out two anti-nausea pills and a paper cup with water. After he drank them down, Nona handed him a lozenge. While he sucked on the lozenge, Ethan, with a woozy fatigue he couldn't shake, looked around.

"Is it a nice place?" he asked.

Nona chuckled.

"You won't believe how televangelists live in their off time," said Nona. "It's beautiful." She slipped another lozenge into Ethan's mouth. "How did you find this place?"

"I spotted it when I downloaded the virus," said Ethan. "Harvey Atwater was using a picture of it for his desktop wallpaper. I figured it would be a good safe house. Nobody would think of it."

Nona helped Ethan from the car and up the stairs into the chalet. In the bedroom, she helped him take off his clothes and led him to the shower, where she scrubbed him down as he sat in a chair. Nona couldn't believe how much weight he had lost and how quickly it had happened. Afterwards, she dressed her emaciated husband in a Hawaiian shirt and cargo pants, and led him downstairs by the hand. While he lay on the couch, Nona tried to feed him, but Ethan declined food and would only drink water while he sucked on more and more lozenges. Nona gazed into his blue eyes for hours as she gently ran her fingers through the hair on the side of his head. He didn't say much because of the pain, but his eyes told her everything she needed to know.

Finally, around seven o'clock, Ethan fell asleep. As he lay on the couch, Nona watched him, and secretly hoped he wouldn't wake up. Not because she didn't love him, but because she did. That afternoon, she could see that he needed more and more lozenges to control the pain, and Nona didn't want her husband to suffer anymore. Then, around nine o'clock, Nona heard something...

"I'm ready now," said Ethan, holding out his hand to the dark figure in the cave.

"Sorry, Ethan," growled the figure, "but there's been a change of plan."

Ethan withdrew his hand.

"But I thought..."

"Things change," interrupted the dark figure. "You, of all people should know that."

"But why?" asked Ethan, staring into the abyss.

"Because," growled the dark figure, "the last mile of a marathon is always the toughest and your race isn't over yet."

"Please take me. Please," begged Ethan, as the figure started to fade. "I don't want Nona to suffer any longer."

"Finish the race, Ethan," said the figure. "I'll see you later."

"Wake up!" shouted a female voice with a Russian accent, while a pair of strong bejeweled hands shook him. "God damn it, wake up!"

A hand slapped his face and Ethan opened his hazy, semi-conscious eyes. Behind Clara stood Boris 1 with his gun drawn, while Boris 2 stood beside Nona tied to a chair. Erika and Harvey hovered next to the kitchen, watching.

Ethan peered upward at Clara.

"Susanna," said a disbelieving Ethan, shaking his delirious head, trying to focus. "I thought we were supposed to meet at the Hofbräuhaus today."

"What the fuck...?" swore a confused Clara in Russian.

She turned to Nona struggling to escape the chair Boris 2 had tied her to.

"Is he stoned?"

"Yes," answered Nona, still struggling.

"What's he on?"

"Fentanyl!"

"Why the fuck is he taking fentanyl?"

"He's dying!" shouted Nona, kicking at Boris 2. "It's for the pain!"

Clara, in shock, looked down at Ethan, looking up at her, trying to focus. She wasn't ready for him to die. He needed to apologize to her for leaving her in Vienna. He needed to beg for her forgiveness. He needed... He...

Suddenly years of pent-up anger and pure unadulterated rage boiled over inside of Clara, and balling up her fists as tightly as she could, she violently punched a helpless Ethan in the face, while Nona screamed and begged for her to stop. Over and over again, she smashed her fist, laden with sharp penetrating jewelry, into his flesh. Blood splattered and flew in the air around the couch as if a bomb had exploded. Finally, Clara, sucking in deep ugly breaths, grew fatigued and standing, she snarled over a groaning Ethan, while her hand dripped with his blood.

Ethan tried to move, but fell off the couch and onto the floor. Clara cocked her leg and furiously kicked him. Ethan moaned in agony as ribs snapped loudly inside his chest.

"Yeah, I'll meet you at the Hofbräuhaus later," screamed Clara as she kicked. "You can tell me how much you love me and how we're going to live happily ever after."

With her final kick she aimed for his face and put all her the force she could muster into it. But it didn't have the desired effect when it connected. Ethan was already unconscious.

"Tie him to a chair," ordered Clara, kicking Ethan a final time. "And make sure his hands are tied to the arm rests!"

Nona sobbed uncontrollably as Boris 2 picked Ethan off the floor and tied him to a chair facing her. Blood covered him and dripped from Ethan's swollen black and blue face onto the floor.

"Leave him alone," sobbed Nona. "He's going to die soon anyway."

"By the time I'm done with him, he'll wish he had died in his sleep this afternoon," growled Clara.

Clara walked to Nona and slapped her face hard with the flat of her hand.

"Where's his pain medication you ugly old cow?" she growled.

Nona hesitated and Clara cocked her hand again.

"In the messenger bag on the coffee table," sobbed Nona, motioning with her head.

Clara turned her attention to the messenger bag and gleefully emptied it onto the coffee table.

"Well, lookey what we have here," said Clara sarcastically, as she picked up Ethan's Glock. "Secret agent man is not going to need this anymore." Clara tossed the gun to Boris 1 and he tucked it inside his belt. Then she piled up Ethan's cash.

"Well, it's not two hundred and fifty million," said Clara, "but I'm going to take it as a down payment." Clara found Ethan's four remaining sheets of lozenges. She went to the sink in the kitchen and, after stuffing them in the drain, she turned on the garbage disposal. After several seconds of grinding, Clara turned it off.

"Now let's see what he feels like when the fentanyl wears off."

Erika cautiously watched the mayhem unfold and decided to fix her grandmother a drink.

In the kitchen, Clara opened the refrigerator and found a large bottle of cold drinking water. Walking to Ethan she poured it over his head. Water and blood drained down his neck as Ethan shook his head and became conscious.

"Wake up, sleeping beauty," taunted Clara. "We're not done yet!"

Reaching into her purse, Clara pulled out a pair of pruning shears. Nona inhaled a deep panicked breath. Clara turned to Ethan and leaning down, she squeezed hard with both hands and chopped off his left index finger at the knuckle. Ethan screamed while Nona shrieked and blood from the stump squirted onto the floor.

Clara slapped Ethan with the back of her hand, further carving up his face.

"Where's the rest of my money, asshole!" shouted Clara. "You owe me two hundred and fifty million."

She slapped him again to get his attention. Groaning, Ethan struggled in the chair from the pain, and Clara suddenly chopped off another finger. Ethan howled and more blood squirted from another stump onto the floor.

"If I have to cut off all your fingers, you are going to tell me what you did with my money!" screamed Clara. "And when I'm done with your fingers, then I'll work on other things!"

Erika rushed over with a dish cloth and the drink. She handed Clara the drink and kneeling down, she held the cloth to Ethan's wounds, to stop the flow of blood.

"Grandma. Stop this!" shouted Erika. "You're never going to get you your money back doing it this way! Look at him. He's in no condition to answer your questions. Wait until the painkillers wear off, otherwise he'll be dead before you can get any answers out of him!"

Blood lust had taken over and Clara, holding the dripping pruning shears, stared at Ethan's fingers.

"If you want your money back, you'll wait a couple of hours," shouted Erika.

Clara continued to stare at Ethan.

"Do you want your money or not?" asked Erika sternly.

"Ok! Ok!" responded Clara, glaring at Erika. She threw the bloody pruning shears onto the coffee table and walked away. "We'll do it your way and wait until he sobers up."

Clara upended the glass and chugged the entire three shots of vodka. Then she went to the bar and poured herself another anger-soaked triple.

While Erika bandaged Ethan's hand, Harvey cowered in the corner, hoping Clara didn't notice him. Clara picked up her glass and the bottle of vodka, and walked to Nona, sitting with her head down, sobbing. Setting the bottle of vodka on the coffee table, Clara pulled up a chair in front of Nona, and sat. Taking a long drink of vodka, she scrutinized Nona's face.

"I wonder what he sees in an old crone like you?" asked Clara.

She reached forward and, lifting Nona's face, she jerked it left and right as Nona frowned.

"It certainly can't be your looks," sneered Clara as she let go.

Clara suddenly spat on her face.

"Did he tell you he loved you?" growled Clara. She finished her drink and poured herself another. "I'll bet he did. You know, he told me the same thing. Said it was him and me for the rest of our lives."

Clara patted Nona hard on the cheek.

"But no happy trails for you two," sputtered Clara, "because once he tells me what I want to know honey—I'm going to kill both of you... slowly... one bloody piece at a time."

Clara grinned sadistically, and forming her index finger and thumb, into the shape of a gun she pointed it at Nona's temple.

"Bang! Bang! No more you or lover boy!"

Clara stood and yawned again.

"It's been a long day," she slurred drunkenly, "and I think I'm going to get some sleep. We'll pick this up in the morning."

She turned to Boris 1 and 2.

"You two take turns on watch tonight."

At the stairs, Clara turned around and cocked her finger at Nona.

"Remember, honey. Tomorrow. Pain, pain, and more pain and then bang! No more you ...or lover boy!"

She looked at Erika still working on Ethan.

"Maybe tomorrow," she mused loud enough, so Nona could hear her, "I'll start by using the pruning shears on the more intimate parts of him, an inch at a time."

She winked at Nona.

"Or maybe I'll begin with you to give him some incentive."

Staggering up the stairs Clara immediately fell asleep in the first bedroom she found.

Around midnight, Erika noticed Ethan becoming conscious. Outside, on the balcony Boris 1 smoked a cigarette, while Boris 2 slept in a bedroom on the first floor, until it was time for his watch. Erika picked up several dish towels and filled a bowl with water. Sitting on a chair in front of Nona, she wiped her face. Nona had cried so much, she couldn't cry anymore, and her cheeks were lined with salt trails from tears that had dried in the last few hours.

"Please stop her," begged Nona softly. "Or have her end it quickly."

Erika finished wiping Nona's face and reached for a nearby bottle of water. She held it up to Nona's mouth.

"Drink," said Erika. "You're probably dehydrated."

As she drank, Nona looked into Erika's eyes.

Erika smiled slightly and Nona nodded.

Moving her chair in front of Ethan, Erika wiped the blood from his swollen face. She could see by his demeanor and the look in his eyes that, although still in a lot of pain, he was more lucid now.

"I won't hurt you and I don't care about the money," said Erika as she worked, "but I need to know the truth about a few things. Can you do that for me?" she asked.

Ethan warily studied her with the eye that wasn't swollen shut.

"That depends," he choked.

Erika held up the water bottle, so that he could drink.

Ethan sucked a long swig of water and then looked at Erika.

"What do you want to know?"

"Did you kill my father?" asked Erika.

"Who was your father?" coughed Ethan.

"Demetri."

Ethan hesitated for a moment while he gathered himself, knowing that the next moment might be his last.

"Yes."

"Why?" asked Erika calmly.

"What did your grandmother tell you?" asked Ethan curiously.

"She said you put him on his knees and viciously shot him in the back of the head," said Erika, wiping the blood from his ears.

"And why did she say I did this?" asked Ethan.

"Because he was laundering money for the Russian mob," replied Erika.

"The truth isn't always that simple." Ethan winced from a sharp pain in his gut. "And is usually a lot more painful than we think."

"I need to know the truth about my family," said Erika. "I promise that I won't hurt you or your wife."

Ethan looked at Nona nodding at him and then into Erika's eyes.

"Your father *and* your grandmother were laundering money through your grandmother's import/export business, but that is not why I was assigned to them," choked Ethan. "Their main business was human trafficking. They specialized in supplying Russian girls and boys as young as ten to wealthy clients and brothels. When I caught up to your father, he was in a hotel room testing out a twelve-year-old girl. I had been ordered by my superiors that when the time came to take him alive, but he decided he wasn't going to go quietly. He fired first and missed."

Erika suddenly stood and stared at Ethan.

"And there's one other thing you might want to know," added Ethan, gasping from the pain reeling through him. "When I started my surveillance, I thought your father was in charge of the operation. But along the way, I learned that it was never Demetri, or your grandfather—it was always your grandmother.

"So, is that the truth you wanted?" asked Ethan, peering upward.

Furious and incensed beyond words, Erika looked around for something to throw, but stopped, knowing it would only attract the attention of Boris 1 and maybe wake her grandmother. Instead, she laid the washcloth on the table, and grabbing her coat, she marched out the front door.

"I'm going for a walk," growled Erika at Boris 1 as she passed him on the balcony.

"Wait," exclaimed Boris 1 waving at her, "boss say you stay in house."

Erika ignored him and strode angrily down the road toward the woods, while Boris 1 wondered what to do. He thought about waking the boss, but Clara might be angry that he let her go. Glancing at Ethan and Nona tied up, he decided to follow her.

The moon shone brightly in the sky that night. However, the world turned a whole lot darker as soon as Erika entered the tree line. She had only walked around twenty meters into the pine shadows when suddenly a hand covered her mouth and she felt a gun jab her in the ribs.

"Shut up!" whispered a voice pulling her behind a tree. "Not a sound."

Boris 1 watched as Erika disappeared into the tree line and swore to himself.

"I never like her. She always give me dirty looks. She troublesome bitch!"

Stopping, Boris 1 surveyed the tall trees in the moonlight and then slowly walked forward into the murky blackness.

"Ms. Barton," shouted Boris 1, as he warily trod down the gravel road. "Your grandmother say you need stay in house."

He looked around him in the chilly pine-scented night.

"Where are you, Ms. Barton?"

Erika stepped from behind a tree.

"You don't have to shout," scolded Erika, drawing his attention.

The last thing Boris 1 felt was a hand over his mouth and a large knife ripping into his spinal column from behind. Struggling slightly, he silently slipped from Janet's hands onto the ground with a *thump*.

A surprised Erika stared downward at Boris 1 for a moment, and then looked up at Janet, wiping the blood from her knife on her black tactical uniform just as René, also dressed in black, stepped from behind the tree.

"Marine Corps. Four years." Janet grinned at Erika. "It was God's plan that he die tonight!"

René tapped Erika on the shoulder to get her attention.

"Hey bitch," reprimanded René, "I've got a bone to pick with you regarding my computer. Do you know how much explaining I had to do to my section tech?"

"Later, later," said Erika, surprising René with a hug. "I'm just so glad to see you. Thank God, you got my text message this afternoon!"

"Ok. Ok," mellowed René, patting Erika on the back. "We'll talk more about the computer later. What's the situation in the house?"

Erika let go of René and the three gathered in a circle.

"I gave my grandmother three extra-strength Ambien in her drink and she is sound asleep upstairs," said Erika. "Ethan and Nona are tied to chairs in the living room. Boris 2 is sleeping in a downstairs bedroom until it's time for his shift. Harvey's asleep on the couch. He's not a problem, so don't hurt him."

René thought for a minute.

"Ok. Here's what we're going to do," said René.

The light in the bedroom suddenly flicked on. Erika ran to Boris 2, sleeping on the bed, and frantically shook him by his shoulder.

"Wake up! Wake up!" she shouted. "There's been an accident."

Boris 2 rolled over.

"Accident?"

"Yes, an accident. Your partner," shouted Erika. "He stumbled off the balcony. I think he's broken his leg and he's been screaming for you."

Picking up his gun from the nightstand, Boris 2 jumped out of bed and quickly followed Erika through the living room and out onto the balcony. Down below he could hear loud groaning. Boris 2 raced to the railing. Boris 1 lay on the driveway gravel below him. But then, puzzled, he scrunched up his face when he noticed drag marks in the gravel driveway leading up to the body...

Thwap! Thwap! Thwap!

René stepped from the darkness behind Boris 2 just as he fell over the railing and joined his partner in the afterlife.

"Never give a bad guy a chance," said René righteously.

Racing up the stairs, Janet rejoined René and Erika on the balcony.

"Well, that was fun," said Janet merrily. "Now let's go pay a visit to your grandmother."

As they walked inside, Erika gently nudged Harvey on the couch. Harvey's eyes opened wide as he looked upward at three ominous women staring down at him. He stared at their guns, and gulped in terror.

Erika pointed towards the door.

"Run, Harvey! Run!" whispered Erika. "And never look back!"

Harvey didn't need to be told twice. He ran full speed out the door, down the stairs past two dead Russians, and escaped into the black of the night with visions of a gentle, soothing beach in Costa Rica on his grateful mind.

Quickly, the women untied Ethan, obviously in a severe amount of pain, and laid him on the couch. Then untying Nona, they led her to Ethan. Sobbing, she lay beside him on the couch, with her arms around him.

Upstairs, Clara, drowsy from the Ambien mixed with vodka, didn't notice being tied to the bed.

"After we get done, I'll call the U.S. Marshals," said René, making sure she tied Clara's arm securely. "She broke her lifetime probation by re-involving herself with the Russian mafia. They intend to put her away for the rest of her hopefully very long life."

Erika looked down at Clara in her dreamlike state.

"Sorry, Grandma," said Erika. "But you were the one who said I had to quit sniveling and be stronger."

Once Clara had been secured, the three women went downstairs. Nona rolled from Ethan groaning, and standing, looked at René.

"He needs painkillers, and we need to leave," said Nona.

"Leave?" exclaimed René. "Leave where? Once I make the call, it won't take the marshals long to get here, and Ethan can get medical help."

"He can't and won't die in a hospital," pleaded Nona, crying. "I know you won't understand this, but we have to get to the Wildey."

"The Wildey? No!" said René. "I can't let you go. You've both been through a traumatic experience. You're not thinking straight."

Erika and Janet took René aside.

"I think we have to help them," said Janet. "He needs to leave. I can't explain it. It's just a feeling I'm having, but he's not supposed to die here."

"I'm feeling the same thing," said Erika. "He needs to get to the Wildey! I don't know why I'm feeling this, but I am."

"What's wrong with you two?" exclaimed René. "Have you both gone nuts?"

Janet looked at Nona and then at Ethan on the couch.

"René," said Janet, looking into her eyes. "I think you're just going to have to have faith that this is the right thing to do."

René sighed and turned to Nona.

"What kind of painkiller does he need?"

"Fentanyl."

Erika thought for a moment.

"I have an idea," she said.

Walking across the room to her grandmother's long black coat Erika held it up for Nona to put on. Nona slipped her arms in and buttoned up. Next Erika picked up Clara's wide-brimmed hat and set it on Nona's head.

"Nope," she thought out loud. "We're going to need to do something about the red hair. Can you tuck it inside the hat?"

With Janet's help and a few hairpins, they managed to hide Nona's hair. Finally, Erika handed Nona Clara's big sunglasses.

"Perfect," said Erika as Nona put them on. "Now you look just like my grandmother."

Chapter 23

Vaya con Dios

2 a.m.
Flagstaff, Arizona

Mattie didn't like the hours at the all-night drugstore. But the pay for the divorced pharmacist was decent and it put food on the table for her two growing children, so she didn't grouse about it. The store at this early hour was empty, and it had been unusually slow for a Saturday night. Mattie glanced at the clock on the wall. When she reached the halfway point of her shift, she started to look forward to having breakfast with her kids in the morning.

Just then, an older woman, wearing a long black coat, a wide-brimmed hat, and sunglasses, walked through the sliding front doors. Mattie thought she looked stylish, but a little odd, wearing sunglasses in the middle of the night.

The woman looked around and then headed straight for Mattie in the pharmacy.

"Hi," greeted Mattie. "Do you have a prescription that needs to be filled?"

"No," said the woman. She raised her hand from her coat pocket to show Mattie that she had a gun. "But I do have a terminally-ill friend who needs painkillers now and I don't have time to go to a doctor."

Mattie gulped when she saw the gun.

"What kind of painkillers does your friend need?" asked Mattie cautiously.

"Fentanyl," said the woman. "The highest dosage you have. He's in a lot of pain."

Mattie saw a tear dribbling down the woman's sunglasses.

"I don't want to see him suffer any more than he has to before he leaves me," said the woman, her voice choking a little. "He had some fentanyl. But some bastards stole it from him. I need enough to make him comfortable for just a little while longer."

Mattie studied the woman and then pointed towards a counter.

"I'm going to have to go back there for a moment," said Mattie. "I promise you that your friend will get what he needs and I won't sound the alarm until thirty seconds after you leave the store."

The woman nodded and Mattie went behind the counter and held up a sheet of lozenges.

"Will one do? Or do you want more?" asked Mattie with her finger on the alarm.

"Just one," said the woman. "He hasn't much time left."

Mattie took her finger off the alarm and returned to the front counter. Slipping the sheet into a bag she stapled it shut, so the cashier up front wouldn't stop her and handed it to the woman.

"I hope this helps your friend," said Mattie.

The woman smiled and to Mattie's surprise laid a hundred-dollar bill on the counter to pay. "Thank you."

True to her word, Mattie didn't sound the alarm until thirty seconds after the woman had left. And for the rest of her life, she fondly remembered the wonderful night that she had been robbed and hoped that someday she would find someone that loved her that much.

Curiously, as a side note, the police were surprised to find that the robber had *accidentally* dropped her purse on her way out of the store. So later that night they issued an arrest warrant for Clara Barton.

Jimmy Bob's Flagstaff Chalet

Clara woke and discovered in her drowsy Ambien-flooded mind that she couldn't move.

"What the hell...?" she muttered.

Tugging at her restraints, Clara also discovered that, though Janet had been a Marine for four years, it didn't mean she knew how to tie a good tight knot.

~

Though René had only seen Ethan in pictures, she barely recognized him on the couch now. One eye had swollen shut in the midst of the extreme bruising on Ethan's disfigured face. By the way he hesitantly inhaled and exhaled, René knew that several of his ribs were broken. With only three fingers, his left hand seemed more of a claw now than a hand and squeezed the air like it had a ball in its grasp. What remained of his body looked pasty and colorless like he was... René's mind stopped... she didn't want to use that word until she had to. She owed Ethan the courtesy.

The painkillers had worn off and Ethan's body was experiencing not only the pain of cancer's endgame, but the full realization of Clara's vicious beating. Ethan groaned in agony, clutching his abdomen, while René, also in agony watching him, wondered what she could do. She laid another cold compress on his swaying forehead and rubbed the top of his hands. It seemed to help a little.

Janet sat nearby, watching. She had seen death in her life, but always quick and sudden or after the fact. She had never witnessed the life slowly drain away from a once proud and able man. She didn't know how much more of his suffering she could bear, but out of respect for the man who once inhabited his body, her spirit refused to leave the room.

Leaning forward Janet tried to comfort her lover and herself by rubbing René's shoulder with her hand.

"Maybe if you talk to him?" said Janet.

René looked down at Ethan and felt her heart bursting.

"Ethan," said René. "Help is on the way. You wouldn't believe what your wife is doing right now to help you."

René glanced at her watch.

"She'll be back any minute," assured René. "With enough painkillers to...well...get you to where you need to go, you know the..."

René looked upward as she thought for a moment.

"I can't remember the name of the theater..." said René.

...the Wildey, whispered a shadowy voice in her ear.

"The Wildey," said René, looking down.

Ethan's good eye stared up at her. Red had flooded the outer areas, but the steel blue in the center still had life.

"Yes...the Wildey," rasped Ethan through the contortions in his face.

"The Wildey." René smiled. "A magical place of red, white, and yellow flashing neon that smells of popcorn, milk duds, Friday and Saturday nights, and afternoon double features. You'll sit in the balcony sharing popcorn and a soda with Nona, while she clings to you when the monster comes on the screen and you'll kiss her when it's gone. And, when the movie is over, you and Nona will walk home in the cooling air of a warm Illinois summer evening, holding each other's hands, while wondering aloud together about the stars, the moon, and the heavens above. Then suddenly as you walk, you'll come upon a street with no lights and you'll look up and see the Milky Way with its billions of stars whirling around in an endless slow dance, and you and Nona will look deep into each other's eyes and think how lucky, in the midst of the infinite universe, you were to have found each other."

René noticed that, despite still being in extreme pain, Ethan had calmed a bit and a slight smile creased his lips.

Just then, a pair of car lights sped up the driveway. Nona, having long since thrown off her disguise, jumped out of Clara's SUV, and with Erika close behind, ran up the front stairway. Once inside, Nona knelt and quickly thrust a lozenge into Ethan's mouth. Slowly, as Nona held him, Ethan's pain melted away. A few minutes later, Nona gave him another. While Ethan sucked on the lozenge, he gazed up at her.

"I heard a sweet voice while you were gone," whispered Ethan.

Nona looked at René.

"Thank you."

René nodded.

"With a little help, I think we can go now," rasped Ethan.

"You sure?" asked Nona.

Ethan nodded.

Erika and Nona gently lifted Ethan, wincing between them, and slowly walked him towards the door.

René quickly ran ahead of them to open it.

"Ethan, before you go, I'm curious about something," asked René as they approached. "There's still billions of dollars unaccounted for. What happened to all that money? I know you and Fernando don't have it, so where is it?"

Ethan suddenly stopped them at the door.

"Billions?"

René studied the puzzled expression on Ethan's face.

"You didn't know did you?" said René, smiling.

"Know what?" asked Ethan. "We only expected maybe a hundred million at most from off-shore banking accounts. I didn't even know Jimmy Bob was involved with the Russian mob until Susanna showed up."

"Well... besides the Russian mob, Jimmy Bob was involved with money laundering for Dim Ping-pong through the bank his church set up," said René, chuckling. You, and your team destroyed the Dear Leader's funding for his nuclear program. The Justice Department is currently freezing every account that my grandfather gave them. The world's a little safer now. But like I mentioned there are still several billion unaccounted for. The math isn't adding up."

A grin spread across Ethan's face.

"So," he said, "there is a God."

"So where is all that money?" asked René.

"It's in an untraceable trust fund in Switzerland," said Ethan, "and is currently being invested, so it can be distributed, in perpetuity, to a hundred different charities and NGOs involved in refugee relief and medical care."

"What?" shrieked Clara.

René looked up. On the stairway stood Clara, pointing a gun at them.

"You gave my money away to charity?" screamed Clara. "You fucking asshole!"

A clap of thunder and the smell of gunpowder sped across the room as she pulled the trigger. René ran to the stairs. Clara tried to fire again, but the gun jammed and in the last jail-free moment of her life, Clara felt René's fist crash against her jaw before she tumbled unconscious down the steps.

Meanwhile, everyone looked around for the bullet. Nona noticed a hole in the glass behind her and wondered for a moment. Conceding that she had been lucky, and that she had ducked at just the right moment, Nona opened the door and with Erika's help, they carefully guided Ethan outside and down the stairs to the Pilot out front. As they laid him in the backseat, Ethan raised his hand to wave at Erika. Erika meekly raised her hand. Nona closed the car door and embraced her.

"I'm really sorry about my grandmother," sobbed Erika.

"Thank you for everything," said Nona, hugging her back. "We'll never forget what you did for us."

René watched from the balcony above as Nona drove away. She believed it was a mistake for them to go, but knew it was their choice to make. She raised her hand one last time as they disappeared into the tree line.

"Vaya con Dios," wished René as she waved goodbye.

When Erika and René returned to the living room, Janet had just finished tying Clara up again. This time with very well-thought-out knots.

"Let's see," said René, thinking out loud to Erika. "First, we need to bury the two heavies. Afterwards I'll call the marshals. It'll take them several hours to get here, so while I wait for them, Janet can take you to the airport. How does that sound?"

"Just fine," said Erika. "But while you two are getting the backhoe in the garage started, I need to do something."

Early that morning when Joanna woke, she checked her cell phone immediately like she always did. Her heart overflowed when she read the text message that she had been waiting for...

–Look forward to seeing your painting of me later today.
XOXOXO
–home forever.

Chapter 24

The Wildey

East of Flagstaff on I-40

"Don't worry my love," said Nona, glancing at Ethan while she sped down the high desert interstate. "I know exactly where you want to go. I'll get you there on time."

Ethan slipped another lozenge into his mouth and sucked while he smiled slightly at Nona.

"A rest stop is coming up," groaned Ethan. "Please get off there."

"But we..."

"Please," rasped Ethan. "It's very important for us to stop."

"Ok, my love," replied Nona.

The blue facilities exit sign came up quickly and Nona got off the highway. Following the arrows, Nona pulled into the auto parking area and parked by a small building that said Men on one side and Women on the other.

Nona turned around in her seat.

"Do you need to go to the bathroom?" asked Nona.

"No," groaned Ethan.

He struggled to sit up. Nona got out of the car to help him. When firmly propped up against the door, Ethan pointed.

"In the women's room," winced Ethan, "you'll find a desperate mother with two hungry children running from her abusive husband. She's been trying to get a ride all day."

Nona stroked Ethan's cheek and didn't question how he knew.

"Don't worry," said Nona, adoring her husband. "I'll make sure they get a ride."

Nona kissed Ethan and closing the car door she quickly walked to the women's room. Inside, on the floor, she found a young woman shivering against the wall wearing a dirty dress and coat and sporting a black eye. Hiding in her arms were two small children no older than five. Nona knelt down, nudged the woman and she opened her eyes.

"Ma'am, do you need a ride?" asked Nona.

The woman nodded.

"Where are you heading?" asked Nona

"Home to my parents in Chicago," replied the woman.

"What a coincidence," said Nona with a smile. "My husband and I have to make one small detour, but after that...well...we can drive you all the way to Chicago."

Nona stood and held out her hand.

"I'm Nona. Come with me."

The grateful young woman woke her two drowsy children and followed Nona to the Pilot. Opening up the back, Nona helped lift the children in. Then Nona and the woman spread a blanket over them as they rested their sleepy heads on the four very comfortable pillows that Barry had included with the car. The kids instantly went back to sleep. Escorting the woman to the passenger side front seat, Nona opened the door and she got in. Looking at Ethan in the back seat she waved.

"Hi, I'm Trudy," said the woman, feeling excited for the first time in days.

Ethan smiled.

"Ethan," he said, "good to meet you."

Trudy's reaction when she saw Ethan confused Nona. She expected her to be horrified.

"I'm curious," asked Nona. "What do you see when you look at my husband?"

Trudy turned towards Ethan, and then back towards Nona.

"A very handsome older man," replied Trudy, a little puzzled. "Why?"

"No reason," said Nona.

Deep in thought, Nona walked to the driver's side but suddenly stopped. Parked thirty meters away gleamed the black SUV that she had seen at the rest stop in California a day earlier. Outside of the car stood a man and woman in dark pinstripe suits and long black coats, smiling at her.

Nona immediately got into the car and drove out of the parking lot past them. In the rearview mirror she watched the couple still standing next to the SUV. Nona breathed a sigh of relief, though still dumbfounded by Trudy's reaction to Ethan.

"What were you staring at?" asked Trudy.

"The black SUV that parked in front of me," replied Nona.

Trudy, perplexed, looked behind them as they drove away. Seeing nothing, she shrugged.

A sign for the Great Meteor Impact Crater came up quick and Nona exited the highway.

"Trudy," said Nona as she turned right onto Meteor Crater Road. "Would you be willing to help me assist my husband when we get to the crater? He's having a hard time walking."

"Sure," said Trudy. "I'm just happy you're giving me and my two kids a ride. I'll help you in any way I can."

"Thank you," replied Nona. "You wouldn't believe the last two..."

Nona almost said days, but then everything Ethan and her had done and been through, both good and bad, flashed through her mind and she said, "Weeks."

"We've had two wonderful weeks," grinned Nona as she glanced back at Ethan.

She changed the subject.

"How did you end up at that rest stop?" asked Nona.

"One day I decided my husband had hit me for the last time," replied Trudy. "And it was either light him on fire while he slept or escape. I chose to do the smart thing for the sake of my children and escaped, rather than go to jail. A man gave us a ride from Barstow, but he ditched us when he asked me for a blow job and I refused. I had been at that rest stop all day trying to get a ride when you came along."

A few minutes later, the Pilot entered the meteor crater visitors center parking lot and Nona parked by the front door. She got out of the Pilot and, with Trudy, they helped Ethan from the backseat. Then, with his arms over their shoulders, foot by foot, the three started slowly walking towards the front door of the visitor's center. Nona suddenly halted.

"Wait, we forgot your pain medication!" said Nona.

Ethan stopped her.

"I won't need it anymore," assured Ethan with a serene smile.

"You sure?" asked Nona.

"I'm sure," replied Ethan, nodding as they continued walking.

Soon, the three stood at the front door. Reaching down, Nona tried to pull it open, but it wouldn't budge.

"It's locked," said Nona.

She looked around for something to break the glass with.

"Try it again," said a female voice beside her.

Turning her head, Nona saw the man and woman from the black SUV standing under a light ten feet away. The woman smiled and pointed. "It's unlocked now."

"Who the hell...?" muttered Nona.

Ethan nudged Nona and she turned towards him.

"They're with me," said Ethan.

Nona turned... but they were gone.

"Who are you two talking about?" asked Trudy, looking around.

"No one," said Nona, as she reached for the door handle and pulled it open.

Step by step, Nona and Trudy helped Ethan up the stairs through the visitor's center to the observation area. A few minutes later, they were outside. On a small hill twenty meters away, shimmered a view area in the twilight, surrounded by a painted metal railing.

"Not far, Ethan," said the dark figure in his mind. "Only a short distance more and your marathon is over."

"Can you take me up there?" asked Ethan, nodding towards the hill. "It's almost time. I need to see it."

"Time for what?" asked Trudy as they turned Ethan towards the knoll.

"Dawn," replied Nona.

Step by very painful step, they helped Ethan climb the hill.

"Keep going," encouraged the dark figure. "You're almost there, Ethan."

With every step he took, Nona cringed as Ethan winced and contorted from pain. Ten feet from the top, Ethan's legs didn't seem to have anything left in them and they buckled. Nona stood behind him and pushed, while Trudy held him up. The closer they got, the more Ethan seemed to lose control, until finally, after one last massive herculean effort, the three reached the top. Then, very carefully, Trudy and Nona lowered Ethan to the cement pavement. When they laid him against the metal railing, he no longer seemed to be in pain. A smile crossed Ethan's face as he gazed towards the meteor crater beckoning to him in the early morning light.

"I'm going to go get my kids," said Trudy, looking toward the half-mile-wide meteor crater appearing before them. "They need to see this. You two going to be ok?"

Nona nodded.

When Trudy left, Nona sat beside Ethan and put her arms around him. Ethan didn't seem to have any strength left. His breathing slowed as he gazed at Nona.

"You know I always wanted to come here," said Ethan softly, "but I just never found the time until now..."

Nona reached for Ethan's hand.

"I want to tell you something before I go," said Ethan.

"What's that, my love?" asked Nona as she squeezed his hand.

"If you had married me first," said Ethan softly, "I would've made sure that you became a doctor."

She kissed his cheek as a tear streamed from the corner of her eye.

"I know that you would've," said Nona. "You're just that kind of man."

Ethan let loose a long sigh.

"Did you have fun?" he asked.

"The best," said Nona, leaning against his shoulder, as they watched the sun peek above the horizon in the distance.

"I'm glad you're here with me," said Ethan.

"I like the dawn," answered Nona, enjoying the sun on her face. "Someone I love once told me, it's like everything is brand new. All the mistakes that you made the day before, or the day before that, are wiped clean, forgiven, and you get another bite at the apple."

Ethan chuckled and inhaled a deep, refreshing breath of morning air into his lungs. Then looking up, he saw the man in the long dark coat smiling down at him from the railing. He reached out his hand to Ethan.

"Nona," whispered Ethan.

"Yes, Ethan," replied Nona.

"It's time to say goodbye."

Nona quickly turned towards Ethan.

"I love you, Ethan," whispered Nona, and closing her eyes her lips met Ethan's one last time. As Nona tenderly kissed Ethan, she felt his life slowly drain from his body. And when Nona opened her eyes, Ethan's were closed. Hugging his limp body against hers as tightly as she could, Nona cried like she had never cried before.

The sun had been up almost an hour when Nona let go of Ethan and stood. She looked down upon his peaceful face in the warm morning sun.

"Goodbye, my love," said Nona. And she walked down the knoll to where Trudy and her kids patiently waited.

As she approached Trudy, Nona held out the Pilot's key fob to her. Trudy looked at the fob that she had just been handed.

"Do you want me to drive?" asked Trudy.

"Yes," replied Nona as she looked beyond Trudy at the smiling woman twenty feet behind her. "The car belongs to you now. If I'm correct, I have alternative transportation waiting for me."

Trudy tried to think of something to say. "Nona, I..."

"When you get to the car, look in the glove compartment," said Nona, fighting back the tears. "I'm sure that you'll find the pink slip has been signed over to you. It's been a wonderful car for Ethan and I, so treat it right. Then I want you to stop at the first open restaurant you see and feed your kids. You'll find plenty of money for gas and food in the messenger bag on the floor in the back."

Trudy embraced Nona.

"How can I ever thank you?" asked Trudy, a tear dribbling from the corner of her eye.

"There's a notebook in the messenger bag," said Nona, letting go. "Inside are all the codes you will need to access an online Swiss bank account. Inside the front cover are the addresses and phone numbers of Artie Thompson and the Kit-Kat twins. From the bank account, make sure Artie has enough money to take care of his wife's health and the Kit-Kat twins have enough money for college. The rest belongs to you."

Nona motioned Trudy away.

"Now get going," she said. "You don't want to be here when they open this place up and find Ethan."

Trudy, overcome with emotion, tried to say something, but Nona shooed her away with her hand.

"Go," said Nona gently, "and take care of your kids."

Nona watched Trudy until her and her children were out of sight inside the building. Then, turning, she walked to the smiling woman.

"Ms. Jones," said the cheerful lady. "It is such a great pleasure to finally meet you. Are you ready to go?"

"Where are we going?" asked Nona hesitantly.

The woman gave Nona a puzzled look and grinned. "Why...to the Wildey of course."

Suddenly, the meteor crater disappeared around Nona and she found herself standing across the street from the Wildey in her and Ethan's hometown of Edwardsville, Illinois. The theater's neon glowed softly against the warm but cooling darkness of the early evening summer sky, while the smell of popcorn drifted in the air, beckoning to Nona, like a fragrant childhood perfume. The woman beside her motioned her forward. Nona hesitated for a moment.

"You need to get your ticket," coaxed the woman gently. "Your movie is about to begin."

Nona crossed the empty street to the red ticket booth in front of the theater.

"Ms. Jones," said the young girl at the ticket booth. "So good to see you. We've been wondering when you would get here. But you know what they say. Better late than never."

"Late?" said Nona.

The ticket girl handed a confused Nona a purple ticket and pointed her towards the glass entry door. "Now you need to see the Ticket Taker."

Nona walked to the front door where a tall man wearing a colorful, immaculate Wildey Theater uniform waited. He took Nona's ticket from her and tearing it, he ceremoniously dropped one half in the glass ticket receptacle next to him and handed the other half to Nona.

Nona stared at the half ticket in her hand, not knowing what to do.

"You have questions?" asked the Ticket Taker, cocking his head.

"Yes," replied Nona. "Am I..."

"Of course," said the Ticket Taker with a delightful chuckle, "or else you wouldn't be here."

"But the ticket girl... she said I was late," recalled Nona.

"You are."

"So, when did I..."

"Two weeks ago." The Ticket Taker grinned. "The night before you..." He waved his hand in the air as he waited for Nona to make the connection. Nona thought for a moment. Suddenly...

"... picked up Ethan," finished Nona, inhaling a deep amazing breath.

"Some people have things they need to do before they get here," said the Ticket Taker wistfully. "It really is a miracle in the Universe to be so powerfully drawn to someone like that. Love that deep is such a rare occurrence."

The Ticket Taker glanced at the clock on the wall.

"Ms. Jones... Nona. Your show is about to begin," announced the Ticket Taker. "Now you don't want to miss the previews of your coming attractions."

"One last question," said Nona.

"Shoot."

"Since I was... well you know... was it all real?" asked Nona.

"Of course, it was real," said the Ticket Taker with a smile. "The joy, the pain, as real as real can be."

Nona started to walk away, but the Ticket Taker held up his hand to stop her.

"Now I'm really not supposed to tell you this," drawled the Ticket Taker. "But this should be a happy occasion and you seem so sad. I suppose it does no harm at this point, all things considered, for you to know."

"Know what?" asked Nona.

The Ticket Taker grinned at Nona. "Ethan was right."

"Ethan was right?" repeated Nona, a bit puzzled. "About what?"

The Ticket Taker continued to grin.

"For you two, it has been decided that what comes afterwards, is very special. It's not a place. It's a time."

Magical, wonderful, electrifying lightning lit up inside Nona. Grinning, she quickly turned towards the theater.

"Don't forget your popcorn and Milk Duds," reminded the Ticket Taker.

The concession lady held out a bag of popcorn and a box of Milk Duds in the air and Nona grabbed them as she danced past her.

"Enjoy your movie," shouted the Ticket Taker as he watched her happily speed away.

At the stairway to the balcony, Nona stopped and thought about the last two weeks for a moment. She glanced to the side at the smiling Ticket Taker urging her on and then, looking upward, she inhaled a deep excited breath, and grinning as much as she possibly could grin, Nona climbed the stairs

Fifty-Five Years Earlier
October 1968, Edwardsville, Illinois

"So, what's playing at the Wildey this weekend?" asked Nona as she pulled her coat from the locker and put it on.

Cynthia shrugged. "Nothing. Just a stupid Three Stooges double feature."

Nona secretly adored the Three Stooges and loved their comedy, but she didn't want to seem uncool to her girlfriend. She was about to say something when she turned and noticed that tall, handsome Ethan Krieger stood behind Cynthia with a big goofy smile on his face.

Staring at each other in wonder, the pair inhaled deep anxious breaths.

"Would the prettiest girl in school like to go with me to the Wildey tonight?" asked Ethan.

"Can we sit in the balcony?" replied Nona, "and have popcorn and Milk Duds?"

"Of course," replied a grinning Ethan. "And you can cling to me when the monster comes on the screen and we can kiss when it goes away."

"Oh, Ethan, I love you," said Nona, tearing up.

"I love you too," said Ethan as they embraced.

Suddenly everyone in the crowded Edwardsville High School hallway stopped what they were doing and turned around to stare curiously at Ethan and Nona passionately kissing.

Cynthia, in total confusion, watched for a moment and then tapped Nona on the shoulder to get her attention.

"When on earth did all this happen?" she asked.

Nona stopped kissing Ethan for a moment and turned towards her friend.

"Around fifty-five years from now," giggled Nona. And she went back to kissing Ethan while Cynthia scratched her head.

Book Covers

All books covers (11x17 high quality) are available for purchase
signed by the author
at
davidkempher.com

Also by David Kempher

Otter Rock Book 1: Julie

March 29, 2022

Escape to the Wildey Book 2: Happy Warriors

May 3, 2022

Otter Rock Book 2: Les Femmes

June 1, 2022

Otter Rock Book 3: Les Enfants

June 29, 2022

Otter Rock Book 4: Wings

August 3, 2022

Otter Rock Book 5: Wings at War

August 30, 2022

Fall 2022

Escape to the Wildey Book 3: Knights Errant

Otter Rock Book 6: Author

2023

The Frosting on her Cake

South on Interstate 12

You can find more information regarding upcoming book releases by David Kempher

at

davidkempher.com

Praise for David Kempher

Too bad I died thirty-four years ago, otherwise, I would probably have something really wonderful to say about my son's book...

— James Kempher (father)

If I could only read, I would probably enjoy 'Escape to the Wildey' more than the laser pointer he had me chase...

— Jazzy (pet English bulldog)

David is a sexy, wonderful, dynamic human being who has a vivid imagination worthy of great praise and...

— oops...just me

About the Author

Currently David is a high school teacher in bush Alaska. During the summer, David travels the west coast of the United States, surfing, camping and generally getting into trouble whenever he can. Sometimes, he likes visiting his sister in the medieval region of the United States known as Kansas and watching local people peer at his Alaska license plates, while trying to figure out why he has a surfboard on top of his car and a University of California sticker on the back window.

His life experiences and the two times he was chased by a moose, not to mention the three times he was abducted by space aliens (not recommended) uniquely qualify him to write about the human experience in isolated bush Alaska, Otter Rock, Oregon (great surfing), and Paris, France. He also loves art, and plans to spend his summer vacation next year in Paris at the entrance to a supermarket parking lot holding up a sign that reads, 'Will teach English, math and history, for a Chagall.'

Made in the USA
Monee, IL
24 April 2023

32356315R00144